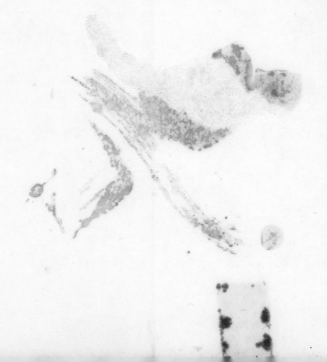

EXECUTION

EXECUTION

BY COLIN McDOUGALL

St Martin's Press
New York

Library of Congress Catalog Card Number: 58-13051

*Printed in the United States of America
by Noble Offset Printers, Inc., N. Y. 3.*

For Diana

BOOK ONE / *The First*

1

THE ISLAND of Sicily.

Sicily—in July, 1943.

Sicily—sun-drenched, war-sick, huddling in her misery.

Sicily, a ripe fruit, fat for plucking. Sicily, the soft underbelly of Europe, pregnant with the peril of invasion.

2

'JESUS,' said Krasnick. 'I ain't gonna shoot no *horses*!'

His ham-red cheek pulled accusingly from the butt of his Bren gun, his eyes flashed wide with indignation. Ewart, his Number Two on the Bren, propped on one elbow, returned the look with disgust; the permanent sneer on his sharp-pointed face became more pronounced. 'Listen, you stupid bastard,' Ewart said in a voice of dispassion. 'You're gonna shoot where you're told—get it?'

Sergeant Mitchell heard them and came sculling across the ground on massive forearms. The reserve section of Ten Platoon was spaced in firing position on a knob of Sicilian parkland, studded with tall, umbrella-topped trees. Four hundred yards distant, on the same level but obscured by trees, was a connected group of stone buildings, identified on the map as Castello Donato; and this was the platoon's first battle objective. At this moment their platoon commander, Lieutenant Adam, was leading the other two sections in a slow, silent advance up the slope which led to the iron gates of the castle. Every eye had been anxiously following his progress.

Corporal Fowler, the section commander, yielded place to Sergeant Mitchell gratefully. Mitchell sat, steadied his elbows on thick thighs, and peered through his binoculars. He had to squint to see beyond the sunlight dappling the grillwork on the ornamental iron gate; then all at once he sat rigid and stopped breathing. For this moment he even forgot to order the section's weapons back on their target.

Here at last, in the afternoon of their first day at war, the enemy was visible; and that enemy consisted of soldiers arrayed in blue and gold, sabres belted at their side, and mounted on horses. *Horses!* Behind the horsemen, in a kind of courtyard, some baggy-panted infantrymen milled about, but there was no mistaking these others: they were cavalry. And *Infantry Section Leading,* which Sergeant Mitchell knew by heart, said not one word about cavalry.

Years before Mitchell's nose had been broken in two places, and when he scowled his nose became flattened to one corner of his mouth. At this moment his scowl made him appear ferocious.

Around him the riflemen of the section were up on their elbows, weapons neglected, mouths agape. But Mitchell was unaware of them. His glance was fixed on the line of advancing men. What the hell was going to happen, Mitchell wondered, when they bumped those cavalry? He watched the lean, stalking form of Lieutenant Adam.

Mitchell longed to be with him too; but he had to recognize his platoon commander's good sense in leaving him back here to organize the covering fire. Lieutenant Adam was competent; during the assault landing last night that was the discovery each man had made about the other. Now, as he watched, Mitchell found himself thinking that in many ways the two of them were much alike— both were solidly built and tough, and recognized a job of work when it had to be done. He's a good man, Mitchell told himself: we're going to make a good team. His glance was appraising as Adam moved through the parkland.

Behind him Krasnick's voice recalled him brusquely to the present moment. 'Horses!' said Krasnick, choking on the word. 'I can't shoot horses!' Krasnick had been raised on a farm in Manitoba. He was considered stolid, almost to the point of stupidity, and he had never before been known to display so much emotion on any subject.

But at once Sergeant Mitchell was in sure control again. 'Get your weapons back on the target!' he hissed savagely to the whole section. Then to Krasnick, as though explaining a point of conduct to a small boy: 'Look, Krasnick, you don't have to shoot the horses. Shoot the men—*off* the horses.'

'Oh.'

Krasnick thought about this and after a moment he seemed satisfied. A moustached giant of a man, sitting astride a white charger, appeared to be delivering an oration to his mounted troops. The muzzle of Krasnick's Bren gun pointed back at the grillwork, steadied, and held firm on the centre of the giant's chest.

Mitchell lay down, poked his own rifle forward, and at once his glance darted anxiously back to Adam. The advancing force was now in the last hundred yards but as yet they could neither see nor be seen from the iron gates of the castle. For an instant Mitchell closed his eyes and willed a message across the parkland to Lieutenant Adam. Just take it easy, he tried to tell him: We'll look after those cavalry for you. Everything's going to be all right. . . .

3

WEAPONS cradled in their arms, Lieutenant Adam and his force moved steadily through the parkland. Their steps were cushioned on pine needles. It was quiet in this forest world; noise from outside, like the far-off clatter of machine-gun fire, sounded muffled and remote. Birds sang from the branches overhead.

Adam's step was sure and alert. His whole being was concentrated on the purpose ahead, but today his mind was so brilliantly quick and alive that not even this hugely important first attack was sufficient to contain it. His mind clamoured with the wonder and excitement of all that had happened since the assault landing last night.

Now, as he paced forward in this parkland, he remembered how the assault boats scribbled white wakes across the sea. On the beach positions flat mushroom flashes announced the burst of bombs; the night air sang with the passage of huge, unimagined weights. Then Pachino burst into rioting flames before them, fired by express command to provide a beacon for the ships and aircraft. John Adam thought of himself as a solid, practical person, not given to fanciful flights, but he found mad grandeur in the concept that cities would be made funeral pyres to accomplish the invaders' purpose. This was a night when irresistibly wild poetry rode at sea.

He remembered the instant their craft struck the sand-bar—the riveting smash of machine-gun fire against the steel door—and the paralysing stab of terror he had known, a knife-thrust of pain. But he dropped into the water and the pain vanished; from that moment he had known only the sense of rising exhilaration which still gripped him now.

He remembered, on the beach, how there had been delay. His Company Commander, Major Bunny Bazin, for whom he felt great affection, was, none the less, constitutionally incapable of reading a map and Adam had to work out their position. At last they advanced inland: through gardens and vineyards, over alien country a-reek with the fumes of Mediterranean sun and sea. There was more delay while they rescued an American paratrooper called Kogan who had been dropped the night before; but then their advance continued—until they reached this forest and glimpsed the outlines of Castello Donato, their objective.

Now, in the parkland, a single bird proclaimed its solo note. Adam's glance flashed along his line of serious-faced men; he could hear the beating of his pulse. Once they emerged from the trees, he knew, there would be no time for anything except a straight charge ahead, to smash inside the courtyard of the castle.

The trees were thinning; then, ahead—thirty yards of open ground. A pause for a fraction of a second——

'Let's go!' roared Adam.

Bayonets and Bren guns flashed from the hip. Every man started to charge across the open ground.

In the same moment the iron gates were flung wide before them. A troop of cavalry, sabres flashing in the sun, came galloping out to charge against the line of infantry. For an unbelieving instant Adam watched while a huge captain of dragoons raised his sabre to cut him down. But before he could even lift his tommy-gun the dragoon went flying from his horse, his sabre tumbling through a flashing arc in the sunlight. Krasnick's Bren gun was firing in short, methodical bursts; under Sergeant Mitchell's expert guidance all the weapons of the reserve section were firing; and in a matter of seconds the cavalry charge was finished. Riderless horses whinnied and kicked their heels in terror.

Ten Platoon's own charge was halted, too. In a daze the men tried to dodge the flying hooves of the horses. Then one soldier slipped to the ground and regarded his bullet-smashed wrist in amazement. A moment later every man was on the ground, crawling forward, firing back at the enemy in the courtyard.

Through the legs of plunging horses Adam caught sight of the Italian infantry as they knelt to fire. Corporal Bell, followed closely by Kogan, the U.S. paratrooper, raced to cover under the castle wall. Two grenades arched high in the air; there was an instantaneous explosion, then clouds of white phosphorous smoke blotted the courtyard and castle from view.

'Come on!' Adam shouted as he ran. 'Everybody into the castle!'

The next few minutes were smoke and shouting and confusion. It seemed a miracle to Adam that so few men were killed or wounded. The Italians only wanted to surrender, but his own men, not knowing that fact, went charging into the smoke and kicking horses, firing at everything that moved. Adam realized at once that the chief danger lay in his own men shooting one another. 'Cease fire!' he roared from the centre of the cobble-stoned courtyard; then he went running about knocking rifle muzzles into the air. The smoke lifted at last and the firing sputtered out. Sergeant Mitchell appeared from somewhere. Stolidly he began to muster a file of prisoners against the stone wall.

Adam stood still and let the action eddy round him. The sun was hot on his face, he wanted a cigarette badly; but there were urgent matters to attend to before the position was secured.

He was still collecting his thoughts when Kogan, the U.S. paratrooper, stopped before him. Kogan jerked a negligent thumb over his shoulder. 'Here's the big brass,' he announced. Behind him, splendid in blue and gold, stood a stout Italian colonel of dragoons. The Colonel shuffled his feet on the cobble-stones, he bobbed and performed a curtsy. His beet-red face dripped with sweat; he wore a wide, ingratiating smile. Adam regarded this sight with astonishment; for a few moments he was unaware of the silver sabre that was extended for him to receive. But then he looked at the sword, he looked in the Colonel's face—like an anxious egg poaching in the sunshine, he thought—he looked at the grinning Kogan, and suddenly he felt an irresistible urge to laugh: he wanted to split his sides laughing. His head went back, his nostrils quivered.

15

But in the same instant he realized that this was a precious moment, too rich to dull in retrospect, and that a certain standard was demanded of himself. Lieutenant Adam choked a little, but his chin came down, and he spoke in the clearest, noblest voice of magnanimity. 'Colonel,' he stated, 'as a brave enemy, it is my desire that you retain your personal weapon.'

With a grave inclination of his head Adam turned and marched quickly away.

4

THE blaze of distant Pachino lighted the night. Several miles at sea the command ship lay idle, its screws just perceptibly churning into the water. Honorary/Captain Philip Doorn, Chaplain of the 2nd Rifles, stood on deck in the darkness. His eyes reflected the flames as he searched longingly, passionately, for some sight of the assault boats and the men they contained.

God go with them, Padre Doorn was praying. His soul was in tumult tonight; he ached with restless, rioting emotions. In appearance he was tall and gaunt, with intense smouldering black eyes. He bore all the outward accoutrements of an avenging prophet, but this was deceptive, since in fact he was a man at peace with himself and his God. Tonight, however, as he stood in the darkness, hands clenched on the ship's rail, his appearance befitted his mood. Go with them, God, he prayed. Those men—*boys* rather: those boys he had shaken hands with before they swung over the side and down the scrambling nets to their small craft— go gently with them, God; spare them this night. . . .

It was sacrilege to think that those strong young bodies, created in God's image, might be smashed or maimed, flung lifeless on a Sicilian beach. In the whites of their eyes tonight he had seen their closeness to God; these were dedicated men, these were crusaders. . . . Like young Adam now—in every respect John Adam was a man. John was his friend, and it was Adam's platoon he had accompanied through the darkness to their rendezvous with the assault boat. At this moment, almost heretically, Padre Doorn longed to be at Adam's side. Despite his cloth, despite his allegiance to the Supreme General, the Padre longed to know the touch of steel in his hand. He longed to storm the beaches with

16

these young valiants, first to set foot on liberated Europe: these true crusaders. . . .

From heaven Padre Doorn lowered his gaze to the dark waters. Dear God, he prayed in the darkness: make me worthy; make me brave to march beside them; help me keep their faith firm. . . .

Behind him, with a total disregard for the blackout, the wardroom door clanged open against the steel bulkhead. A gigantic figure stooped and emerged on deck. In the centre of a moon-massive face a cigar glowed redly; the figure moved deliberately across the deck.

'Ah, Padre——'

Brigadier Ian Kildare announced his presence. He stood affably close, and allowed the rail to support the weight of his six-foot-four-inch, two-hundred-and-fifty-pound body.

In the darkness Padre Doorn assumed an unseen and ludicrous attitude of attention. He was never at ease in the presence of this man. There were things about the Army, he conceded in moments of private despair, that his training at Diocesan College and his few years of pastoral work simply did not equip him to understand —and the chief of all these mysteries was Brigadier Ian Kildare. The man's leadership ability was unquestioned, unmistakable, but equally so was his—ah, coarseness. Worst of all, however, the Padre could not understand the kind of faith that moved the Brigadier; he only knew that it differed radically from his own friendly relationship with God; and it was this fact that made him more nervous than anything else.

The Brigadier drew on his cigar; the glow lighted his jowls and bull-like neck. Perched jauntily on his head the Padre could see the familiar Balmoral cap, with its green knob and badge—the silver badge of the Hart Rampant, symbol of the Scottish Borderers, now a-wink in the flamelight of Pachino. Although this headgear was strictly against regulations the Brigadier never wore any other.

This was a tiny part of the whole mystery which the Padre could never comprehend. It appeared—so informants in various officers' messes had tried to explain to the Padre—that, despite his rank, Brigadier Kildare was not a regular Army officer. He had not attended the Royal Military College, and therefore did not possess one of the mystic numbers which qualified the recipient for lifetime membership in a sort of mutual-benefit club. Instead, in civilian life the Brigadier had been president of a lumber company in Vancouver, where he devoted his evenings to the command of a reserve Army unit known as the Scottish Borderers. This unit was quite without distinction of any kind; for one thing, it had never even been called on active service. But—so the Padre was told—since Ian Kildare was its Commanding Officer, it became *ipso facto* a regiment with noble and honoured traditions—and beware the man who spoke the contrary! Major Bazin, one of the Rifles' company commanders, and another mystery in his own right, had once tried to sum it up for him. Brigadier Kildare, he told the Padre, exalted the Scottish Borderers as a subtle means of humbling the regular officers under him and infuriating those above. Then Major Bazin smiled gently at the Padre's puzzlement and told him not to worry if it didn't make sense; so many things did not after all.

One thing, at least, which the Padre understood was the crushing burden of responsibility that this man bore. As they stood at the rail together, in this moment of crisis, the Padre could imagine the stern look on the face beside him, those blue eyes clouded in sombre reflection of the next terrible decision to be made.

The Brigadier tapped his cigar ash upon the rail. 'Got 'em by the balls, Padre?' he inquired courteously.

As always, the Padre was struck dumb by this salutation. The Brigadier waited in companionable silence while the Padre cleared his throat and made mumbling noises. After several seconds of such noises the Padre knew he must speak and he decided to communicate some of the genuine excitement seething inside him. 'Have you seen Pachino on fire, sir?' the Padre asked.

Brigadier Kildare laughed, in excellent good humour. 'That's only the first, Padre. Soon we'll have all Sicily burning. Then, in good season—Rome; and after that, Berlin.'

The Brigadier puffed contentment through his cigar.

Behind them a voice coughed. The Padre recognized the nervous and customary greeting of his Commanding Officer, Lieutenant-Colonel Charles Dodd, who was standing, steel-helmeted, in the darkness.

The Brigadier turned and glanced toward the new arrival. He did not seem pleased with what he made out in the darkness because his voice bristled with sudden irritation: 'Charley—for God's sake stop worrying! You're going to get the Rifles ashore without a casualty.'

As always, the Brigadier spoke as though from some profound and superhuman depth of knowledge. It was impossible to doubt the calm assurance of the Brigadier's voice, and now despite themselves both men felt some of their anxiety lifted.

All three stood at the rail together and watched the tell-tale flash and thunder on the shore. Pachino was now irretrievably ablaze. The explosions on shore thudded through the water and vibrated the steel plates of the ship. Here on deck at sea they had the illusion that the land lifted and fell each time that it was hit.

The Brigadier cocked his head in appreciation. 'There's music for you,' he said. 'Fifteen-inchers—from the monitors.' Overhead two small cities seemed to be ripping holes in the sky.

Colonel Dodd's voice remained tense and anxious. 'Their ack-ack seems to have stopped.'

'Of course.' The Brigadier nodded in the darkness. 'The defences are saturated. That's Phase One, successfully completed.'

Colonel Dodd pushed himself away from the rail and peered unhappily down at the choppy Mediterranean. 'My headquarters boat is loaded, sir,' he announced without conviction.

'All right.'

'Think I'd better push.'

'All right.'

The Brigadier remained staring out over the water and still Colonel Dodd made no move to go. He stood as though rooted to the deck. Padre Doorn understood this particular mystery, at least. Charley Dodd was an insurance broker from Toronto, an excellent desk man who might have made a good staff officer. Instead, however, the dictates of war had made him commander of an infantry battalion; and Charley Dodd was simply not the man for midnight adventures on a tossing sea. The Padre could visualize the vexed look of indecision which must now possess his face.

'Sir—' Padre Doorn took advantage of the lengthening pause to address his Commanding Officer. 'May I go in the first boat?'

Colonel Dodd's response was curt and immediate. 'No,' he said. 'Your place is with rear headquarters.'

The Brigadier swung massively from the rail. 'Never mind, Padre,' he said. 'I'll save you a place beside me. Now Charley—for Christ's sake shake the lead out and get cracking.'

When Colonel Dodd had departed at last the Brigadier clapped a hand on the Padre's shoulder and pulled him companionably close at the rail. He was fairly rumbling with good spirits. 'You know, Padre,' he declared, 'in one important respect our two jobs are really much alike: you give the troops God—and *I* give them hell!'

The Brigadier's huge body shook with laughter for several seconds; then gradually the sound petered out. The two men stood silent again in the darkness, and now the Brigadier was breathing heavily, fretfully, as though undergoing a complete and unexpected change of mood. After another few moments the stub of his cigar red-traced down to the water. 'And before they're finished,' the Brigadier added, in a sombre tone, 'maybe God will give the poor buggers hell, too.'

The Padre was astonished; he looked up quickly. Objectionable though the words might be, this was a new tone: one he had never heard before. Perhaps this was his chance to penetrate the mystery at last, to speak to this man, to make communication. . . . He searched in his mind for the words; and he started to open his mouth.

But the Brigadier's hand had dropped from his shoulder. Already the hulking figure was half-way to the ward-room door. 'Got to get back to my bloody radio,' Brigadier Kildare explained, and stooped to go inside.

5

THE little world of Castello Donato was secure. Adam felt proud of the terse message conveyed in his first situation-report. 'Objective Snug,' this report ran. 'Five enemy killed, twenty-seven P.W., including cavalry. Own casualties: two wounded.' Elated, Major Bazin had signalled congratulations from his rear position.

The 'castle' turned out to be a group of stone farm buildings, its five-foot walls the only evidence of a war-like past. Adam busied himself for some minutes attending to the wounded, checking ammunition, and assigning arcs of fire to the sections outside the walls.

At last he sat down on the cobble-stones. Gratefully he eased his equipment off; he leaned back in the sun and lighted his first cigarette. The courtyard had a busy housekeeping air: fires sputtered under mess-tins, the wounded were getting fussy attention. Adam pulled deeply on his cigarette; he glowed with a warmth of virtue and content.

Sergeant Mitchell walked over, rifle and bandolier of ammunition slung on one shoulder. His rugged face was a beam of satisfaction. 'I've got news,' said Mitchell; and grinning he sat down at Adam's side.

Outside the courtyard there was a single rifle shot, a pause, then another. Quickly Adam started to his feet but Sergeant Mitchell's big hand detained him. 'It's only Krasnick,' Mitchell explained. 'He's shooting the wounded horses.'

'Oh.'

Adam sank back on the cobble-stones again.

'One of the cellars,' Mitchell went on, 'is full of wine. Nothing but vats of *vino* from floor to ceiling. And—it's not bad.'

Adam looked at him sharply. Mitchell's report was delivered in a detached, objective tone, but it was plain that he waited to see his platoon commander's reaction.

'Well,' Adam said, after a thoughtful pause. 'Let's go and see.' The two men stood up.

The cellar was cool, sunk in the depths of the earth, lighted by sunshine which filtered through a latticed door. A lance-corporal called Harrison, noted as the platoon's only teetotaller, stood before a vat of *vino* with a tin cup. Beside him, squatting on his heels, was a wizened-up little Italian, and it was plain that this old man had elected himself wine-steward-in-chief. It was also plain that men of the platoon were passing and pausing at the vat in relays. Well, Adam thought then: why not? Every man in the platoon had certainly earned a cup of wine today. He sat down on a cask and accepted the tin cup from Harrison's hand. The cool air of the cellar washed soothingly on his sweat-encrusted body.

Adam swirled the wine in his cup. One crimson drop spilled out, splashed on his bare knee and ran down to his boots and puttees. Adam tasted. The wine was tart and earthy, rich with full-bodied grape, cooler than any drink he had ever known. He put his head back and drained the cup.

The little Italian bobbed before him and scraped his boots on the cellar floor. *'Buona?'* he shrilled, peering into Adam's face as though seized by some frenzy of doubt. *'Buona, signore?'* he pleaded.

Adam seemed to reflect. Then he handed the cup back to Harrison. *'Buona,'* he pronounced. 'Let's have some more.'

Time seemed to be suspended in that earthy cellar. Lieutenant Adam and Sergeant Mitchell sat on the ground with their backs against a cask; they sipped from the tin cup and they talked about their first battle, their first day at war. It was the calm, contented talk of competent men satisfied with a good day's job of work. Adam gazed proudly, benignly, as each of his sweat-stained men stepped up to the vat of *vino*. And after a little he began to see this cellar populated by a new breed of bravest men: warriors—soldiers drinking the wine of conquerors. . . . Each passing moment he filled with a greater warmth of peace and contentment. He was also filling, quite rapidly, with *vino rosso*.

6

B UON A P A R T E could not have looked more imperial, Montgomery more lordly, nor MacArthur more godly. Brigadier Ian Kildare stepped from the Landing Craft, Infantry, into two feet of water without a glance for his footing. Three implacable steps and he stood planted on the shore of Sicily. His blue eyes flashed in the sunlight; his glance over the beach was imperious, yet judicious, as though he had still to decide if this land lay ordered in the condition he had prescribed.

Prosecution of the campaign was suspended while Brigadier Kildare paused to make survey. The members of his staff had to halt behind him; this meant they stood in a damp semicircle, water lapping over their boot tops, waiting patiently to proceed. On the Brigadier's Balmoral cap the silver Hart Rampant glittered like an unsheathed sword in the sunlight. It remained only for a gillie to rush forward and plant a standard in the sand. There should have been the skirling of bagpipes and the clashing of claymores.

At last the Brigadier stirred. Padre Doorn who stood one pace to the rear thought that he heard the words 'So be it,' uttered in

22

a solemn tone, but the Brigadier may only have been clearing his throat. The Padre was overjoyed at finding himself here..As a member of the Brigadier's party, instead of staying with rear headquarters as Colonel Dodd had ordered, he would get forward to the fighting troops much faster.

The Brigadier strode firmly across the sand to a track where two jeeps with engines running stood waiting. His staff officers squelched wetly behind him.

Brigadier Kildare hoisted his big frame into the front seat of a jeep. He regarded his Brigade Major, a melancholy little man named Hunter.

'I shall go at once to the Rifles' forward company,' the Brigadier announced. 'Get Brigade Headquarters established and report to me by wireless.'

He settled back and laid a cocked tommy-gun across his ham-like knees. With any luck, the Brigadier was thinking, today I shall earn the first of my D.S.O.s. The jeep started forward and the staff officers jumped to attention. Their wrists banged painfully against their foreheads in a smart and prescribed salute known privately inside the Brigade as the 'Hart Rampant Special'.

7

PRIVATE-FIRST-CLASS Joseph Kogan was a happy soldier. But he was a happy soldier with a conscience. These Canadians were good guys, he'd had a good day with them, and he was feeling really fine, but now—before the darkness fell—it was time to set forth and find his paratroop buddies of the 505th Combat Team. And after much difficult thought he had at last decided on his method of progression over the Italian countryside. In the courtyard of the castle he was busy adjusting the saddle on the Italian colonel's white charger. It was not easy though: for one thing he had never before ridden a horse; and also, for some reason, his fingers seemed unaccountably clumsy with the straps and fastenings. None the less he hummed a tune while he worked.

Lieutenant Adam emerged from the door of the wine cellar and walked over to stand beside him. 'Ah, Kogan,' he observed pleasantly. 'Off for a ride?'

Adam wore his helmet and had his tommy-gun slung on one shoulder. He was on his way to inspect the section positions in the half-hour remaining before last light. This was the period of stand-to when every soldier manned his fighting post.

Kogan straightened and he beamed at Adam affectionately. The big charger stayed placid under his hands. This was a damn good lootenant, Kogan thought to himself, a good man to have back with the combat team. If only there was some tangible way he could show his appreciation for this officer's worth— Suddenly he was overwhelmed by the immense generosity he had in his power to dispense. 'Lootenant,' Kogan said, 'I will wait. *You* take the horse, and ride it round on your inspection.'

At once Adam perceived the logic of the proposal, and saw how appropriate it would be to use the captured mount for this purpose. He was moved by the huge sacrifice Kogan was making on his behalf. 'Thanks, Kogan,' he said simply. 'Help me up.'

But once Adam was mounted in the saddle the charger seemed to sway with his weight and he suddenly realized how far away the ground was. A pin-wheel of dizziness went off; it took every effort of will to maintain his seat. Kogan tugged at the horse's reins, and Adam began to feel ill as well as dizzy. A new and startling realization swirled into his mind: My God, he thought, with sudden dismay, that *vino*—I've gone and got myself utterly plastered. . . .

8

R IFLEMAN Jones was the sentry posted at the castle gates. Sergeant Mitchell had placed him there deliberately: on the side away from the enemy where, presumably, he could cause least harm.

Rifleman Jones was known in the platoon as Jonesy or young Jones, and it was quite accidental that he *looked* the ideal soldier. He was a handsome boy with a strong, well-muscled body, a flawless blue gaze, and a shock of golden, corn-bright hair. He possessed a permanent smile—like a perennial grown from seed.

Unfortunately his flawless blue gaze could appear unfocused at times. Jonesy could look at an object as though he perceived something quite different from the thing regarded by any other person. The medical officers, of course, should never have passed him in the beginning; probably they were deceived by his superb physique and appearance. The fact was that Jonesy's mind had

24

simply not ripened at the same rate as his body; he retained the innocence of a child; he trusted everything in the world, and he would do anything he was told.

He was still a good enough soldier, however, as long as someone did tell him what to do. Long ago he had ceased to be the butt of the platoon; instead each man accepted the fact that Jonesy was theirs and that he had to be looked after.

Today no one had thought to tell Jonesy that sentry duty in the face of the enemy differed in any respect from the type of guard duty that had been drilled into him at barracks in England. Consequently he wore full battle-order and he stood in rigid at-ease position in front of the iron gates. Sergeant Mitchell's last words had been: 'Come and tell me at once if you see anything move along that road.' Jonesy had nodded his handsome head, flashed his blue eyes intelligently, and forgotten the instructions at once because he had never been issued their like before.

Now he watched with interest as two jeeps raced toward him through spiralling tunnels of dust. Slow gears of thought began to mesh in his mind; he was working out the mechanics of his proper military greeting.

In the front jeep with Brigadier Kildare rode Major Bazin and the Brigade Intelligence Officer. Padre Doorn had managed to install himself with the Signals Officer in the second jeep. These were the first vehicles to get this far forward and they moved at high speed to defeat the aim of enemy gunners.

The Brigadier's jeep squealed to a stop in front of the stalwart-looking sentry. There was a wild glint in Jonesy's eyes, but his mouth was grim with determination. Click, and his boots snapped together, rifle hard into his side. One, two, three, and he sloped arms. Pause—One, two, again, and he presented arms. Jonesy had done this a thousand times before on the parade square at Aldershot.

'Hah,' said the Brigadier, turning to Major Bazin in the back of the jeep. 'See that? A damn fine soldier!'

Major Bazin felt the sweat prickling his face. He knew Jonesy well: he was the last man in the Company he would have selected for this present duty.

'You, boy,' commanded the Brigadier. 'What's your name?'

Jonesy remained locked in the present-arms position. The

Brigadier began to frown as long seconds of silence ticked by. Then, suddenly, Rifleman Jones was galvanized into action. Down his rifle smashed to the on-guard position, bayonet point quivering within an inch of the Brigadier's face. 'Desert Rats!' snarled Jonesy, in a voice of most blood-curdling menace.

'Eh?'

The Brigadier pulled his head back.

Major Bazin closed his eyes.

For day after day on shipboard the challenge and reply had been drilled and re-drilled into Jonesy's head. Sergeant Mitchell had made him memorize it. 'Desert Rats!' was the challenge, the reply was——

'Kill Italians,' said the Brigadier, with less than the usual conviction in his voice.

But as they drove into the courtyard the Brigadier was smiling again. 'Must compliment you, Bazin—really, you've got your men at a fine fighting pitch. What *is* that fellow's name?'

'Jones, sir.'

'Good. I'll remember that.'

Adam, Kogan and Sergeant Mitchell stood grouped about the white charger. Mitchell was first to see the jeep and he jolted his elbow into Adam's ribs. Adam took one look and reacted. 'Number Ten Platoon,' he shouted. ''Shun!' Every man in the courtyard, including a number of interested Italian prisoners, jumped to rigid attention. Adam's wrist banged to his forehead and hit upon the edge of his helmet. He faced the jeep, his eyes focusing on the Brigadier's moon-like face. 'Sah!' Adam shouted, with the full power of his lungs.

In addition to his prescribed salute the Brigadier made it understood that the most soldierly acknowledgement of authority, as demonstrated in the drill-halls of the Scottish Borderers, was the word 'Sah!' delivered in a loud, decisive tone.

The Brigadier unloaded his massive frame from the jeep, his face beaming. 'Splendid,' he said. 'Splendid. You have all done magnificent work today. . . .' Then the white charger in the centre of the group finally registered in his mind. His eyes opened wide; eagerly Brigadier Kildare advanced upon Adam and the horse.

But the Signals Officer stood importuning at his side. 'Urgent message from Division, sir.'

The Brigadier took the piece of paper and read. The smile slipped from his face to be replaced by a frown of utmost gravity. He looked up and gazed sternly round the courtyard, still unaware that the most breathlessly interested members of his audience wore Italian uniforms. 'Men,' the Brigadier proclaimed, 'I want you to be the first to hear this message from Division. Message reads as follows: "Warn all units dig in. Expect German counter-attacks during night." '

On needed occasions Brigadier Kildare was an actor; and now his air of gravity was quite assumed. In point of fact he knew this message to be rubbish—a matter of Division getting itself in the usual flap. *He* knew that if any Germans were within striking distance they would already have struck. And, as it happened, the Brigadier was right: he usually was in matters of this kind. Still, he thought now, the Brigade would have to dig in real earnest soon enough—they might as well get some useful practice tonight.

Again he allowed his good spirits to emerge. 'Get out your entrenching tools,' the Brigadier cried, in a tone of gay invitation. He turned and peered toward Lieutenant Adam expectantly. Sergeant Mitchell suddenly made off in the direction of the gate.

'Yes, sir,' Adam answered automatically.

His eyelids were heavy; he was finding it difficult to keep his eyes propped open. Major Bazin regarded him with an unmistakable look of disfavour.

'Come, Bazin.' The Brigadier turned back to his jeep.

'Sir—' Adam rallied himself for a final effort. 'When the Germans come—we'll get 'em by the balls!'

The Brigadier chuckled. His body rumbled with huge appreciation. 'Good fellow,' he cried; and he patted Major Bazin's shoulder, as though to confirm his affection for Ten Platoon and all its good fighting men.

When the jeep passed through the castle gates again Rifleman Jones had disappeared. In his place Lance-Corporal Harrison stood in a most decorous position of attention.

9

AND they dug. Every man in the Brigade dug. With nothing but the short, back-breaking entrenching tools they wore on their belts they broke savagely into the hard Sicilian soil.

The men of Ten Platoon dug deeper and harder than any. They sweated the *vino* they had drunk through their pores and back into the ground from which it had sprung; they rained the ground with weariness. They dug through stand-to, and while a carnival red moon scaled the sky. No man needed urging—because the Germans were coming.

The Italians did not matter. They were happy conscripts who came blinking from their holes, glad to welcome the new overlords who would replace the hated *tedesci*. The Italians were pure comic-opera; already they were fond of them.

But the Germans—the mere name was enough.

The Germans were the men they had come these thousands of miles to meet. Unsmiling men whose faces they knew only by photographs: grim, unrelenting faces framed in coal-scuttle helmets or peaked baseball caps; lean, sun-tanned professionals, superbly arrogant. Clad in paratroop smocks, or camouflage-daubed tunics; driving half-track vehicles or ominous square-hulled tanks, towing their 88-mm. guns, manning their deadly mortars—the Germans, the professionals, the tough guys. . . .

They dug because the Germans were coming.

At last, in the loud moonlight, with their trenches knee deep, the order came to move. Men came out of their trenches cursing; blisters were broken as hands fumbled in the dark to fasten tools back on their web equipment.

Now the Germans were *not* coming. Corps and Division had established their headquarters ashore and realized what Brigadier Kildare had known from the beginning: there were no Germans within fifty miles; it was therefore essential to press forward at all speed while opportunity still offered. From every point of the beach-head perimeter battalions and companies of infantry began to group themselves; ribboned into snake-like columns they surged along every road leading north.

10

HONORARY/CAPTAIN Philip Doorn, Chaplain of the 2nd Rifles, marched at the rear of Battalion Headquarters. Even in this third hour of marching he felt no weariness. Instead he found pleasure in the cadenced ring of his steel-shod boots on the road, in the eager response of all his muscles.

Back at the Start Point there had been immense confusion: units piling up on one another, guides running about, officers poring over maps by flashlight, company sergeant-majors swearing at their men to get the hell on or off the road. No one paid the Padre any attention, and he took advantage of that fact to place himself here where he would be safely out of his Colonel's way. Lieutenant-Colonel Dodd, he knew, was not at all pleased about the Padre's forward expedition with the Brigadier.

Ahead there was a muffled curse as two men bumped together and the Padre smiled to himself. When men blasphemed in his presence they were embarrassed, quick to apologize; but the Padre only felt touched at such innocence. He believed that he knew these men well: he was not being at all fanciful when he thought of them as crusaders. They were here in a just cause, doing God's work. It was the basis of the Padre's faith that man had God inside himself, that he expressed God by being good; and a man who was true to his cause was true to God. At church parades the Padre had often wanted to tell the men these things, but good sense assured him they were better left unexpressed.

Now there was silence on the line of march; breath was too precious to be wasted. The only sound was the rhythmic beat of boots on the roadbed, the occasional clank of rifle or bayonet against mess-tin. The Padre felt a deep and grateful sense of kinship with the marching men around him. It came as a joy to share the corporate pain of marching, to suffer the same degree of ache and fatigue.

Now they were mounting into the range of coastal hills and each step demanded extra effort. The road spiralled; they marched through the first smashed town, in the same silence, without stopping. In places men had to break step in order to pick their way over scattered debris. Shutters and bricks lay in the street; moonlight peeped through a pierced wall. There was a reek of high explosive in the streets, the sickly sweet smell of spilled *vino,* or something freshly dead.

The Padre tried to summon up pity, or even the regret he had expected to feel, but he could not succeed. This was war, after all, he was thinking, and in war towns have to be destroyed.

In the darkness Padre Doorn found himself flushing, ashamed at his own lack of outrage. It had been the same at that Castello

Donato place today. In the first moment, when he saw the dead horses and the dead Italian soldiers in the courtyard, he had known a quick choke of apology. But next he saw John Adam, his friend, standing with his captured charger, surrounded by his victory-flushed men, and admiration swelled inside him to the exclusion of everything else. The affair became something exhilarating. This attack, he knew, would occupy an honoured place in the Regiment's history: the day a platoon of the 2nd Rifles routed a squadron of cavalry, and captured a castle.

No, the Padre told himself, he could not be a hypocrite and pretend regret. They were all here on God's errand, and they were doing men's work. These were exciting times, and he was glad to be living them.

The Padre squared his shoulders and leaned his weight forward. They were through the town. Now they were starting to climb a forested hillside.

11

WHEN can I decently get into my jeep? Lieutenant-Colonel Dodd was wondering, as he limped bitterly along. I'm tired now and each additional damned-fool step is taking more out of me. It's all very well to talk about setting an example, but I've done that already: I've marched with my men for the last three hours and shared all their discomfort. And now, like any intelligent, sensible commander I should conserve my strength. I should get into that jeep and start working on my administration: bivouac arrangements, food and ammunition supply, tomorrow's order of march; and a thousand other urgent matters. If only that Brigadier would drive by and see me here marching, *then* I could get into my jeep. . . .

He limped ahead in pinched-lip silence. Beside him Ramsay, his Adjutant, had difficulty matching his erratic step. The trouble was, Colonel Dodd decided in a flash of insight, that Brigadier Kildare knew him too well. He recognized his administrative competence, his grasp of detail—but at the same time the Brigadier doubted his endurance and his power to command under stress. Worst of all, he had to agree with the Brigadier's estimate: he should *not* be here. He should be in some 'A' or 'Q' job back at Division, or better still, at a static headquarters. This forced march into alien country on a dark night: the whole affair was simply too—disorganized. His mind liked orderly patterns; he wanted all the given factors of a situation arranged and classified before he plucked out the carefully prepared decision.

His teeth were clenched tight; his feet were two burning localities of pain. He could visualize the sores, blisters—even blood, perhaps—on the soles of his feet. And a commander, he told himself angrily, forfeits reasoning ability when he is physically exhausted. If only that goddamned Brigadier would drive past . . .

Suddenly Colonel Dodd stepped out of the moving column. Captain Ramsay collided with two men behind him as he scrambled to reach his side. At the edge of the road Commanding Officer and Adjutant watched the plodding files of soldiers march by. 'Ramsay,' Colonel Dodd ordered at last. 'Ca^l\ my jeep forward.'

12

THE next few days were a blur of tortured, aching marching.

On the east coast, near Catania, the British attack was resisted viciously; in the west the Germans withdrew slowly before the advancing Americans. The time was ideal therefore for the Canadians to smash north, up the middle of the island, and penetrate the enemy's centre. Speed was essential; but lacking vehicles they had to push painfully ahead by forced marches.

These inland mountains were a merciless furnace; the sun split the stones and made the stubble crackle. The soldiers were bleached by dust, stifled by heat and clogged by thirst. At last they outdistanced the flow of supplies from the beach-head, and it was necessary to stop for two blessed days of rest and sleep; bleeding feet were eased out of cracked boots for the first time.

When they set out again they were leaner and harder; they knew what to expect from this burning wasteland. Useless equipment was junked. Each man became a self-contained unit, pared down to fighting trim, his water-bottle the most important single piece of equipment.

Tanks and guns and trucks began to move among the columns of infantry. The whole mass surged ahead, reckless and eager to make first contact with the enemy. But still, the only enemy they met were occasional bands of Italian soldiers, marching in parallel directions, attempting to go home. The vast bulk of the Italian

Army in Sicily streamed happily into prisoner-of-war cages; but there were some, of sterner breed, who elected the long march home and were prepared to fight if anyone tried to stop them. These men were known as deserters; they threw their uniforms away but they kept their rifles. Some of them killed, and in turn were killed.

The invaders marched on, from one harsh mountain ridge to the next, coming ever closer, and wondering if the Germans ever would appear.

In fact, of course, the Germans were already there. At this moment advanced detachments were mining roads and siting ambushes. These professionals set about their work with calm, unhurried competence. First, bridges and vulnerable road points were blown. Then the 88s were sited to ambush the oncoming tanks or armoured cars. These vehicles would be permitted to turn the elbow of a mountain road, the first and last tanks would be picked off, and the others blasted in succession. If infantry led the plan was just as simple: the point men would be hit by concentrated machine-gun fire, the following troops would have to deploy into cover already registered by zeroed-in mortars. The Germans were there all right, and waiting.

Brigadier Kildare observed the first ambush that was sprung. Across a mountain valley he focused his binoculars; his eyes recorded the sight of a flaming scout car; but at once his mind leaped to locations on the map ten and twenty kilometres ahead. It was there, he knew, that the real battles would begin.

13

HIGH on a hillside Lieutenant John Adam shared the only bush in Sicily with a lizard. Man and lizard had come to recognize the sun as their mutual enemy, the bush as a common friend, and they lived together companionably. Farther down this reverse slope the men of Ten Platoon were digging slit trenches. An occasional stick of black explosions parading down the crest urged them on with their work.

Adam lay on his side and peered downhill, searching anxiously for the water detail. At the foot of the hill the stubble of a once-yellow wheat field was burned with black, ugly patches. In the full fury of noonday sun they had attacked across this fire-scorched space.

After more minutes of watching, Adam observed three figures toiling through the stubble: two civilians, joined by a wooden yoke on their shoulders, with an escorting soldier behind. These were big Jim and little Joe, their two Italian volunteers, followed by Corporal DiCicco; and now the trio paused a moment before commencing the long trek uphill. Even at this distance sight of the wooden cask swinging from its yoke brought an impotent spasm of saliva to Adam's mouth. A drink, Adam thought then, simply a deep unending drink of water—and man had heaven in his grasp.... At last he forced his glance away.

By raising his eyes two degrees Adam looked down the muzzles of a troop of twenty-five-pounders in the field beyond, and the guns chose that moment to fire. Concussion shook the hillside; the lizard flopped from underneath the bush, its eyes beaded red with indignation. Quickly Adam rolled onto his belly and reached for his binoculars. He wanted to observe the strike of shells on the village across the valley. That village, and the cemetery which guarded its approaches, was where the Germans were installed in force.

On the same hillside, bush-shirt wrapped round his head like a turban, Sergeant Mitchell also watched the approaching water carriers. He watched with satisfaction and proprietary pride. The two impressed Italians had been his idea.

Yesterday, when they were ready to move off, young Jones was missing. Mitchell found him—after a blasphemous five minutes— sunning himself behind a stone fence. Sitting on each side of him, chewing ravenously at the hard-tack and bully beef they had been given, were two young Italians clad in ragged civilian clothing. Instinctively Mitchell swung up his rifle and took the first pressure. He knew they could only be deserters, and the order from Division was quite clear: every deserter, as a suspected sniper, was to be shot on sight. But Mitchell looked in those terror-struck faces; he estimated their years—twenty, perhaps, the same as Jonesy; he saw the little cardboard suit-case that lay between them. . . . What the hell, he thought then: they're only boys, kids really, and they could provide the platoon with useful labour. His rifle dropped and the two Italians came clutching at his ankles with

33

dog-like gratitude. He fell them in at the rear of the platoon, and gave them a load of extra rations and ammunition to carry. Both youths had olive-soft complexions and white, flashing grins; one was short and one was tall. At once, therefore, somebody named them big Jim and little Joe.

Lieutenant Adam made no objection. No one mentioned the word 'deserter'; and in any event the men of the platoon had more sympathy for the so-called deserters than for those who occupied the P.W. cages. These men, at least, were doing their damnedest to get home; and it took guts to try to pass through the German lines. By the end of the day the two boys had been adopted by the platoon. And now Sergeant Mitchell watched with satisfaction as they came toiling up the hillside with their load of water.

From his high perch Adam kept his binoculars searching the village and the cemetery for signs of enemy movement. Soon the battalion was going to launch a full-scale attack on those objectives; there they would come to grips with the German infantry for the first time. After every attack thus far they had found nothing but sour German souvenirs on the objective: spent cartridge casings and empty mortar boxes. The Germans stayed just long enough to inflict maximum casualties, and then withdrew untouched.

Adam stared at that village with its hidden horde of enemy, and he felt a slow pulse of anticipation begin to beat inside him. He was angry and eager. He burned with impatience to try himself against this enemy; and it was the same, he knew, for every other Canadian soldier on the hillside. They were sick of marching and skirmishing; they wanted to get at the Germans and fight. That was why they had come here after all.

Ever since the landing Adam had been swept away on a flooding tide of exhilaration. He had never felt more alive; until now he had never known his senses fully engaged by life. There had been that cup of wine back in the captured castle, the first Sicilian dawn, strange fruits and purple mountain tops, the reek of high explosive, smashed towns at midnight, the cheering populace—all these things, and the hard competence of his manhood proved each day. And always there was the possibility of death lurking round each corner, close enough to make doubly precious each moment of living.

34

Adam looked the red-eyed lizard in the face. He felt almost drunk with the day's bright sunshine. 'Bring on the Germans,' he wanted to yell at his lizard. 'Bring them on—that's what we're here for!'

But then he laughed at his intensity and shook his head to clear it. He picked up the binoculars again. Each little cemetery vault was painted in dazzling designs and colours, resembling bathing-huts gaily clustered on a beach of green. He watched as the 25-pound shells went marching in among the vaults, blowing graves and bones into the wind no doubt; but still adding a gay, Saturday-afternoon-at-the-fair appearance to the scene.

He drank deeply from his freshly-filled water-bottle. If this is war, Adam thought, then maybe the Germans have something, maybe the Germans are right. Maybe it is good to be young and to be at war. . . .

14

MAJOR Bunny Bazin strolled back from the cemetery whistling. He had the face of a benevolent, if slightly cynical, horse, and today his long jaw was a canoe of contentment. He had been visiting the forward company of the 'Scots' to reconnoitre the ground over which 'B' Company would attack. Before the Rifles could assault, however, the Scots would have to clear the ground they were on and the tanks would have to firm up the approaches. He sauntered down the centre of the road, the sun hot on his face, enjoying the sensory impressions which flashed parrot-bright in his mind. He paid no heed to the occasional black explosions which blossomed nearby.

Major Bazin was a perma ient force officer but unfortunately for him the physical world was his foe. He could not read a map, he had no sense of ground, and invariably he saw a host of solutions to a military problem when, in fact, there could be only one. Long ago he had catalogued his military deficiencies and accepted the fact that he would never rise beyond his present rank. And long ago he had ceased to care.

He continued on his way, whistling.

Half a mile back Major Bazin stopped to visit Ten Platoon. They had moved down from the hillside, and were now sheltered behind an embankment. In front of a shattered stone hut men sat in the sunshine cleaning their weapons. Fires sputtered under two biscuit tins which spewed a rich odour of meat and vegetable stew into the air. Major Bazin cocked his head and sniffed appreciatively. Then Adam stood beside him, spoon and mess-tin in hand; he had been sampling the first batch of stew.

'Will you stay for dinner, sir?'

'No thanks.' Major Bazin's nostrils quivered regretfully. 'Got to get back to Battalion for an "O" group. But that "M and V" smells good!'

'Yes,' said Adam, with pride. 'We have two imported cooks.'

Grinning, he pointed toward big Jim and little Joe. The two Italians were stripped to the waist, standing over the biscuit tins and stirring with vigour. Egged on by the surrounding men they made great play of adding imaginary spices and flavourings. They were like children on a Sunday picnic, behaving extravagantly, yet knowing themselves protected by parental indulgence. At that moment a Bren gunner named Simpson tossed a tin in the air which little Joe fielded with a stabbing catch. 'Try that one, too,' Simpson ordered. 'It's haricot ox-tail—then we'll have the whole bloody Compo ration in.' The men of the platoon laughed their delight.

But Major Bazin no longer smiled; his face was dark and stormy. 'These men are Italians,' he accused harshly.

Adam looked up with surprise. 'Yes,' he said. 'They're Italian. Good workers too.'

'Have you looked at their boots?' The Major shot this question out.

Adam followed the cold glance of Major Bazin's eyes. It was obvious that the boots worn by the two Italians had once been issued by some army quartermaster's store.

'Well—' Adam began.

'Have you searched them? For identity cards, hidden ammunition, any other articles of army issue?'

Adam flushed. 'All right,' he said. 'So maybe they're deserters—'

'John—you bloody fool! The order from Division is that deserters are to be shot on sight. Did you know that a Scots sergeant-major was killed by a sniper last night?'

'No,' Adam admitted. 'I didn't know that.'

36

'Well, he's the fourth in the Brigade. The Brigadier is hopping mad. He'd shoot *you* if he saw you palling it up with these two here.'

Every man in the platoon was sitting up, watching, listening. Quietly Sergeant Mitchell came to his feet, he shouldered the two Italians away from the steaming tins, as though to make them less conspicuous.

Major Bazin's long face became mournful as he watched big Jim and little Joe try to efface themselves in the background. 'Hell,' he said then. 'They certainly look harmless enough. Still, I suppose we'll have to take them back to Battalion for interrogation at least. Who found them?'

'Sergeant Mitchell and Jones, sir.'

'All right. Let's go. You, Mitchell, Jones, and your two friends.'

Mitchell already had the two boys pulling on their shirts while he buckled the belt of his own web equipment. Then little Joe picked up the small cardboard suit-case to signify that they were ready. This was the first time Major Bazin had seen the suit-case; at once his glance darkened. 'Open up,' he commanded sharply.

Big Jim got down on his knees to assist his companion; for a moment as they knelt together on the ground they looked like pitchmen getting ready to display their wares. But the suit-case had little to reveal: a ragged shirt, a comb, two razors, some snapshots of a girl—amazingly, a bottle of ink—and an Italian Army water-bottle.

'All right—pack it up,' Adam commanded curtly.

No man in the platoon smiled now; and Adam himself looked grim as their small party moved out to the roadway.

15

BATTALION Headquarters was in a stone farm-house. Major Bazin went inside to find Lieutenant-Colonel Dodd, and left Adam standing in a sprawling, cobble-stoned courtyard, crowded with men and vehicles. At one end a picket gate led into a barn-yard; from there a pungency of fresh manure flowed forth to flavour the afternoon air. The sun felt like a flat weight, heavy and pressing.

Adam watched while his two charges sat on the cobble-stones, leaned their backs against a wall and lighted cigarettes which Jonesy—for whom this had turned out to be a wonderfully exciting outing—was quick to provide. Adam kept one eye cocked on the door which Major Bazin had entered, and strolled round the courtyard looking for any news which might affect Ten Platoon's immediate fortunes. He picked his way between parked trucks and carriers until he came to a stop beside the Signals jeep. He knew this would be the likeliest place to wait. He nodded to the sergeant who was listening on the Brigade net.

In this courtyard there was no urgency of time: instead there was a sense of lazy well-being and relaxation. In one corner some men brewed a steaming tin of tea. A few yards away from Adam a hairy sergeant, stripped to his underwear shorts, was sitting down to shave; between scrapes of his razor he hummed a tune in complete self-absorption. Adam could not put a name to the tune, but the melody was one that he knew well and it eddied through his mind.

Across the courtyard Adam saw that his two Italians had become the centre of attraction. Men crowded round curiously, staring, pressing on them cigarettes and chocolate bars. Jonesy was a proud master of ceremonies; he was explaining how the two had been named big Jim and little Joe.

'Well, Joe—whadda ya know?' called one of the soldiers.

Little Joe rolled his eyes comically; he made a quick circling gesture with thumb and forefinger. Both of them were sitting erect now, alert, laughing, smiles flashing from their teeth; anxious to please in any way they could. They understood and would go right along with this kidding. It was the same in any army, they knew: there were always the jokes which were not so much intended to be funny as to serve as a kind of greeting, or a wry acknowledgment of shared discomfort. There was always the incessant marching and countermarching, then the waiting while one of the officer-gods decided what to do with them next. They were thoroughly familiar with all this. They much preferred their young *Tenente* to the horse-faced *Maggiore* who had brought them here; they would much rather be back eating 'M and V' stew with Ten Platoon; but for the present it was pleasant to sit here in the sunshine and smoke tailor-made cigarettes, and talk and laugh a little. Their little suit-case lay on the cobble-stones before them; soon they would be told to pick it up and go to some other place, and in due course—if God was willing—they would even reach their distant homes in Italy one day.

Now it was big Jim's turn to vie for the onlookers' approval. He thumped his balled fists hard upon his chest. '*Canadese— buona!*' he declaimed, and he made as though to stuff a chocolate bar, paper wrapping and all, down his throat.

Adam saw that Sergeant Krebs of the Regimental Police had strolled over and was now looking down at the pair. Krebs was a big man, almost too fat to ride his motor cycle; and he had no friend in the Battalion. He stood watching the two Italians sourly and his glance fastened on big Jim's chocolate bar. 'Yeah,' Sergeant Krebs observed. 'Better eat it while you can—you stupid bastard.'

'Cut it out, Krebs—they're *my* prisoners.'

Sergeant Mitchell elbowed his way into the group, his glance cold and hard on Krebs' fat face.

Adam clambered to his feet; but before he could move toward the prisoners the lean, agitated form of Padre Doorn was bustling round him. The Padre's gaunt face was filled with immense concern. He plucked at his friend's arm. 'I just heard about this, John,' he said. 'Is it serious? Is there anything I can do?'

'Hell, no,' Adam replied. 'All I want to do is get rid of these two goons and get back to my platoon.'

Sergeant Mitchell now had a space cleared round the prisoners. As soon as Adam approached the two Italian youths jumped to their feet and stood at quivering positions of attention. Jonesy stood up with them, but as usual several seconds too late. Brooding, Adam regarded his three charges. 'Oh, sit down,' he said at last. 'Every damn one of you is more trouble than you're worth.'

Then he heard his name called. He turned and saw Captain Ramsay, the Adjutant, standing by the Signals jeep. As he started back he heard the Padre open a laboured conversation in Italian while more chocolate bars appeared in his hand. But Adam's main concern at the moment was how his platoon was faring with only Corporal Fowler in charge. He wanted to get back to them.

Since Major Bazin was still inside the farm-house with the C.O. he asked Captain Ramsay about this. 'You'd better wait,' Ramsay replied. 'The C.O. is sending your two Wop friends back to Brigade. I've just put the message on the air——'

'Sir!' The Signals Sergeant had his earphones off; his voice crackled with urgency. 'Bring Sunray to set!'

'Hell,' said Ramsay. He wheeled about and started to run toward the farm-house door.

'Sunray' was the code name for a unit commander. This meant that the next highest Sunray—the Brigadier—wanted to speak to Colonel Dodd personally. Adam walked round to the far side of the jeep. He stationed himself as close to the crackling earphones as he could get.

Colonel Dodd emerged from the house at a slow march of dignity; he made a point of not hurrying his pace. He wore a studious, concentrated look on his face, as though to denote he was only temporarily coming away from more urgent business to which he would presently return. At last he came to a halt at the jeep, adjusted the earphones on his head, and picked up the microphone. 'Sunray Two Baker on set,' Colonel Dodd announced firmly, after clearing his throat.

Adam was close enough to see the flecks in Colonel Dodd's eyes, to observe the vertical bob of his prominent Adam's apple. He was close enough also to hear the powerful voice which now rattled the diaphragms. 'I do not choose,' this voice crackled loudly, 'to be bothered with administrative detail when I am fighting a battle. Shoot these deserters at once. And bloody well smarten up if you wish to keep your command. Report when my order is carried out.'

The Brigadier had violated wireless security. An enemy monitoring set would recognize this message at once as an order from Brigadier to Battalion Commander. The Brigadier considered, of course, that wireless, like other procedures, was devised for him, and not the reverse.

Colonel Dodd stood with the microphone in his hand as though he was holding a deadly serpent. 'Wilco' was the only answer allowed him; after gulping for several seconds he forced his words out, and made the breach of security complete. 'Wilco, *sir*,' Colonel Dodd replied.

With exaggerated care the Colonel placed the microphone down on the hood of the jeep. He walked on stiff legs round the front of the jeep where he paused, as though surprised to see so many soldiers filling the courtyard. Everyone at once looked away from him; each person pretended to be busy with whatever he had been doing before. Even the Sergeant who had been shaving picked up his razor again, although this time he hummed no tune. The Colonel had his own lips puckered slightly as though he might take up humming himself. He rocked back and forth on his heels, looking at everything and everybody. His glance passed over the two prisoners, still grouped with the Padre and Jonesy, touched momentarily upon Major Bazin, Sergeant Mitchell, Lieutenant Adam, and all the others in the courtyard, continuing panoramically, without pause and without recognition. The sun was even hotter now, pressing flatly on the cobble-stones, expanding upward and outward, to fill the space with thick humid silence. Lieutenant-Colonel Charley Dodd, the insurance broker from Toronto, looked around the Sicilian courtyard for an eternal moment of silence. Then his heels came flat on the ground. He cleared his throat with great vigour.

'*Mister* Adam.' The Colonel's voice undoubtedly sounded louder than he had intended.

'Sir?'

Adam stepped forward, tommy-gun still slung at his shoulder.

'These two deserters you captured—you made a mistake which you will now remedy. Shoot them at once!'

The silence became hollow, like a huge emptiness waiting to be filled. For this moment Adam could not speak, nor could anyone else. The glance of every man in the courtyard flashed instinctively to the two Italians, still sitting on the cobble-stones. Both now leaned alertly forward, the smiles fallen from their olive-soft faces; they knew that something important concerning themselves was under discussion.

Adam flashed a glance of wild appeal toward Major Bazin 'Sir?' he stammered; and Major Bazin stepped forward to his side. 'Sir!' he protested angrily.

But Colonel Dodd looked at a point somewhere between their shoulders. There was no bottom to the depth of silence which overflowed the farm-yard. A tremendous weight of reluctance, a slow heavy burden of unwillingness settled down on each person's shoulders. It had now penetrated to every soldier in that place, with the possible exception of Rifleman Jones, that the two Italians were going to be executed, and that within a matter of minutes. And this thought required some preparation in their minds. Perhaps this was a reasonable and not unusual demand in war, perhaps the same thing was happening all along the front. But they were still new to war—this was something new in *their* experience. They had seen some of their friends die, of course, but that had been in the midst of explosions or the angry lash of machine-gun fire—not in a lazy, sun-filled courtyard. This might be a matter of military necessity, this farm-yard affair might have to be done; but they did not like it: their unwillingness was almost palpable in the sun-drunk silence. Big Jim and little Joe sat nervously on the cobble-stones; the worst part for them must have been the way no one would meet their questing glances.

The first look of shock had passed from Adam's face. He stood, white and trembling, at attention before Colonel Dodd. Full cognizance of the order he had received cleaved him, and left him incapacitated like a gigantic wound. He watched with dream-like fascination while Major Bazin spoke in the Colonel's ear. Ramsay too had stepped forward and the three of them whispered together urgently. He watched each one glance at him in turn as the discussion went on. Adam was thinking, with desperation: Is there any way out? Have I the guts to refuse the order? Or—he was shameless now—is there anyone else I could stick with the job? Mitchell? Could I ever look Mitchell in the face again?

The discussion ended; the three officers drew themselves up. Then Sergeant Krebs was standing before them. Adam's presence seemed to be forgotten. He swayed slightly and he closed his eyes.

'Listen, Krebs,' Colonel Dodd was saying, 'I want to get this thing over with as quickly as possible. March them into the barnyard and do it there.'

'Yes, sir.'

Sergeant Krebs saluted. There was no change of expression on his beefy jowls. It was as though this was the sort of normal order which he might expect to receive in the course of the day. He wheeled about and started across the cobble-stones toward the two prisoners. The fingernails of his right hand scratched lightly against the revolver case strapped to his side.

There was a sudden flurry of motion. The lean, agitated figure of Padre Doorn came bounding past Krebs, to halt impetuously before the Colonel. The Padre's face was alive with his feeling;

all that he had ever been, or ever might be, was posted on his face as though affixed to a bulletin-board, and subject to the same public injury. The Padre was open and defenceless; he looked fragile, as though his being might easily shatter into nothingness.

'Sir,' the Padre said, his eyes burning candles on the Colonel's face. 'Are you really going to shoot these two boys?'

'Yes,' said Colonel Dodd, looking beyond him. 'Do you wish to provide spiritual assistance?'

Padre Doorn choked with the force of his outrage. 'That would be mockery—'

'In that case, Padre—kindly get the hell out of the way!'

The Padre stood in anguish, his fists balled at his side. Then he turned his head slightly and saw his friend Adam. Their glances locked: they shared a long, aching moment of examination. Then the Padre's gaze dropped to the ground. He looked at the ground as though he would never again wish to look toward heaven.

Sergeant Krebs had the prisoners on their feet now; he forced them before him over the cobble-stones. The two boys looked frightened; their feet were clumsy and uncertain as they walked. Little Joe held the suit-case clenched tightly in both fists, so that it dangled in front of his crotch. They cast quick glances behind them; once big Jim stumbled and almost fell. The most frightening part must have been the grim faces everywhere they turned, the glances that slid away and refused recognition. Sergeant Krebs prodded them on, and now he had his revolver drawn.

When they came abreast with the officers in the centre of the farm-yard a voice spoke. It was Colonel Dodd, the insurance broker from Toronto, trying to reduce the affair to a mere matter of soldierly toughness, to inject a note of hard-boiled humour. His voice sounded hoarse, and intolerably ugly.

'You can put that suit-case down, bud,' the Colonel said. 'You won't need it where you're going.'

Little Joe, knowing no English, glanced once toward the voice, clutched the suit-case more tightly to him, and scurried ahead. There was not the least stir of response in the farm-yard. It was as though there had been no interruption to the silence; as though the remark had never been made. Colonel Dodd flushed deeper red, his teeth bit into his lip. Adam felt strong fingers grip his arm; it was Sergeant Mitchell who stood beside him.

As soon as they passed through the picket gate Sergeant Krebs fired a shot which hit little Joe in the back. Little Joe squealed with pain. He fell forward onto the manure, the suit-case flew from his hands, and its meagre contents scattered all around him. Big Jim turned about; he went down on his knees, his hands came together beneath his chin as though he would pray—not to his executioner, but, for a moment, to God. Sergeant Krebs fired again and shot him in the shoulder. Then both men were squealing at once; Sergeant Krebs fired his remaining four rounds into their bodies. But they were both still alive, both flopping despairingly in the manure. Sergeant Krebs broke his pistol and began, laboriously, to load another six rounds in the cylinder.

'For Christ's sake!'

It was a cry torn from Adam's throat, and being. He started to run; as he ran he ripped the tommy-gun from his shoulder with painful force. He went plunging forward, through the picket gate and into the barn-yard. Half a second behind Sergeant Mitchell came charging after him. Mitchell jostled Sergeant Krebs to one side; his hands reached out toward his platoon commander's weapon. But then the summer afternoon was perforated by sharp, surgical bursts of sub-machine-gun fire. Adam emptied his magazine. In the barn-yard there were floating wisps of smoke, then silence again. Adam turned about. He tramped back, his boots heavy with manure; Sergeant Mitchell came plodding behind. They halted in front of the waiting officers. For several seconds the entire group remained locked in the same attitude: heavy, immovable, borne down with the weight of sun and thick silence. Colonel Dodd's glance was still fixed blankly on the barn-yard.

Adam pulled at the sling on his shoulder and addressed his request jointly to Colonel Dodd and Major Bazin. 'Permission to rejoin my platoon, sir?'

Colonel Dodd made no answer. His eyes were glazed, his breath laboured. At his side Padre Doorn's glance was lowered; he held one hand as a shield over his face. Major Bazin made a silent gesture then. Go on, this gesture and the whole weary length of his face seemed to say: Yes, go on—get the hell back and rejoin your platoon.

Adam and Mitchell about-turned and marched in step across

44

the cobble-stones. Jonesy was waiting for them, his face working with violent emotion; he opened his mouth to speak.

'Come on, Jones,' Mitchell ordered quickly. 'Fall in behind.' Rifleman Jones obeyed. Their boots rang a metal tune on the cobble-stones as the three men marched out of the farm-yard.

Out on the road the sun was still shining. Somewhere ahead of them, from the direction of the cemetery, there came the hollow crump of mortar bombs, the uninterrupted lashing of German machine-guns; it sounded like a counter-attack in force. They marched toward this sound, and toward the approaching night and the German infantry, now attacking.

It was not cold in this sunlight, but Adam began to shiver. He had the impression that formless shapes grouped and squatted and disported themselves at the roadside; and as he saw them the fear came. This was the real fear, quite unlike the momentary pang of terror he had known in the assault boat. This was the sick, vulture fear which chained itself to one's shoulder for ever.

Adam felt violated; as he walked he wanted to cry out for his lost innocence. It was like the time, he remembered, that first time when he was seventeen and he walked away one rainy night from visiting a brothel. Fear was wanton at the roadside; and *now* there was certainly no exhilaration in war. There was only this marching, ever closer, toward fear in the night.

The three men walked on in silence. The battle noises became louder as they drew close to the platoon position.

Jonesy felt saddened and disturbed; but he was not sure why, and he translated his worry into one he could readily understand. 'Say,' Jonesy remarked. 'I hope the boys haven't gone and eaten all that "M and V"!'

For an instant Adam could actually see the full mess-tin of meat and vegetable stew he had held in his hands a short time before. The thick, meaty taste came like grease to his mouth.

'Shut your stupid trap, Jones.' But Sergeant Mitchell did not look his way. Instead, he was watching Adam anxiously. He held one hand below his elbow; he marched close beside him.

They walked on a few more steps before they had to halt. Then Adam left them. He moved away and vomited at the roadside.

16

THE attacking enemy fought the Canadians by gun-flash and moonlight; the cemetery and the village changed hands several times that night. In the morning the Brigade launched a final assault and captured the objectives. Casualties were heavy on both sides.

After that came other villages, other hills and pockmarks of Sicily to storm and capture. The Canadians attacked and attacked, getting leaner and harder and more efficient at their job each day, until at last they pushed the enemy onto the slopes of Mount Etna; and there the defence collapsed. The Germans fled across the straits of Messina, leaving their dead and prisoners behind. In thirty-eight days the campaign was over, the battle won.

The Canadian force moved to the parched hillsides of central Sicily to rest and regroup. At once a ruthless new broom of efficiency swept the incompetents away. Of the 2nd Rifles Lieutenant-Colonel Charley Dodd was the first to go. He departed one night in thin-lipped silence, without farewells or regrets, for a base unit in North Africa. His successor was a permanent force officer named McNabb, an efficient and decisive man in every way. Major Bazin was shifted to the command of 'D' Company. Lieutenant John Adam, considered one of the best officers in the Battalion, was promoted to Captain and the vacant command of 'B' Company. Reinforcements arrived to fill the depleted ranks.

And then, pared down to fighting trim, the infantry battalions started to train. Within days their preparations became obvious and unmistakable. The least astute soldier among them knew they were about to cross the straits of Messina and invade Italy.

BOOK TWO / *More*

1

'D' COMPANY of the 2nd Rifles was to attack in one hour; during this interval there was nothing to do but wait.

Major Bunny Bazin, commander of 'D' Company for the past five months, lay on his back, head pillowed on friendly grass. Within his range of sight pan-like clouds tilted blue-white on Apennine peaks. To him it seemed a kind of afternoon floor-show performed for his private enjoyment.

Dear God, but I'm contented, sighed Major Bazin's one self to the other. A charge of voluptuous pleasure coursed and tingled the length of his body. He stretched; his toes wriggled happily inside his boots.

This afternoon his mind was liberated and all-powerful—a separate free-self—functioning like a precision machine to attain any ordered conclusion, but pausing the while to hold friendly parley with his workaday body-self. Long ago he had finished his daily task of positioning himself in relation to the rest of the world. Today there had only been the same familiar problem to consider: the matter of his friends John Adam and Padre Doorn. Adam had turned out to be a first-rate company commander; the trouble was that he tried to fill the aching emptiness inside himself with nothing but efficiency. . . . As for Padre Philip Doorn, the man had simply become a graveyard ghoul. . . . In each case, of course, the cause dated back to that afternoon in the Sicilian barn-yard. Each one of them had been changed—himself least of the three because there was less in him to change: *he* had lost his saints when he was very young; long ago he had made his com-promises. . . .

But his mind had duly processed and registered these concerns; at this moment he knew nothing but contentment. His liberated self went ranging forth with intoxicating freedom of power to survey the whole broad world of possibilities. Today the process of thought itself lay bared to him; any concept was capable of exact definition; no truth was too impossible to discover. Major Bazin was experiencing a state of grace.

'What shall I name this state?' Bazin's apart-self demanded. And his other self responded with a quick, interior chuckle. 'Name it Bazin's Mystique of Battle,' it declared. 'Mark One, for use while awaiting a—say, an imminent action. . . .'

'And of what does it consist?' his self persisted.

'Simply, it is a state of serenity before battle, a condition of bliss, or near-grace, which can be obtained no other way—'

His face showed diamond white in the glare of distant mountains; but a frown marred his glance. That was the paradox, he thought: man fully realized himself as man, attained fulfilment, only under the savage scourge of war. This state of present bliss, the way men risked and expended their lives, the humbling, even lovely, spark of compassion which flowed between them in times of extremity—these things were created by, and only made possible by war.

Major Bazin sighed. A melancholy thought for the social scientists, perhaps—but there it was. At this moment the only reason he was able to perceive truth revealed was because his life was placed in forfeit. Today it was quite possible he would be killed. For that reason, and during this interval only, he was granted dispensation. It was a hard way to buy peace with oneself, but the *only* way. . . . All his self-doubts, his inadequacies, his ignobilities, the impossible search for meaning in life, his own tiny, fractional share in the human predicament—all these were cancelled, or suspended at least, for the duration of the interval.

But, Major Bazin reasoned: if I cease to exist, then will not all unresolvable problems cease to exist also? A smile touched his face; he rubbed his shoulder blades into the comfortable ground.

All problems, he thought: all human strivings and gropings are based on continuity; they are predicated on the fact that the agent will continue living; but if he ceases to exist—then, *ergo,* everything else also ceases to exist. What an infinitely soothing conclusion this was. . . .

He shifted his weight to one elbow. Am I saying, he asked, that objects possess only subjective existence? Yes, he decided—damned well right I am! And a tremendous truth suddenly rushed into his consciousness: It must follow as inexorable consequence that if *I* cease to exist, then the war itself will cease to exist. If I die today—*the war will be over!*

Major Bazin pulled this discovery round him like a blanket of rapture. What magnificence! What an intelligent, perspicacious being he was. . . . Here, lying on this ground during his own granted interval, watching the afternoon floor-show of the Apennines, he had solved the world's gravest single problem. *Any* man could end the war, any time he wanted. . . . Judiciously Major Bazin pursed his lips. Now, perhaps, it would be well to state the principle in formal terms. . . .

Bazin heard the interior laughter mocking deep inside him, but he did not care. He was utterly happy at this moment; and in a special, almost tender, sense, he believed he actually had found a new aspect of truth. At least there was enough truth in this new truth to render him happy.

'Take a Memorandum,' his mind dictated. 'To: All Corps and Divisional Commanders. Subject: Bazin's Infallible Plan to End the War. . . .'

But I couldn't sign it 'Bazin', he thought, with a moment's dismay: I haven't sufficient rank. Who *could* originate the message?

Then he marvelled at himself anew: this latest discovery was brilliant, supreme, unsurpassable. . . . Of course, he told himself: there could only be one possible originator. He continued rapid dictation. 'All Acknowledge,' he ordered. 'Signed "God".'

Some of the cloud-load spilled from the tilted pans and splashed like candy fluff on the mountain peaks. This Apennine floor-show was only just beginning. If it had not threatened to interrupt his serenity of thought Major Bazin would have sat up to clap his hands in applause.

2

'BLESSED be the name of the Lord,' the voice of Padre Philip Doorn intoned sternly. 'Amen. Where's the next?'

Two men—drivers unwillingly conscripted from Headquarters Company—laboured toward him through the clinging mist and drizzle. Their boots were weighted with mud; between them was suspended a body wrapped in a gas-cape. They laid their burden along the raw lips of a freshly-spaded grave; then, at a signal from the Padre, they eased the body into its resting-place. They stepped back a pace and removed their helmets.

'I am the resurrection and the life—'

The Padre's voice was at once a rapid, insistent drone. His dark glance was fixed unwaveringly on the crumbling earth. This was his fifth burial today; he had worked out the required timing to a nicety; and he was probably breaking all records for a regimental chaplain. Most other Padres were content to wait until the battle ended before they performed their final offices—but *he* was following on the heels of the rifle companies as they advanced. Sometimes it was a mere matter of minutes before he and his assistants had readied a dead soldier for interment.

'I became dumb, and opened not my mouth—'

As he spoke the Padre stole quick glances at the watch on his wrist. His long, enveloping trench coat was caked with mud. He had not shaved; his eyes were black thumb-prints of sleeplessness.

'For I am a stranger with thee.'

The Padre rattled the words off, then he became aware that one of his assistants was plucking nervously at his sleeve, that he had been standing there doing so for several moments.

'Sir,' the soldier whispered unhappily. 'The one you've got now is an R.C.'

There was only the shortest pause, then the Padre's voice took up its drone again. 'Make him the companion of the holy Angels in heaven,' he commanded.

It made little difference what words he used. In point of fact he had been delving into Roman Catholic liturgy recently because in many respects it was more satisfactory: everything was provided for; he found there an authority and prescription which was lacking in his own. When there was time he intended to investigate these rites and sacraments at greater length.

'Amen,' said the Padre. 'Fill in the grave.'

The Padre watched impatiently while the two men shovelled earth. His head was cocked toward the drumfire of guns up ahead. He kicked the mud from his boots; it was time they were moving on.

Padre Doorn turned, he peered through tufting mist in the direction of the battle noises. His glance encompassed the whole sweep of ground, but went no higher; now he never looked higher than the junction point of earth and sky. Even, it had been observed, the strafing of enemy aircraft was not sufficient to draw his glance upwards.

'Pick up your tools,' the Padre commanded, without turning his head.

His unwilling assistants fell in behind him. Shouldering their picks and shovels they shuffled forward. With the Padre's gaunt figure in the lead the little band formed a gloomy silhouette on the sodden landscape.

3

THE old man who owned the farm performed a shuffling clog-dance in the mud. The men of Ten Platoon watched with interest. They rested on their elbows, propped up by their packs, weapons lying across their knees. The sun of Sicily was only a pale memory on their cheeks now; their faces were white with December, and with the occupational whiteness of men who are going into action. Up ahead the battle noises were loud on their axis of advance. They shivered in the morning mist.

'Give 'em hell, Pop,' one of the men encouraged. Any kind of a joke would be welcome on a morning like this.

'*Tedesci—tutto robbare!*' declaimed the little man, as he hopped violently from one foot to the other.

The old man saw himself in the framework of his history; the magnitude of his suffering must be made explicit. He meant that the *tedesci* had robbed him of everything; and in this he was not strictly correct, because the farm-yard where the men now rested was littered with dead animals who were unmistakably and offensively present. Still, they had been killed by *tedesci* fire, and perhaps it came to the same thing.

Ewart flicked his invariable cigarette stub to one corner of his mouth and spat. The saliva missile struck expertly against the flanks of a rib-scarred cow. Winter flies scattered and buzzed their annoyance.

The old man found hopping difficult in the heavy mud so now he planted himself, feet wide apart. At his side his sixteen-year-old

51

son, of identical shape and features, with immense calf-brown eyes, regarded him solemnly, obviously ready to play the part of straight-man in his father's comedy production.

The old man's eyes began to pop. He blew into his leathery cheeks until they swelled like two tethered balloons. The index finger of his right hand rotated in menace, then it stabbed. The balloons were punctured; his breath escaped in a fierce, sibilant whistle. This noise he created to punctuate his feelings about the *tedesci*.

Young Jones laughed guilelessly; the other men, even stolid Krasnick, and Simpson the tough Bren gunner, grinned in appreciation.

The men had discovered that these southern Italians possessed such a complete vocabulary of gesture that whole conversations could be effected without speech. There was the universal and expressive sign for hunger: five spread fingers raked across the neck and throat. Sometimes this was accompanied by the word *'Mangiare!'* but more often the communication was made in silence and became more terrible and importunate for that reason. There was the extended finger rotated loosely from the wrist, signifying *'Niente*—Nothing', and this, depending on the message conveyed by the face, could indicate anything from simple 'No' to the bottom-most depths of futility, the last relinquishment of striving. There was the exquisite courtesy of 'good-bye': four horizontal fingers fanned lightly on the thumb. There was—

'Cover!' roared Sergeant Mitchell. His voice blasted the morning mist like a fog-horn.

Each man rolled flat on his belly, forearms cushioning his cheeks, helmet covering the nape of his neck. With the tearing howl in the sky each man started to count, each in his fashion prayed. Heavy stuff was falling back here; it was up ahead, in the fields they had to cross in a few minutes, that mortar bombs puckered the ground like steel hail. The shell whined over their heads and struck a hundred yards to the rear, causing a dull, black explosion. Several seconds later wet clods of earth came tumbling from the sky to land with hollow plops on the men and dead animals in the farm-yard.

The men sat up, grinning their relief; fingers fumbled to retrieve dropped cigarettes. In their midst the old man stood choking with the immensity of his rage. He peered at the heavens, that impersonal source of death and destruction, and he shook his fists in a gesture of implacable vengeance. The boy still cowered on the ground, eyes wide with terror; but his father's awful gesture must have seemed some kind of assurance because now he sat up and shook his own fists in a puny effort of imitation. The father watched approvingly; he roughed one hand through his son's mop of tousled hair.

Sergeant Mitchell stopped watching them. He could see the aerial of a signaller's wireless set one hundred yards away on the left flank; and from time to time he caught sight of Captain Adam's rangy form moving among the Company Headquarters group. His glance kept careful watch on the aerial, alert for the warning order to move.

Sergeant Mitchell was platoon commander today. Their new reinforcement lieutenant was L.O.B.—Left Out of Battle. The L.O.B. system meant that no matter how heavy the casualties in a given action there always remained a core of trained officers and N.C.O.s to come forward and reconstitute the rifle companies if need be. And, Sergeant Mitchell now thought morosely, this time they were sure as hell going to need their L.O.B.s. Judging from the battle reports, and from the present weight of shelling, it was plain the Germans intended to hold the line guarding Ortona with all strength at their command.

Again Sergeant Mitchell looked at the two Italians as they stood in the ruins of their farm-yard, and the glance of his nose-flattened face was sympathetic—things were tough for these poor buggers too. . . . Corporal DiCicco, acting as interpreter, sat beside the old man translating his remarks for the amusement of the platoon. Mitchell stuck another cigarette in his mouth; he was certainly in no hurry: the longer they stayed here the better he would like it.

Through spiralling cigarette smoke he looked in the faces of the men of Ten Platoon. It was a good platoon—even with their few problem cases like Jonesy and shifty little Ewart. Against these were the others. . . . Corporal Bell, who broke up the attack on that castle back in Sicily, only twenty years old, but real fighting man all through. Simpson, the Number One Bren gunner, the best man with a Bren he had ever seen. Simpson had a little ditty which he sang when he fired his gun in earnest. Brrrrt—a sharp burst; and there was Simpson squinting down his sights, singing through clenched teeth: 'Maybe it itches, but it kills the sons of the bitches. . . .' That was as much of the refrain as anyone had ever made out. And Frazer, baby-faced Frazer who for two years in England spent most of his time in arrest or detention—but perhaps the only man Mitchell had ever met who really merited the term 'fearless'. Frazer maintained that he never entered a Wop house, anywhere, without throwing a grenade in first.

Oh, it was a good enough platoon, Mitchell knew. The sad part was the way their ranks had been thinned since Sicily; and today there were bound to be others left lying in those fields ahead. . . . But, hell—Sergeant Mitchell flicked his cigarette away and stopped thinking these thoughts. He looked up in answer to Corporal DiCicco's voice.

This promised to be the biggest laugh of all. DiCicco's ugly face was dead-pan as he announced to the platoon that the old man had just made them a free gift of all his dead livestock. Beside him the old man sat in benign triumph, waiting to experience the full flood of their gratitude.

The men looked at the gaunt scarecrow cow, at the flies parading its ramrod legs, and they laughed. The old man took their chuckles as an expression of appreciation. He bowed and nodded, all a-smile.

'Tell him thanks, Joe,' Mitchell said, stifling his laughter. 'But we'll go along with our bully beef and hard-tack.'

There was a quick exchange of Italian, some voluble gestures, followed by a sudden flash of interest on DiCicco's face. 'Say,' DiCicco announced. 'He says there are some chickens—fresh killed this morning.'

Every man sat up straight. Chickens were something else. Chickens could be tied to one's belt and carried away; there would always be time, somehow, to cook chickens. Corporal Bell jumped to his feet, eyes gleaming, his strong young face alight. He strode over to the old man, seething with nervous energy. 'Where are these chickens?' he demanded. '*Dove*, Papa—*dove* the bloody chickens?'

Papa beamed at him proudly.

'The boy will show you,' Corporal DiCicco said, after glancing

54

toward Mitchell for approval. The youth with the calf-like eyes danced to his feet and tugged at Corporal Bell's sleeve. At a trot the two of them set out toward a shed at one end of the farm-yard.

'Krasnick,' Mitchell ordered, 'You go too, and see if they're any good.' Obediently Krasnick lumbered to his feet. Corporal Bell and the boy were already stooping over at the shed.

They all heard the gun's report and the banshee howl in the air at the same instant. 'It's an 88!' somebody yelled, and then each one of them was hugging the ground.

There was a crash and one edge of the shed disintegrated. A large piece of board went floating through the air, struck the side of the farm-house, and dropped clattering to the ground. Then there was silence: a second's vacuum of silence, with the reek of high explosive creeping in.

Sergeant Mitchell was first on his feet, and he went charging toward the place where the shed had been. There was no noise at all, no plaint or terrible, testing call of one suddenly wounded. Mitchell stood over Corporal Bell and saw that the left side of his body had been carved away. Bell had taken the force of the explosion; the Italian boy lay a few feet away, dead also, but marked only on the forehead where a steel splinter had entered his brain. The old man was hopping about in Mitchell's way. He brushed him aside and peered round the farm-yard.

'Harrison,' Sergeant Mitchell called.

Lance-Corporal Harrison stepped forward. Mitchell looked somewhere in the direction of his right shoulder; Harrison had been Corporal Bell's closest friend.

'Harry,' Mitchell said. 'It's your section—take his tommy-gun, and anything else you need.'

'O.K., Mitch.'

Harrison spoke in a low tone. He was equally careful to avoid looking in the other's eyes.

The R.A.P. man had unstrapped his own gas-cape, and now he was pulling it over Corporal Bell. He turned to minister to the other corpse.

A screech of unbearable anguish split the silence of the farm-yard. The noise issued from the old man, who was now kneeling at his son's body. One convulsed hand plucked at the boy's head, fingers rumpling the shock of thick hair. As he stroked the dead body the old man's throat was lifted sufficiently to allow the screech to emerge—like a whistle blast, strident, sustained at an ear-shattering pitch.

The men were sitting in the same places they had occupied before the shell exploded. Now they shifted their feet and looked away, as though embarrassed. Mitchell went and stood beside the old man. He touched him clumsily between the shoulder blades, and peered anxiously round for Corporal DiCicco. Then the two of them stood over the old man, touching him with ineffectual patting gestures. The same unremitting screech continued; it became a throbbing ache in the eardrums.

'All right, Papa,' Mitchell kept saying, trying to pierce the torrent of noise. 'All right, Papa—just take it easy.'

Between them Mitchell and DiCicco raised the old man to his feet. The screech halted for a moment but then it was replaced by staccato bursts of sobbing which were even worse. DiCicco spoke urgently in the old man's ear but his words had no effect. Papa broke away from their grasp. He ran to the centre of the farm-yard, threw his head back, and drummed his fists upon his chest. *'Mio bambino,'* the old man shouted, *'Morte! Morte!'* He kneeled down in a position of prayer and he began to pound his head upon the ground. Each time his head lifted the accusing shout of *'Morte!'* rose and smashed echoing through the farm-yard. Somehow this wail seemed worse even than the screech or the sobbing had been.

'For Christ's sake stop him!'

This was Lance-Corporal Harrison, calling angrily to Corporal DiCicco. He was kneeling at Corporal Bell's cape-covered body, trying to pull personal belongings from a pocket.

All the men were now stirring uneasily. The noise made by the old man was a rasping scrape on their nerves.

Papa stood up. He ran back to his son's body, peered down for a moment, and then he started to run in a wide circle round the farm-yard. He came to a halt in front of Krasnick, whose ears were still ringing from the shell explosion. *'Morte!'* the old man shouted accusingly at Krasnick. Krasnick did not budge; he stared back at the old man unblinkingly. Probably in his mind, after seeing all the dead animals, Krasnick thought that nothing much worse could happen today.

56

Papa moved on. He commenced a grotesque, flopping pilgrimage round the farm-yard. The men found something grating, unpleasant, even insulting in this sight. They became restless; they eyed him coldly.

The old man stopped in front of big Simpson. '*Morte!*' he shouted at him. Simpson returned the glare; he shifted the Bren gun on his knees.

'Shut your face,' said Simpson, in a flat, level voice.

For the men this was simply too great a display of grief, more than the conditions warranted—an over-generosity of grief. All right, so the old man's son was dead. That was tough—but this was war, and things were tough all over. And there was Bell's body too, lying among the dead animals. No one was splitting a gut over Bell. . . .

But still the wail of '*Morte!*' rose and fell. The old man went hopping from man to man, launching anew his accusation of grief.

Mitchell shared the mood of his men. After all, the old man had something left: he had his own life. Whereas Bell was going to stay behind in this farm-yard; and in the mortar-lashed fields ahead others among them were going to die. All he wanted to do now was to stop that wail; he felt like shouting himself. 'Shut up, you old fool,' he wanted to yell. 'At least you've got your own life left. . . .' Mitchell made an angry sign to Corporal DiCicco.

DiCicco's face was stern and set. He caught the old man from behind and held his elbows.

'*Morte!*' The old man broke loose and spat at DiCicco.

DiCicco slapped his face, hard.

Then a new look, a tired, comprehending kind of look formed and settled on the old man's face. Quietly now he sat down, and he sobbed; but it was quiet weeping, as though to himself; a crippled kind of sobbing, as though he realized at last he must hobble his grief and not allow it to importune these others.

Sergeant Mitchell saw the aerial moving at Company Headquarters; and he caught the hand signal from Captain Adam. He gestured his men to their feet. The men stood up, buckling the belts of their equipment.

Then Ewart came over to stand in front of Corporal DiCicco. It was as though he had felt nothing, understood nothing of all

57

that had taken place. 'Hey,' he said to DiCicco. 'What about those chickens?'

For an instant it seemed certain that DiCicco would smash his fist in Ewart's face. But then, abruptly, he turned on his heel.

DiCicco walked back to the place where the old man sat; he hesitated a moment, then he touched him once on the shoulder. When he moved away the sound of sobbing had become low and indistinguishable.

Corporal Fowler's section took the lead. The men fell into step, settling themselves to the weight of weapons and equipment.

Lance-Corporal Harrison moved forward to walk alongside Sergeant Mitchell. They walked several paces in silence, then Mitchell spoke, without turning his head. 'Never mind about that, Harry,' he said. 'They'll be along to bury him later.'

In the fields ahead the explosion of mortar bombs sounded louder and closer.

4

'THERE are your D.F.s,' said the Forward Observation Officer, better known as Foo, as he drew the last circle on his talc-covered map.

Captain Adam seized the map-board greedily; he feasted his eyes on the neatly numbered circles which completely ringed the village of Caielli. Each one represented a Defensive Fire task, a concentrated blast of artillery on a registered piece of ground. Now Adam could call down these D.F.s like a steel ring round his company position.

'Thanks, Foo.' Adam grinned at the artillery officer. 'That makes me feel a lot better.'

'Me too,' said Foo, grinning in return.

Adam was nervous. Last night's attack had been almost too easy. The Battalion had walked into this enemy strong point and captured it practically unopposed. Soon the Germans must wake up to the fact that their vital defence line in front of Ortona had been pierced; when they did they would undoubtedly counter-attack violently. And now it was already first light.

'Just give me the word,' Foo went on, 'and we'll dump the whole Div Arty around you.'

But Adam had already started away. 'Thanks again,' he called over his shoulder. 'I've got to go and tie in with that Limey tank commander.'

Adam crossed the ground with quick, powerful strides, looking every inch the competent infantry officer. And sometimes he was even able to forget that there was nothing inside him except this competence. Each morning when he wakened the emptiness was there, like an aching void. So was the vulture fear; but this had become so familiar, so customary a part of him that now it went unrecognized, almost unsuffered. The emptiness was the horror; and he tried to fill it with his competence—with that, and a burning concern for the soldiers under his command. He did not understand what had happened to him; he only knew it had something to do with the two Italians who were killed in that Sicilian barn-yard. He simply tried to force the whole horror from his mind; and at times like this, when action was imminent, he was partially successful.

Now, as he strode over the ground, he wondered anew at the unexpected success of last night's attack. In silent columns they had clambered through a scrub-choked valley, then climbed the cliff-like slopes of this village. They were in among the houses before a shot was fired; the Germans were still tumbling from their blankets when the first grenades went booming in amongst them. Some German battalion commander, Adam thought with grim satisfaction, was going to have one hell of a lot of explaining to do. . . .

The best part of last night's work was the force of tanks installed inside the battalion perimeter. Six of the supporting British tanks had been able to scale the almost impassable slope. So now, at least, they had these tanks and the artillery D.F.s to sustain them.

Adam found the British tank commander at 'B' Company's forward position. He was a stout, ruddy-faced Major, wearing a turtle-necked sweater. His plump jowls were exquisitely shaven; his face had a pinkish tinge, as though he had come fresh from his tub and toilet lotions. In one hand he sloshed a mug of tea; the other directed the movements of two British troopers who were setting up a Besa machine-gun.

'Hello, old boy.' The Major greeted him warmly, waving the mug in his hand. 'Thought I'd site a few spare guns on the ground to thicken up your defences.'

'Good show!' Adam declared at once.

Half-jokingly he had adopted the other's jargon. He liked this British Major. He also liked the way the little British troopers handled themselves; they knew their business. And these guns sited along the sunken roadbed would be useful indeed.

The two officers discussed technicalities of supporting fire. 'B' Company had one platoon straddling this sunken lateral road, the other two sited in houses of the village which overlooked the road and its approaches. An open field extended for some two hundred yards beyond the sunken road until it merged into bush and sparse forest.

'Nice killing ground—what, old chap?' the Major asked.

'Top-hole,' Adam replied without hesitation.

'Now,' said the Major, serious for a moment, 'all we can do is wait.'

But his face cleared at once; his pink cheeks glowed with good humour. 'Tell you what, old boy,' he confided in a husky whisper. 'I've a bottle of whisky in my tank. When the party's over come and have a splash with me.'

Adam smiled. 'Thanks, old man,' he said. 'I'll be there. You can count on that.'

Both men were grinning broadly as Adam turned to walk back to his Company Headquarters.

5

IN THE village of Caielli Lieutenant-Colonel McNabb, Commanding Officer of the 2nd Rifles, sat at a kitchen table. A cigarette, unheeded, burned almost to the flesh of his fingers.

He ignored the map-boards spread before him. His glance kept darting to the door; he was waiting, with mounting impatience, for the report of his Signals Officer. It was essential to get the field telephone connected and pass his message to Brigadier Kildare. This probing attack had been successful beyond expectation. The Rifles now held the only bridge-head across the river; and if they were reinforced in time to meet the coming counter-attack the whole Divisional assault might be switched. But if they were not reinforced—

Colonel McNabb watched the second-hand of the wrist-watch

propped on the table. By now the enemy must surely be forming up; already this delay was ominous. . . .

'Sir—'

Vipond, the Intelligence Officer, broke in on his thoughts. 'Padre Doorn is here. He says it's urgent. Something about two "S" cases in the R.A.P. who want to rejoin their companies.'

Vipond got this out in an apologetic rush; plainly he had spoken only at the Padre's insistence. An 'S' case was a soldier suffering from 'exhaustion', diagnosed by a Medical Officer as too sick to fight.

A look of thunder touched the Colonel's face. He wheeled toward the doorway. There he discerned the Padre's figure, blocking the light, shrouded in a loose trench coat. The long figure started to advance.

'Padre—' The Colonel's voice stopped him like a lash. 'The R.A.P. happens to be no goddamned business of yours. Henceforth I'll trouble you to attend to your own proper duties. Good day.'

Colonel McNabb turned his back. For a moment the shadowy form hesitated, but the barely-controlled fury in the C.O.'s voice was unmistakable. In the doorway there was a shapeless shuffle of a salute, and the figure vanished.

The Colonel sat down again, aching with anger. He had grown to detest this ghoul of a Padre. Now, at a time like this, speaking to soldiers in the R.A.P., trying to recall their sick minds to some impossible vision of duty; when instead he should be out passing round cigarettes. . . . Why, the man even *looked* like a ghoul, in that flapping trench coat, flopping round the company positions looking for corpses—happy only when he had a burial service to conduct. . . . Well, by God, once this action was over—

'Phone's in, sir!' sang Vipond's excited voice.

Three minutes later the Colonel laid the receiver down. His fingers drummed on the kitchen table. 'Vipond,' he said. 'If there's time I want an "O" group. Call the Companies at once.'

He answered the urgent question in Vipond's face. 'The Division is committed to the attack on the coast. But we're ordered to hold this bridge-head at any cost.'

'Yes, sir.' Vipond reached for the battalion telephone.

But in the same instant both men froze, heads cocked in an odd, arrested motion as they listened to the mortaring on the forward positions. They detected a new note in the sound: the bombs were falling in a sustained, saturating pattern. Then from the far left, from 'B' Company's position, came the loud lashing roll of machine-guns. The Colonel sat down again. Vipond's hand dropped from the telephone.

6

THE mortar concentration lasted three minutes. Behind came the German tanks and infantry: waves of infantry, rolling through the forest and out on to the open killing-ground. They were following closely, perhaps only fifty yards, behind their mortar barrage. The men of the Rifles saw this, and despite the interdicting fire they stayed at the top of their slit trenches or their windows, and they kept on firing.

The first attack was beaten off. Lumbering in blind the German Mark 4s were easily picked off by the hull-down British tanks. The infantry were cut down by machine-guns and the blasts of 25-pounders, far in the rear, firing their concentrated D.F.s. But after such a show of force it was plain the enemy would come again: this had been a full battalion attack launched against each flank of the Rifles' position.

When the lull came the men of Ten Platoon looked out of the windows of the two stone houses they occupied and saw the battle litter they had helped create. Five German tanks were burning; the dead were spread, in lumps and bundles, over the ground. At the sunken roadbed Twelve Platoon had suffered most. Wounded men lay on the banks of the road, crying out terribly for help. Among them the furthest-advanced German tank wore the body of its dead commander draped like a pennant round its turret.

Corporal DiCicco stirred angrily at Sergeant Mitchell's side. 'Can't we help those guys?' he said, pointing to the wounded.

Mitchell's own face was an ugly scowl. 'Wait,' he said.

And a moment later they saw Captain Adam out on the ground directing stretcher-bearers. The unwounded men of Twelve Platoon came walking back to the houses, their faces white, carrying extra weapons and bandoliers of ammunition. Sergeant Mitchell moved about assigning them new fire positions at the windows.

Then the artillery concentration hit the village. The men held to the quaking floors of their houses as though there was danger they might fall off. When the mortaring began again they knew the infantry were coming, so they stood up and went back to their windows.

Sergeant Mitchell directed the platoon's fire from an upstairs window. Kneeling beside him, firing his Bren gun, was Simpson. Unbelievably, the front edge of Simpson's helmet had been smashed flat. His hands, caked with dried blood, ministered expertly to his gun. The barrel was over-heated and Simpson had to fire in very short bursts. As he fired he sang his song. 'Maybe it itches,' his voice croaked. Then a short burst. 'But—' Another burst of three rounds—'It kills the sons of the bitches!' Final burst, magazine off, new magazine flicked on; finger gentling on the trigger again, and the fire and the song continued. It would continue, Mitchell knew, as long as there were men to fire at, or until the barrel burst.

Mitchell's thoughts were grim as he fired his own rifle. There simply were not enough Simpsons, not enough Bren guns, to stop this kind of attack. The tanks were firing high-explosive shells in their windows; the houses were slowly collapsing. Two British tanks were burning. And some of the German infantry had got beyond the sunken roadbed.

Simpson rolled from his window and fell to the floor. 'Stopped!' he bellowed. 'Can't get another round through the bloody barrel.'

He lay on the floor swearing. A moment later Mitchell dropped himself as a burst ripped the wood-work and lodged a jagged splinter in his cheek. He lay within inches of Simpson's sweat-caked face. The two men regarded one another solemnly; their lips blasphemed in slow unison. Suddenly Simpson started to laugh. 'Yeah,' he said. 'Things are sure tough all over. Give me a rifle and let's get the show back on the road.'

But Mitchell was already on his feet. At one window he saw Corporal DiCicco lobbing grenades as fast as he could pull the pins. That meant that the infantry were all around them.

'Back to the windows!' Mitchell roared.

He seized a tommy-gun, raced to DiCicco's window, poked his head and shoulders through, aimed, and started to fire.

7

AT FIRST the silence was not quite believable. Before there had been a torrent of thought-devouring noise but now there was nothing: no mortaring, no shelling—nothing but silence. At first men spoke in the loud, half-shouting tone they had used to pierce the previous volume of sound, but once the silence was accepted their voices dropped to a whisper, as though they hoped by this means to avert the onset of invading noise again.

It was ten o'clock in the morning; the sun was well up, the day was hot. Adam and Sergeant Mitchell stood together looking out of a window. From the field, with its dead bodies and burning tanks, vapours of heat steamed from the ground. There was only one question in everyone's mind.

'Will they come again?' Mitchell asked, in the low voice all had adopted.

'Maybe not,' said Adam.

In reality he was sure the enemy would attack again, but there were reasons why they might not and it did good to speak them aloud. 'After all,' he said, 'they've lost all their tanks, what amounts to two battalions of infantry. Unless they have more tanks, and more men—'

'Good,' declared Simpson, speaking from the floor. 'The bugger will fire now.' He clicked the retaining catch on the barrel of his Bren, and looked up at Adam. 'What about ammunition, sir?' he asked. 'I've only got one magazine left.'

'It's coming up from B.H.Q.,' Adam replied. 'Whatever there is left.'

He turned to Sergeant Mitchell. 'Everyone might as well stand down. We'll know soon enough if they're coming again.'

Adam set out to tour his defensive position. His whole force, including British troopers from the burned-out tanks, now occupied only three houses. In the street, sheltered between the houses, N.C.O.s were doling out the last precious rounds of ammunition. Stretcher-bearers lifted their burdens with painful care over the rubble and debris. Some of the men sat cleaning their weapons; others picked at opened tins of bully beef, or simply sprawled in the sun.

Every man Adam spoke to replied in the same quiet voice which had become the universal speech of Caielli. And everywhere, with no orders given, men were working: moving bricks to strengthen fire positions, or helping to carry the dead and wounded. When orders were necessary these were mere gestures or soft-spoken words. There was no voice of command, and certainly no voice of anger heard in Caielli.

There was a gentleness about every soldier in Caielli. Each man was considerate toward his fellows. Faults and meannesses which at other times would have drawn quick anger were overlooked, or even ceased to exist. Even little Ewart, Adam now noted with surprise, cigarette dangling from his lip, was helping to lift a body over the rubble, although he could have been taking his ease alone somewhere. In times of extremity Adam had seen this same thing before. There was tenderness in the streets of Caielli.

At the sunken road Adam found the British tank Major. His body lay half out of his tank turret. Adam looked, and he thought with a pang of sorrow: We'll never drink that bottle of whisky now. . . . It must have been an A.P. shell because the Major had no head: there was only the red, meaty stump of his neck. Adam closed his eyes. The sunlight burned his eyelids; the smell of charred flesh was stifling, choking. Quickly he turned away.

Adam called his platoon commanders together, although there was little to deliver in the way of orders. They sat on the brick floor of a cellar: Sergeant Mitchell from Ten Platoon, a corporal representing Twelve Platoon, and Lieutenant Venner, an experienced officer, commanding Eleven Platoon. At one end of the cellar a ramped door had been ripped off. Sunlight and rubble dust filtered through.

Their small affairs of business were soon concluded, but long after there was reason to do so they continued to sit together on the brick floor. It was cool and restful here. For a moment Adam's thoughts drifted back to that other cellar, the first cellar—at the Castello Donato in Sicily. He looked at Mitchell and he started to grin.

But suddenly every glance darted to the beamed ceiling of the cellar. An immense whoosh of sound possessed the sky; each one of them knew at once that some huge projectile was hurtling toward them.

Instinctively each man rolled flat on the bricks and started to count. Adam peered in Mitchell's face which lay within inches of his own. 'Twelve seconds!' he said in a voice of awe.

The sky was strangling in a noose of noise, then the shell struck upon the south slope of the village. Every brick and stone in Caielli was loosened; the brick floor they lay on trembled with concussion.

Lieutenant Venner was the first to speak. 'Big enough to be 280-millimetre,' he said, in a tone of objective appraisal.

'May be a good sign,' Adam remarked. 'It could be a hate stonk if they're not going to attack again.'

The bombardment continued. With each explosion the cellar shook; masonry tumbled outside. Adam found the brick pleasantly cool on his cheek. Around him his men held to the quaking floor, smoking cigarettes, listening and waiting. In the doorway a swirling cloud of rubble dust almost obscured the sun.

Then, for an instant, this dim light was blotted from view. A gaunt figure loomed in the opening, crashed through, and rolled on the floor before them. The figure was enveloped in a loose, hampering garment; there was a thrashing struggle until it was launched to its feet. The garment turned out to be a trench coat. The figure was Padre Philip Doorn.

The Padre stood on his feet and faced them. As he moved flakes of debris snowed from his head and shoulders; his face was pasty-white. Only his eyes were alive: two coal-black eyes burned in the white mask of rubble. One arm of the trench coat lifted. His mouth was a black gash.

'Back to your posts, men!' cried the Padre, in a voice of sternest doom. 'The enemy has overrun your position.'

The men on the floor stared at the accusing figure. They could read battle noises like a musical score; they knew there was no enemy attack; yet here came this alien creature flopping among them, reviling, accusing. He brought with him a new and ugly passion, quite foreign to the spirit of Caielli which they had all earned and shared between them this day. The men on the floor looked and felt anger flare inside them.

Adam came to his feet; he made a noise in his throat and he started forward. But Sergeant Mitchell caught him from behind. 'The man's demented!' Mitchell hissed in his ear.

Adam stopped and looked at Sergeant Mitchell with surprise

—not at what Mitchell said, but at the word he chose to use. Adam's arms dropped to his side. He moved out of the way.

Mitchell and Lieutenant Venner exchanged a glance. Then they started to advance, shoulder to shoulder. On their faces they wore broad, reassuring smiles. Together they moved upon the erect, monumental figure. Slowly, carefully, they closed in on Padre Doorn.

8

THERE was a third attack, but it was a minor affair: a mere matter of spite which accomplished nothing except to add to the toll of dead on both sides.

Then, at five o'clock in the afternoon, a battalion of Punjabi infantry marched into Caielli to relieve the 2nd Rifles. The danger of any further attack had lessened to the extent that both Commanding Officers agreed to effect the relief while it was still daylight.

The little Indian soldiers, jaunty, high-stepping, marched in behind their British officers; they stared at the devastated village, the unburied bodies, the awful spent force of battle everywhere; and their faces grew solemn. The men of the Rifles were moving out in small, patchy columns: sections of two or three men weighted down with the weapons of their dead comrades. In numbers a Punjabi platoon seemed a strong company compared to these straggling groups. The Indians looked at the Canadians with respect.

A British subaltern stood with the Punjabi's Adjutant outside Battalion Headquarters. He frowned thoughtfully as he watched; he bit at his blond moustache. 'Where are they going now?' he asked.

'Don't suppose they'll ever catch it worse than they did here,' the Adjutant replied. 'They're moving over for the Ortona attack.'

9

SOME weeks later Brigadier Ian Kildare, D.S.O., was being driven in his jeep through the streets of Ortona. At the wheel was Hunter, his melancholy Brigade Major; in the back of the jeep sat a morose, black-visaged man with intense smouldering eyes. This was Corporal Fergus, who served as the Brigadier's combination orderly, bodyguard, and bagpiper.

The Brigadier's silver badge, the Hart Rampant, winked bravely in the January sun; his glance was serene as he surveyed the rubble-cleared streets. The battle for Ortona had been won a week before; now his victorious Brigade occupied the town for a period of rest. He was mildly surprised to observe how many houses remained undamaged. Whole sections of the town, of course, were smashed flat—by guns and tanks, and where his men had mouse-holed with explosive charges from one house to the next, and then fought the German paratroopers from attic to cellar and out onto the rubble piles again. Still, there were streets the fighting never reached; and since all the inhabitants had been killed or evacuated there was ample space to accommodate his three infantry battalions.

Brigadier Kildare gazed through a rich screen of cigar smoke. In appearance he was as unassailably majestic, as infallibly Jovian, as he had ever been. In fact, however, his personal fortunes were by no means secure. He had discovered that a hard core of resistance had formed to oppose his inevitable promotion to Major-General.

In honesty no one could deny his military competence. His battle sense was intuitive genius; he was swift in executing each tactic. He was the first, for instance, to use tanks—successfully—forward of infantry in an area of anti-tank guns; first to send columns of infantry infiltrating through enemy defences at night. His ability to foresee the enemy's intention was uncanny. He anticipated the only major counter-attack that was made, and so disposed his fire power that the chosen killing-ground was littered with dead Germans.

In that case why should he not go on to command the Division, the Corps, and even an Army in due course?

There were many reasons, but chief of these was the lack of obligation he felt to conceal his contempt from others less gifted. To a 'G' staff which had spent laborious weeks manufacturing an operation order for crossing the straits of Messina came Brigadier Kildare to leaf negligently through their pages. 'Useful for the latrine,' he observed, 'if nothing else.' And in the end the planners hated him no less because he happened to be right.

It was the glowering Fergus, however, who really sealed his doom. When Brigadier Kildare arrived at a Divisional 'O' Group insultingly arrayed in the regimentals of the mythical Scottish Borderers, that was bad enough. But then to be followed by this hangdog, personal piper—the other senior commanders looked at each other wordlessly and made a vow: Kildare would only command the Division over the heap of their dead bodies. . . . Fergus was the unforgivable insult.

Little was known about this mysterious Fergus, although it was said that he came from a Glasgow slum. He followed everywhere in his master's footsteps like a vicious dog, owning allegiance only to his Brigadier. In fact, Kildare had discovered him by chance one day in a British holding unit, piping like an angel, looking like a devil; and by bribery or intimidation he had effected his transfer to the Canadian Army and an honoured place on his personal staff.

The Brigadier accurately appreciated the enmity of the others, the threat to his ambitions, but he showed no least sign of perturbation. If anything he only showered more favours on Fergus. He promoted him corporal. And each evening Fergus piped the Brigadier to dinner; the air around Brigade Headquarters pulsated with wild bagpipe dissonance as Fergus strutted up and down, paining out his marches, his pibrochs and laments. When the keening was done the Highlander from Vancouver and the Highlander from Glasgow would sit down to drink a solemn dram together. No, the Brigadier was not in the least perturbed. To the end he would follow his destiny, and it appeared that Fergus would follow close behind.

Now, on the rubbled street, the jeep squeezed past a chugging bulldozer. The Brigadier's mind catalogued details about the billets they drove past, but he was here with more definite purpose than that. He was driving toward 'B' Company of the 2nd Rifles and Captain John Adam, to bear him certain intelligence. His high affection for Captain Adam dated back to the first day in Sicily.

The jeep turned sharply into a square. Ahead the Brigadier saw a sweep of blue Adriatic, glinting in sunlight hundreds of feet below. On one hand was a ruined castle, on the other a church—even more devastated, but with ruins soaring upward to heaven where its vast dome was sliced vertically in half. Sticking from the rubble at the base of the church was a sign fixed on a stake. 'Twelve Platoon Latrine,' this sign announced.

The Brigadier signalled Hunter to stop. From the sign on the ground his gaze travelled upward, flowing with the flaring buttresses. Seagulls flapped whitely round the opened dome; on the inside, suddenly and delightfully exposed to heaven, painted saints and cherubim seemed to swim gaily in the sky. It made one giddy to look.

For several moments the Brigadier's glance shuttled from Twelve Platoon's latrine to the airborne saints and seagulls. Then he chuckled; it was a rumble of warmest pleasure.

'D' ye see that, Fergus, man?' the Brigadier demanded.

Fergus made no reply, until it was plain one was awaited. 'Aye, sir,' he grunted, without raising his glance.

'Hunter,' the Brigadier went on, seeking more active appreciation. 'Here, revealed before us, is the junction point of heaven and most earthy earth!'

Hunter produced an adequate noise of laughter, and the Brigadier's chuckle rumbled on. His gaze followed the pink cherubs with affection as they breast-stroked their way among the soaring gulls. He blew contented clouds of smoke from his cigar.

10

'GOOD morning, sir.'

Captain Adam saluted and stood at attention beside the jeep. His battle-dress was freshly creased, his belt and revolver holster blancoed, his boots brilliantly polished—in every way he looked the alert, well-turned-out officer. In fact, however, Adam suffered from a mild hang-over; and he was impatient to return with Mitchell, his newly-promoted Company Sergeant-Major, to the Company's training area. He only wanted to get this unexpected visit from the Brigadier over with, and get back to his work.

'Good morning, sir,' Captain Adam said again, vying for the Brigadier's attention. Brigadier Kildare still feasted his gaze on the happy juxtaposition of latrine and heaven.

The Brigadier turned at last, his face a massive smile. 'Ah,' he stated. 'Adam. Have you got 'em by the balls?'

'Yes, sir.'

Adam spoke with no change of expression. Gone were the days of the barked word 'Sah!', the wrist-breaking Hart Rampant salute. Adam stood waiting.

Regally Brigadier Kildare descended from his jeep. On the pavement his unlimbered frame towered like a monument. He took Adam by one arm and marched him several paces toward the centre of the square.

'Let's not waste time,' the Brigadier said. 'I've two things to tell you: First, your M.C.'s approved—you can put the ribbon up any time. Second, your majority has also come through. This is advance information. McNabb will be telling you later today.'

Adam looked up at the big, moon-like face. It was beaming; and he fancied there a look very close to affection. Why, he thought with surprise, he came all this way to tell me himself—

'Congratulations,' the Brigadier added as an afterthought.

'Thank you, sir,' said Adam.

Once, Adam remembered, in the long-ago before Sicily, he had day-dreamed of how he might feel at a moment like this. But now the news brought him no sense of elation. When confirmed, a company commander automatically became a major; the men of his company had earned him that Military Cross, and more. . . .

'One other thing, Adam. Want you to advise me on—'

The Brigadier looked serious; the butt of his cigar smouldered unheeded between his fingers. 'It's that Padre fellow—Doorn.'

Adam glanced quickly away. This was the last thing he wanted to think about this morning. He only wanted to get back and see how his reinforcements were mastering their grenade drill. But the Brigadier stood waiting for his comment.

'The Padre?' Adam asked.

'Yes. McNabb wants me to fire him. What do *you* think?'

Adam stood silent.

'It was in your company position that the man caused some kind of disturbance and had to be restrained. I'm going to abide by your judgment as to whether he should be dismissed or not.'

Adam became more conscious of his hang-over; his thought processes were sluggish and unwilling. Deliberately, he had forced this problem from his mind. For some time now—and it was not only that affair in Caielli—he had sensed something frightening, even evil perhaps, about his former friend Padre Doorn. Yes, for

71

the good of everyone the man probably should be fired, and yet—
who was *he* to pass judgment? Especially since he felt himself
yoked to the other by an inescapable bond that had been forged
in that Sicilian barn-yard, when big Jim and little Joe were
executed. He would never forget the awful moment when he and
the Padre looked at each other, and knew that neither one would
do anything to stop the execution; their glance said something
that was never finished, perhaps because it never could be
finished. . . .

'Well?' The Brigadier tapped on his cigar case.

Recently Adam had heard that the Padre was going quietly
about his affairs, as though anxious to avoid notice, eager to hold
his job.

'Well, sir,' said Adam, with heavy effort, 'they say he's doing
a proper job now.'

'Yes,' said the Brigadier. 'Even McNabb admits that. And
chaplains are bloody scarce—at the moment there's no replacement available. That's why I ask: keep him or fire him?'

'You require my opinion, sir?'

'*Yes*, dammit! That's what I said—it's up to you.'

There was silence. For an instant Adam closed his eyes; then he
looked up again. 'Keep him,' he said, in a voice that was barely
audible.

'All right.' Brigadier Kildare turned back to his jeep, the matter
at once erased from his mind.

'Now, Adam,' he went on, as the two men walked slowly across
the square. 'I consider you the best company commander in my
Brigade—if not in the whole of Italy. Henceforth I want you to
come to me directly with any problems you may have.'

Adam could not prevent the surprise from showing on his face.
Then, after a moment, he thought that he understood. Together
he and the Brigadier had overruled Colonel McNabb on the subject of the Padre's dismissal. And hence there was to be a
reciprocal bond between them too. . . . But this was absurd: there
was no one he respected more than Colonel McNabb. Adam
gulped; he opened his mouth to speak.

'No—' The Brigadier shook his head. 'Never mind bothering
me with thanks, Adam.'

The jeep sagged heavily as the Brigadier climbed aboard. 'One last thing. Starting tomorrow five days' leave will be granted to all ranks. Up to one-half your strength may be away at any one time.'

Adam's response was immediate. 'That's going to play hell with our training, sir.'

Since the Battalion moved into rest he had been so obsessed with the urgency of training his reinforcements that the possibility of leave had never occurred to him. A trained soldier stood a greater chance of living, and it had become Adam's whole purpose in life to prevent as many of his men as possible from being killed. This news made him uneasy—with half his strength away at one time the Company would cease to be wholly under his command.

Settled in his seat, the Brigadier was sucking billowing plumes of smoke from a new cigar. Hunter held the jeep in gear. Fergus stared indifferently at the back of his master's neck. Adam stood on the pavement, frowning.

Suddenly the Brigadier looked up. 'Who commands Twelve Platoon?' he demanded.

'Lieutenant Venner, sir.'

'Well—my compliments to Mr. Venner, and my congratulations on owning the most religious latrine in all Italy!'

But Adam was thinking about what this leave business would mean; and he did not even remember to smile. He was still frowning as he saluted and the jeep pulled away.

11

IT WAS like coming to the city after a winter spent in the bush or on the farm. The streets of Bari loomed as large and magnificent as those of London, or New York, or Montreal.

On this first morning of leave the men from Ten Platoon followed obediently in Sergeant DiCicco's footsteps, almost as though marching to some Company duty. For the moment, until they were oriented, they felt safer bunched together. They wore fresh uniforms, with bright unit and Divisional flashes agleam on their sleeves. They walked with the stiff gait and curiosity of new-landed tourists. To them the seaport city appeared much vaster than it was; when they saw street-car tracks, although no street-cars were running, they stopped and nudged one another with delight. Bari was cream white in January sunshine, the Adriatic a dancing, cobalt blue; and the sparkle shone in all their eyes. Their mood of holiday excitement grew fiercer every moment.

DiCicco wanted to get away from these others. He knew exactly how he planned to spend *his* leave. He was going to find a family, preferably in some remote, outlying part of the town, a family with a dark-haired, amply-fleshed daughter, and for five days he was going to live as the son-in-law of that family. It was the simple family life DiCicco wanted. No whoring or drunken dissipation for him— he just wanted to put his feet up somewhere with a dark-haired girl beside him. And since he could speak Italian his plan was quite feasible. His plans were clear enough, all right; but now DiCicco's ugly, good-natured face was set in a scowl of worry. It was not really his concern what happened to the men who accompanied him, and yet—there was young Jones. *Somebody* had to look after Jonesy.

There was no doubt that Frazer and Simpson would be able to look after themselves. DiCicco glanced over his shoulder; he sighed as he saw Frazer swaggering along at big Simpson's side, clutching a mysterious, paper-wrapped parcel under one arm. If anyone, it was the Military Police who should worry with those two on the prowl.

Krasnick, he knew, would report regularly to the Rest Camp to eat the dinners of anyone missing as well as his own; the rest of his time he would spend sleeping or picking his teeth. Shifty little Ewart would disappear at once about some dubious business of his own. But Jonesy—who would do anything he was told, who was utterly vulnerable without someone to guard him. . . . DiCicco bit his lips; his scowl grew blacker as the little band marched on behind him.

On the Corso Vittorio Emanuele the sidewalks were crowded. Soldiers on leave and soldiers from base installations, with their bright Army flashes, wove in and out among the swarming Italians. It was a happy, bustling crowd. Despite all the vicissitudes of war the citizens of Bari still appeared gay and zestful. They were content with the strange condition of peace that had descended on them, content too with the fresh-printed Allied currency temporarily crinkling in the pockets of the foreign soldiery. It was noticeable, however, that the only women on the sidewalks were either very old or very young. Frazer and Simpson exchanged a quick glance; this was an important factor in their planning. Last night they had agreed that in the morning they should do no more than 'case the joint'.

DiCicco had called Krasnick to his side, and the two men talked together as they walked. The little detachment formed a compact file as it paraded the Corso. Palm trees lined both sides of the street; now they were in the centre of the shopping district.

At first the street appeared a bustling Fifth Avenue, but it was soon evident the merchants had little to sell. The stores, with their plate-glass and marble facings, had everything in their windows, but that everything turned out to be pitifully little. One jeweller's window had paste jewels and trinkets; to fill the remaining space there were bottles of hair tonic, shoe laces, belt buckles, and even an illuminated manuscript. Still, a plate-glass window in itself was a novelty, and many soldiers stood with their noses to the glass, studying each item in the sparse array. Every ten feet or so an olive-hued shoe-shine boy clamoured for business; and every fourth doorway led into a barber shop. There were restaurants selling real ice-cream and sweet glasses of syrup. Gay-looking wine shops dotted the street.

DiCicco halted at one of the palm trees and called his band in a circle round him.

'I'm leaving you guys here,' DiCicco announced, slowly looking each one in the face. 'Now get this—'

He stared first at Frazer and Simpson. 'If you two get yourselves arrested, you'll have me and Mitchell to worry about when the M.P.s are finished working you over.' His gaze shifted. 'Ewart—'

The cigarette flicked to the opposite corner of Ewart's mouth. 'Ewart, you do what you damn well want. And Krasnick here has the job of looking after Jonesy.'

DiCicco stared into Jonesy's shining blue eyes, and noted the excitement flushing his handsome face. With both hands he seized the front of the boy's tunic and pulled him within inches of his face. 'Understand, kid? Krasnick here is taking care of you. You do everything that Krasnick says.'

Jonesy bobbed his head up and down in eager agreement.

DiCicco turned. 'O.K. on that, Krasnick? Don't take him no place he can get in trouble.'

'O.K.,' said Krasnick, with no change of expression on his moon-like face.

'Well,' said DiCicco. 'All right then.'

He knew that Krasnick, if dumb, was reliable, and it was the best that he could do. Now he was anxious to get away. 'So long, you guys,' said DiCicco. And he marched quickly away, heading toward a less frequented street.

At the palm tree Frazer and Simpson hung behind for a moment. They had their own consciences to satisfy too. 'Sure you'll be O.K.?' Simpson said to Krasnick.

'Yeah.'

'So long,' said Simpson and Frazer in one voice, as they turned away together.

But Ewart piped up then. 'Hey, Frazer—what you got in that paper parcel?'

Frazer and Simpson hesitated. They looked at each other and they started to grin. They were far too proud of themselves to keep this master-stroke a secret. Frazer undid one end of the paper parcel and the others saw a sleeve of a battle-dress tunic, with a sergeant's stripes and an 8th-Army flash sewn to the arm.

To Ewart this still did not figure. 'What gives?' he demanded.

'Eighth Army Mobile Bath Unit,' Simpson answered proudly.

Ewart's little eyes were round Os of anger; he still did not understand. Krasnick and Jonesy simply looked blank; probably they never would understand.

'Look, you dope,' Frazer explained. 'We lifted these tunics from the Rest Camp last night. The M.P.s start chasing us—see? They're looking for two Canadians—see? That's when we blow the joint and join the Mobile Bath Unit—whatever the hell that is!'

Ewart was shaken into an admission of deep respect. 'Say— that's sharp. That's real sharp.' He leaned against the palm tree; and he was still shaking his head in admiration as Frazer and Simpson left them, moving into the current of pedestrians flowing along the sidewalk.

The three men remaining looked at one another, at a loss to know what they should do next. Jonesy was smiling, flushed and excited at the endless good time that stretched ahead. Krasnick and Ewart simply ignored each other's presence. For the past year Ewart had been Krasnick's Number Two on the Bren gun, but neither man had ever felt impelled to speak except for some clear and urgent reason, such as indicating a target, or clearing a stoppage on the gun. They stood under the palm tree, eyeing one another for a full minute; finally Krasnick clamped a huge hand on Jonesy's arm, and with no glance for Ewart, moved onto the sidewalk. After a moment Ewart followed behind; temporarily at least he had his own reason for staying with these two.

For an hour they window-shopped. Jonesy, of course, was entranced; he cried out his pleasure at each glittering object he saw. 'Gee,' he exclaimed, for the tenth time. 'Can't I buy that one?'

'No,' Krasnick replied at once. And his heavy hand pulled Jonesy along.

But a moment later Krasnick came to a stop himself, his attention riveted on an object in one of the bright windows. Ewart took advantage of this fact to sidle up beside Jonesy. 'Come with me, kid, and I'll show you a real good time,' he muttered from one corner of his mouth, his cigarette dangling from the other.

Ewart knew that like himself Jonesy had ten crisp 100-lire notes folded in his pocket, received from the Camp Paymaster that very morning. It was his plan to extract the 1,000 lire from Jonesy before proceeding to his other business. This was an easy way to double his original ante. It was a poor leave, Ewart figured, if he did not return a richer man than when he started.

Krasnick's fingers still gripped Jonesy in a clamp of steel, but he stood motionless, mouth agape, all his awareness concentrated on the object in the window. Ewart had never known the stolid Krasnick to display such interest before; he peered over his shoulder to discover the cause. It was a belt Krasnick was looking at—a black and red leather belt, richly tooled and embossed. On closer inspection Ewart made it out to be a money-belt.

'Find out how much!' Krasnick spoke without turning his head. In the same way he might have ordered: 'Load another magazine.'

Ewart shrugged and moved to obey. A few moments later he emerged from the store. 'Six hundred lire,' he reported.

With no further word Krasnick turned on his heel, pulling Jonesy along behind him. It was as though he had been told that the belt was a millionaire's possession, and had at once dismissed all thought of it from his mind.

12

EWART was not pleased with the restaurant Krasnick had selected for lunch. His glance darted angrily round the spacious, well-lighted room, at the Britishers filling the scrubbed-oak tables and swarming at the bar. They were the only Canadians present and there was not an Italian in the place. Ewart had vainly tried to lead the way into a dimly-lit wine shop where instinct told him he would be bound to meet accommodating citizens who shared his interest in financial transaction. For one thing he wanted to get a quick market appraisal of the sackful of supplies he had cached back at the Rest Camp. But Krasnick had stopped a British transport corporal, asked his advice, and here they were.

The three of them had one of the large oak tables to themselves. They sat and stared with unabashed curiosity at the other customers present. All these soldiers from the base establishments seemed to know one another; cheery greetings were called across the room; each table was spread with small, unlabelled bottles of white wine. The food on the zinc-covered bar looked tasty and different: there was bread and *pasta,* and numerous little bowls containing sauces. Ewart's eyes lighted a little when he observed one plate which displayed indisputable slabs of Army bully beef.

While they were still gawking a waiter placed three of the little wine bottles on their table. Jonesy's glance was sheer rapture; his look pleaded; and after a moment Krasnick decided to allow him this treat. Ewart touched Jonesy on the arm and gestured to the waiter. 'Jonesy,' he said. 'Give the man some money.'

'No,' said Krasnick, with a black look. 'We pay our share.'

From a pocket deep inside his tunic Krasnick pulled out a purse, one of faded leather, shiny with use, locked with a substantial metal clasp. Ewart, who slept and fought beside this man, had never seen the purse before. *Now* he understood Krasnick's passion of adoration for that money-belt back in the shop window.

The waiter departed after each man handed over a hundred-lire note. No one touched the wine until the change had been returned and distributed. Ewart sipped gloomily at his glass.

The room was a blue haze of cigarette smoke; more Britishers were coming in each minute. Two soldiers halted at Krasnick's shoulder. 'Mind if we join you, mates?' asked the older one, a man with a darkly humorous face. He snapped his fingers for wine and both men sat down. The second Englishman was a frail-looking, fair-haired boy about twenty years old. 'Here's how,' said the dark one. They drained their glasses, and again the older man snapped his fingers.

The three Canadians stared at the new arrivals in silence. Jonesy was eager to talk, of course, but did not know how to begin; and the others talked only when there was some clear reason for doing so. Accordingly the three of them sat in silence and raked the Englishmen with their stares. The two Britishers grew restive under this unwavering regard. They thought, of course, that these were any three ordinary Canadian soldiers; they could not know what a very un-average trio they had by chance encountered.

Finally it was the older man who broke the silence. He regarded the three solemn, fish-eyed, unblinking faces. 'Well,' he said. 'You three chaps off on a hell-raising spree?'

His remark only produced more searching stares.

By now Ewart was about ready to give up; Jonesy's 1,000 lire was being too closely guarded. But before he left it occurred to him these two characters might give him some useful gen.

'What outfit you guys with?' Ewart demanded, speaking to the older of the two men.

'Sanitation,' the man replied shortly.

He and his companion stirred in their seats; they looked round the room to see if any other tables were vacant. The attitude of these Canadian infantrymen convinced them that trouble was about to develop. Base troops were sensitive, and these others seemed spoiling for a fight.

'Sanitation,' the older man said again, in a firm ringing tone.

'Yeah?' Ewart's sneer expressed interest, although the two men could not know that fact. 'What sort of racket is that?'

'Sanitation!' Jonesy suddenly burbled out, delighted to pass such a difficult word over his tongue.

Krasnick stared and said nothing.

'We spray houses with D.D.T.,' said the younger, fair-haired boy. His mouth was a quivering line of truculence.

'What the hell's D.D.T.?' The cigarette dangled in one corner of Ewart's mouth; actually his curiosity was fading fast.

'Sanitation!' Again Jonesy rolled out the word in triumph.

'Yes,' the older man said savagely. 'And what's it to you? For

your information D.D.T. stands for dichlorodiphen-something. . . .
Anyway, when this war's over it's going to revolutionize
agriculture!'

The Sanitation man spoke on, in firm, emphatic tones, explaining the works and wonders of D.D.T. And then—if these three
continued to stare at him insultingly *he* was going to strike the
first blow.

Jonesy and Ewart did not even pretend to listen; and Ewart
started to stand up. But Krasnick had shifted in his chair. He sat
forward, his eyes opened wide, and he drank in every word. For
the first time he allowed his hand to drop from the back of Jonesy's
chair.

'Look,' Krasnick suddenly interrupted. 'You take a quarter
section of wheat—'

His whole attention was focused on the man opposite him;
unthinking, he drained his glass of wine. The Sanitation men
warmed to this new interest; both Britishers nodded and smiled.

Ewart's little eyes narrowed and he sat down again. The discussion continued; more wine arrived on the table; and every
moment the room became more crowded, more clogged with
smoke. Half an hour later Krasnick did not even turn his head
when Jonesy and Ewart stood up and slipped away from the table.

13

IN A corner of the city refuse dump, warmed by the afternoon
sun, with the blue-white Adriatic lisping below, Frazer tried to
control his giggling long enough to receive the bottle of cognac
from Simpson. Then, with the bottle safely in his hands, Frazer
leaned back and hooted. Tears rained down his cheeks, he was
going to choke with laughter. At his side big Simpson held both
hands to his belly and howled. Affrighted, the rats of the dump
put down their tails and ran.

'It's a secret weapon—that's what it is, Sim!' Frazer barely got
the words out before he started to strangle again.

'And the old bag's face!' Simpson's hand struck hard on Frazer's
knee. Both men rolled in the dirt, laughing with fierce,
uncontrollable sobs.

Frazer and Simpson had pulled off the coup of their lives. They
had visited, made effective use of the facilities of a brothel, and

then walked out without paying. When it came time to depart from their respective rooms there had been an exchange of knocks on the wall. Then, in place of two Canadian soldiers, out strode a sergeant and a private of the 8th Army Mobile Bath Unit. The sergeant brushed by the gaping madam with a curt nod of dismissal, ushering his smaller companion into much more sanitary surroundings.

Struggling, the two men subdued their fit of laughter. The memory of their feat swirled round them, as warm and glowing as the cognac that they drank.

'Sim,' said Frazer, with a happy sigh, 'you sure earned your three stripes the hard way.'

They laughed again, but this time with a gentle, spent kind of reminiscence. Lying on the refuse dump they filled with tired content. Below them they heard the lapping Adriatic; out at sea black smoke clouds tugged behind a racing destroyer. It was late afternoon now; dusk was not far away. They were warmed with cognac and satisfaction, and four golden days of leave still stretched ahead.

'Pass the bottle,' Simpson said. The two men settled back comfortably on their refuse pile.

'*Mille grazie,*' said DiCicco, accepting the chair in front of the fire which the old man offered. He sat down gratefully; as he took the cup of wine from the old man's hand his smile was pure bliss.

From her corner the dark-haired daughter of the house smiled once, then quickly lowered her eyes. They had met in a small nearby square, where DiCicco at once took the burden of kindling from her arms and explained in gentle Italian that such labour was not for a beautiful creature like her. From that moment an attraction like a physical warmth of touch had flowed between them.

DiCicco gave the old man a cigarette. On the kitchen table were stacked the tins of bully beef he had brought from the Rest Camp. The family did not yet understand that he was *Canadese,* not *Americano;* perhaps they never would, and he couldn't care less. There were going to be much more important things to occupy him during the next four days. He leaned back in his chair and pushed his boots closer to the fire. DiCicco sighed happily and unhooked his collar. He was at home.

The Military Police patrol found Jonesy peacefully asleep in an alley-way. The M.P. corporal tugged at Jonesy's limp body until he had him propped in a sitting position, illuminated by the harsh headlights of the jeep. Jonesy blinked, and opened his eyes sleepily. 'Hi,' he said.

His uniform looked as though it had been trampled by horses in a field of mud; dried blood clotted his hair and caked his face; but Jonesy was quite happy. He had learned one tune; and when he got drunk it was his habit to sing this one snatch of song interminably. He opened his mouth.

'Maybe it itches,' Jonesy's voice croaked. Then, more confidently, and with a sudden burst of power: 'Kills the sons of the bitches!' The words went booming down the hollow alley-way, and Jonesy giggled. He was feeling fine.

'Hospital or guard-house?' called the driver of the jeep in weary tones.

'Oh—guard-house, I suppose.'

The corporal was gloomy. He did not like this neighbourhood; he wanted to be back where there were lights. The whole area was out of bounds, each alley-way was honeycombed with dangerous dives. Just now he had imagined the sound of a door opening; he hated to turn his back on any of these dark doorways. But now he had his burden tottering on its feet; Jonesy flung an affectionate arm round his neck. They started toward the jeep.

'Corporal—I say, Corporal!'

This hail came in an English accent. Then a sergeant, his 8th-Army patch bright in the glare of the jeep's headlights, stepped into view. Behind him was another British soldier who strolled over to the driver of the jeep.

The sergeant—he was a big man, properly dressed except that he wore no hat, and seemed to have suffered some bruises on his cheek—stepped to the corporal's side and peered into Jonesy's bloodied face. 'Why, I believe that I know this poor chap,' the sergeant declared. He spoke with the precisely rounded phonetics of a British Broadcasting Corporation announcer.

The corporal, still holding Jonesy at his shoulder, regarded him

82

coldly. The sergeant's companion was lighting cigarettes with the driver of the jeep.

When he spoke the corporal's voice was as cold as his stare. 'Sergeant, I'll ask for your name, unit and number—'

The sergeant blinked. 'But of course. It's Sergeant, ah—Ian Kildare; 8th Army Mobile Bath Unit. Now, about this poor fellow here—been in a nasty accident, looks like. Thought I could take him to the Canadian Rest Camp in my—vehicle.'

The sergeant's tongue tripped on the word 'vehicle'; indeed, his whole accent had become oddly slurred. He blinked in the bright light and he stared at the corporal owlishly.

'Sergeant, you're out of bounds here—'

The headlights were suddenly extinguished. There was a strangled cry from the jeep, and in the same instant the sound of fist smashing hard upon bone. The corporal buckled quietly at the knees. The sergeant caught hold of Jonesy's swaying body. 'Frazer,' he yelled. 'Come and get him on the other side!' Then there was the sound of heavy boots clattering down the alley-way.

Minutes later, in a still darker alley, three men lay hidden behind a comfortable pile of paving stones. In the darkness Frazer was attempting to place the mouth of a bottle at Jonesy's lips. Beside him big Simpson, the dignity of his sergeant's stripes concealed by the dark, made gasping noises as he sucked at an injured fist. 'I know they didn't have time to fire,' Simpson got out, after a moment, 'but why the hell didn't they drive after us?'

Frazer let Jonesy's body sink back to the cobble-stones. He put the bottle to his own mouth and he swallowed noisily. When he spoke his voice was heavy with reproach.

'Sim,' he said. 'You know better than that. I took the ignition key.'

A back alley of Bari erupted suddenly with the choking gurgles of two men who had to laugh desperately without making noise.

14

THE convoy was being marshalled on the main square fronting the seaport of Bari; beyond the sea-wall the harbour was dotted with squat cargo ships and clean-hulled naval vessels. Tired soldiers dozed inside their trucks, waiting for the long drive back to Ortona to begin. N.C.O.s went up and down the column checking names against nominal rolls.

Lieutenant Venner was racked by arid fever; he had the sere, withered feeling of a man who has survived five days of intolerably satisfying leave; all he wanted in the world now was to crawl into the cab of one of the trucks and go to sleep. But two of his men were missing. Krasnick had brought young Jones in from the Rest Camp where apparently he had been holding him under lock and key; but Frazer and Simpson were unaccounted for. And he had to report this fact to Major Drake, the fearsome officer in charge of the convoy.

'What about the M.P.s?' Lieutenant Venner demanded from Sergeant DiCicco, who stood pallid and gloomy at his side. 'Do they know anything about them?'

'I imagine they know a lot, sir,' DiCicco answered grimly. 'Except where they are right now.'

'*Mister* Venner!' It was Major Drake again, bellowing from the head of the column.

'Well, here goes,' said Venner. 'It's their own damned fault.'

He started to walk forward but DiCicco caught at his arm and pointed out to sea. Three aircraft were sweeping in low, almost touching the water; and there was something indefinably wrong about these planes. Then, at the moment they saw the black crosses on the wings they heard the hollow throttling of machine-guns. Venner fell on top of DiCicco's body as the first explosion rocked the square, hurling pieces of pavement into the air. Venner rolled free and the two men lay side by side, arms over their heads, while more bombs dropped around them. Belatedly the ack-ack guns pounded their piston-slaps of noise into the general din. Venner peered into DiCicco's face close beside his own. 'Thank God,' Venner groaned. 'For a moment I thought it was just my head.'

The sneak raid was over in a matter of seconds; the three planes went skimming out to sea again. Men picked themselves from the ground, swearing a little, dusting and patting their limbs to discover any injury. In the harbour black smoke poured from one of the cargo vessels; the centre vehicle of their own convoy lay smashed on its side, but nobody seemed to be hurt. One man clambered from the damaged truck and stood brushing himself off. 'Hell, sir,' he said to Venner. 'Let's get back to the front where it's safe.'

Half an hour was spent rearranging the truck loads under the lash of Major Drake's booming voice. Some time during this interval Sergeant DiCicco looked up to find Frazer and Simpson both standing helpfully at his elbow. Bits of pavement and masonry clung to them, their faces were pale, but their uniforms seemed surprisingly clean and fresh. DiCicco gave them a look second in ferocity only to the glare that Lieutenant Venner unloosed a moment later. Frazer and Simpson banged their heels together; they stood at quiveringly erect attention. Lieutenant Venner opened his mouth—to speak, to blast, to annihilate.

'*Mister* Venner!' Once again Major Drake was calling from the head of the column. Once again the trucks were loaded and waiting.

Venner stood quite still and thought for a moment. At last he gave the two men a lingering look, and he turned away. Lieutenant Venner cupped his hands. 'All present and accounted for, sir!' he shouted back.

15

THE Padre's utility truck bounced on every bump in the rough, dirt road; its springs twanged a constant rattle of complaint.

Padre Doorn's glance on the pock-marked road was fixed and stern; his knuckles showed white on the steering-wheel. In the cab beside him young Jones, recently appointed to the job of Chaplain's helper, braced his feet against the floor-boards.

Today's objective was in sight ahead: a shining mirage of a village, part way up a mountain-side, where it seemed to squat on top of spiralling entrails of white-gashed track.

The truck bounced, the Padre scowled more fiercely. Jonesy, as the pitching permitted, sniffed at the smell and feel of early spring in the air today. Heat steamed from the fields on both sides; the hedges were white with marguerite, pinkening with dogwood. Jonesy possessed elemental senses: he had never grown far away from nature, and his being was subtly attuned to changes in season. With the same instinct of animals in the nearby fields Jonesy knew this to be the first day of spring. As they drove his nostrils continued to quiver with pleasure.

Padre Philip Doorn only knew that it was later than he thought; he wished he had a jeep instead of this fifteen-hundredweight in order to cover more ground more quickly. But that would have meant seeking Colonel McNabb's permission, and therefore he contented himself with this truck and the fact that his Commanding Officer asked no questions about his long absences from Ortona. The Padre was embarked on a search. Systematically, according to plan, he was visiting a selected list of towns and villages far in the rear of the fighting front.

As the truck's windshield dipped and rose the Padre kept measuring the distant village in his glance. Some time ago he had picked out the Byzantine dome of its blue-white church. This was the church of San Giacomo—today's objective; still miles away. And each day more time was running out; the end of his search was no closer in hand. The Padre clenched his teeth against the bumps; his foot rode the accelerator.

An hour later the truck nosed on to the spiralling track. 'Jones,' the Padre asked, 'what time is it?'

Jonesy answered at once, happily, heedlessly; not even turning his head. 'It's growing time,' said Jonesy.

'What?'

The remark was so much at variance, so grotesquely unrelated to the Padre's own thoughts, that his mind was startled into considering the literal meaning of Jonesy's words. Sometimes the classic simplicity of the things the boy said had this effect. The Padre's glance darted to his new assistant. Through the cab window Jonesy was staring at the flawless sky above; his blue eyes reflected the glow.

'Jones,' the Padre ordered harshly, 'get your eyes back on the road.'

'Yes, sir,' said Jonesy, obeying at once.

The Padre drove on, threading the road's spirals, feeling a new ache of pain in his breast. He had selected young Jones specifically because of his limited intelligence, his unquestioning obedience: these qualities made him the ideal assistant for his present purpose. He had taken advantage of Major Adam's absence on leave to approach the Battalion second-in-command; once, apparently, Adam had asked to have Jonesy transferred to a safer job, and hence the posting was easily arranged. Yes, Jones was ideal for his purpose, but—

There was something about the boy—his moods of quick, soaring elation, his unabashed joy in being alive, the way he had gazed at the sky just now—that reminded the Padre of his own self, as he had once been. The Padre drove on, a desolating pain of sadness in his heart.

When he was a boy, Philip Doorn remembered, he would waken each morning and rush to his window to see if the world had changed overnight. This was quite possible, after all: each day was a miracle; unguessed adventures lay in wait behind each corner and each daybreak. Being alive in itself was an unbearably exciting thing. He lived in the country; his father's house was swaddled in gentle Ontario farmland. And any morning from his window he might discover the mill-pond changed to a glittering sea, the tiny hills swollen into emerald mountains. Each morning, with his first glance at the sky, he drank in huge draughts of happiness.

It remained the same when he grew older. At college, before breakfast and before chapel, he would hurry outdoors as soon as he could; and his first invariable act was to fling his glance upward to the welcoming sky. This was a moment of glory—he was alone with, and in the presence of, his Friend. . . .

The Padre twisted in his seat; his teeth grated together. What sacrilege this seemed now! And yet, at one time, *once* it had been true; so true and so right. . . . Each morning he *spoke* to his Friend; they held quiet communion together. He was vouchsafed calm certainty in the rightness of the world, and he went to his day's work refreshed. Never did he lose his sense of gentle wonder at being alive. And never—until that barn-yard in Sicily—had he felt alone when he stood beneath the sky.

His *Friend*. . . .

The Padre made a noise as if in pain; it was a choking sound which made Jonesy turn in alarm. But he saw only that the gaunt, frightening man beside him was clearing his throat in violence and anger.

'We're here,' Padre Doorn said a moment later, as the truck bounced on the first paving stones. 'This is San Giacomo.'

The Padre paid no heed to the children, the dogs and the

bleating goats that swarmed around the truck. The church lay at the far end of the village and he drove a slow, cleaving path ahead. He had eyes only for this church, but without real expectation: it was simply another to be checked from his list. He guessed he would only find what he had found a dozen times before. . . . The church, ancient and mouldy. Inside, a priest with dirty soutane and stained breviary; a buzzing of sleepy flies, a rank odour of incense and melted wax. Then the laborious greeting, the halting talk in Italian, although he had become quite fluent now; the diseased-looking sexton called in for consultation. And, at last, the regretful shrugging of shoulders; and an invitation to partake of vinegar-tart wine.

No, Padre Doorn held little hope that his search would end today. Not today, perhaps. Not this time, perhaps. But some time—soon. . . .

16

IN THE back of another truck, his body tossing on a sea of piled kit-bags, Adam was returning from his leave in Bari. This morning he had missed the departing convoy, and had hitch-hiked this ride instead. His hands held tight to the tarpaulin straps; but his mind was unaware of his body's bumps and bruises.

On the kit-bags his body lay spent and exhausted, but his mind inhabited a separate existence: detached, it hovered above him, refusing to recognize or even take interest in the animal ache of his body.

He had been the last to go on leave. As long as he could he stayed with the Company, taking over the first static position in the line north of Ortona, fussing over the leave roster of others, afraid to leave the Company deprived of his presence. But now, five days later, the words 'B' Company meant nothing to him. The men under his command—indeed, the whole war and his place in it— had become a remote, shadowy concept without importance or reality. As the truck bumped over the hundred and fifty miles separating Bari from Ortona the only existence his mind recognized was the life he had lived yesterday and last night.

This was an existence with a girl called Elena.

In the bar-room of the Officers' Hotel a drinking companion from the night before called him to his table. In bright morning sunlight the table was aflash with glasses and bottles. There were several British officers, all hung-over, some drunk again already —and three Italian girls. Two of these were unimportant: they looked like, and probably were, tarts. The third was Elena.

Adam sat down with his drink and watched her. Alone of those present he perceived after a moment how artificial her gaiety was; how she laughed to avoid flinching when the meaty hand of the Colonel beside her squeezed the bare flesh of her arm. She laughed when the two tarts did, copying what came to them naturally; but her brown eyes were a hundred times more expressive, and sadder too.

She was attractive, Adam thought: she could even be beautiful; but at the moment her mouth was enlarged and too red with lipstick; there were inadequately powdered circles under her eyes. Adam alone saw that her smile was contrived; once it slipped from her small, oval face she would look as frightened as she actually was. And yet, she made the Italian music of her voice ring more loudly, more vivaciously than the laughter of the old pros.

Hell, Adam thought then as he drank his drink: maybe she *is* new to the game; but if she chooses to play in a league like this she deserves whatever it is she gets. . . .

For the first time their glances met: there was a surprised moment of mutual recognition. Sometimes two strangers will look at one another, and know at once that each will respond to the other if circumstances bring them into relationship; moreover, each will be vulnerable to the other. So it was then in the glance that Adam and the girl Elena exchanged.

Elena was first to drop her gaze; she flushed and moved in her chair so that the Colonel's hand was forced to fall from her arm. Adam went on drinking and watching.

She doesn't like herself, he thought. She doesn't like what she is doing, what she has or may become, and—this came with a flash of unpleasant knowledge—perhaps that is the element common to us both. . . . But he dismissed such thoughts as mere idleness. From the first instant he saw the girl, Adam now realized, he had determined to have her. He wanted her, and he would have her.

And Adam did have her. He took her away from that hotel bar-room, from the other officers, with the same efficiency he displayed in a Company attack. He had her in her own bedroom that afternoon, in half darkness with the shutters closed, while her parents and brothers sat gravely in other rooms of the apartment; then in his hotel room all during the night, with the door barricaded against the prowling world outside.

That first time, as they sat together on her bed, his hands feeling the texture of her flesh, Adam wondered for a fantastic instant if the parents in the rooms outside waited for the creak and groan of bedsprings, and how they planned to spend his 1,000-lire note. There had even been a formal offer of wine; and that—for a blazing moment—sent Adam blindly, furiously mad with anger. The daughter of the house represented the family's capital: they sent her out to earn the food they must eat. . . . But Adam's anger cooled. What the hell, he thought: much worse things than this happen in wartime. . . . He declined the offer of wine and followed Elena into her room.

When their naked bodies touched he felt her thin frame tremble, the smile fixed on her face had become pathetic. But Adam was in a mood of what-the-hell. He stroked her small breasts; experimentally he kissed the hollow of her shoulder. Hell, he thought: she *does* seem new to the game; the forced smile wavered, then her mask of jauntiness cracked, as though for ever. She spoke more English than he did Italian, but now:

'*Ti amo*,' Elena said. 'I love you.'

Adam ignored this. Unresisted, his hand voyaged up and down her trembling body.

'Say it,' she said, half moaning, half tearful. 'Say—*Io ti amo*—'

'Go to hell,' said Adam, going on with what he was doing.

He felt her sobbing under his hands. Then Adam looked into her eyes; he saw the magnitude of her shame, and suddenly he understood. She may have done this before; for all he knew successions of drunken officers may have had her on this very bed. But however often it had happened—and that part did not matter—it had never been more than drunken rutting. She had become a commodity, or the instrument rather, which provided a living for the waiting family outside. But between them there had been that moment of recognition, that flash of communion. And she wanted to pretend that the act they were about to consummate was more than a mere fusion of bodies: that two human beings were concerned, doing this together because they both wanted it so. She wanted to pretend that he was the man who might, under other, better circumstances, have been her lover.

Adam went on looking in her eyes, his hands cupped on her shoulders. She turned her head away and Adam saw her trying to fit the false smile to her face again. Suddenly he was engulfed by an overpowering wave of sadness and pity; the hard lust receded in his body; he hated himself for the thing he had said a moment before. In the shuttered darkness he became aware of his nakedness. Then he took her chin, he forced her face back to his; and he felt like cursing when he saw that bar-room smile of jauntiness trying to remuster itself.

'Elena,' he said. He spoke softly; it was the first time he had used her name. 'Elena. All right. All right then—*Io ti amo.*'

He looked away from the new light in her eyes. It was as easy as that: he had only to pretend, say those words. It was pretence, but he had given her something; and, oddly, he felt better at once, as though he had also given something to himself.

Quickly she pressed her body against his. She kissed him, a kiss that started as a quest of innocent gratitude, but then she was quivering at his touch; her own small hands went to his body, and she was whispering a hot, broken melody of Italian.

It was a night when each one said '*Ti amo*' many times. It was a night of soft agonies, caresses, surrenders, and consummation. And during that night, when their bodies lay stilled, passion for the moment spent, they were aware of themselves as two human beings, aching toward communion: striving toward the impossible union of selves.

It was eight o'clock in the morning when Adam finally got Elena back to her apartment. Then he stopped the first north-bound truck; and flung himself into the back, on top of these kit-bags.

Now as the truck bounced and bumped his body suffered, but without concurrence from his mind. His mind still dwelt apart, reconstructing and rearranging in wonder the words *Io ti amo*. . . . He knew they meant something of immense significance; at this moment they were the only words in the world that mattered. If someone had said to him: ' "B" Company—the 2nd Rifles', that phrase would have come with no more force than a mathematical abstraction.

It was late afternoon when the truck rolled to a bumping stop

outside Battalion Headquarters in Ortona. Adam spoke to no
one. He went directly inside, and fell asleep on the first cot he
stumbled upon.

17

NEXT morning Adam wakened early. The instant he opened his
eyes his mind raced back to yesterday's world: the world of Bari,
and Elena, and the new possibility of existence. He was filled with
restless energy. Snores still sounded from the cots around him as
he dressed, buckled on his belt, and went out into the streets.

A new day of war was beginning. Here, in Ortona's morning
streets, the trained ear could detect each tone and overtone as
instruments tuned for the day's orchestration. In the rear one gun
from a battery of mediums eructated an exploring round; closer,
a troop of twenty-five-pounders banged angrily in unison; a heavy
mortar tube throated metallically, regurgitating its first bomb
before breakfast. Behind the front men would be rolling from
their pup tents; in forward positions they would be standing-to,
weapons cocked, eyes peering into unfolding waves of light. Only
hundreds of yards behind would be the clatter of cook trucks,
the rattle of mess-tins, soldiers whistling, the smell of steaming
porridge. Everywhere men were starting their morning chores:
machine-gunners firing last night's belt to clear their gun; flat
trajectory gunners checking lines of fire; crews carrying bombs to
the mortar sites. Like day labourers the soldiers were moving to
their tasks, tools on their shoulders. Everywhere the day's work
was beginning.

Adam had heard every note of war before; he knew each passage
and the full score; but this morning the sounds glanced from his
mind. Only two miles ahead, at this moment, his Company was
standing-down from its battle positions, but even that fact had
no meaning. His mind was 150 miles away. He existed in another
world called Bari, where *Io ti amo* was the language spoken.

He walked slowly, head down, picking his way between the
neat-swept piles of rubble. He walked the streets of Ortona like
an indifferent visitor who passes time between trains.

By chance he had followed the main street to the western limit
of the town, and now before him he saw, with a thrust of surprise,
the ruined apartment building which 'B' Company had once

attacked and captured. He was forced to remember then, with a pain of recollection. Some of his men had died going through that gaping doorway; then, from those windows, they had fired and thrown grenades at the attacking paratroopers.

Adam stared at the building for several seconds; his mind darted forth on an anxious patrol of thought. Abruptly he turned about.

At the Headquarters mess he ate breakfast by himself, at one end of the table. The other officers glanced once at his drawn face, his air of brooding silence, and left him alone.

Later Adam made his way to the rear H.Q. building. Captain Ramsay, the Adjutant, looked in Adam's face and at once he grinned. 'Say, Johnny,' he remarked, 'next time I'm going to get me a leave like the one you must have had!'

Adam did not reply. He moved to the window and hunched his shoulders as he stood looking down at the street.

'Well,' said Ramsay, suddenly businesslike. 'There's not much new to report. "B" Company's in the same position. Bazin just took over the hot-spot—Point 69—for the next two weeks. A few casualties from shelling. And about the same patrol activity.'

His back turned, Adam still stared from the window.

'Let me know when you want a jeep,' Ramsay continued. 'Bill Begg wants to get back here tonight for sure.'

Adam started to nod. Bill Begg was his second-in-command: he was due to go on leave tomorrow. But his head stayed cocked with an arrested motion. This time he *heard* the single round fired somewhere in the rear. He heard the whistle overhead, and the sound tugged him back a little closer to present reality.

'Here is "B" Company's nominal roll. You'll be pleased to see you're almost up to strength now.'

Adam turned. He walked, as though with effort, to Ramsay's desk. He sat down and took the sheet of paper in his hands. In that instant the familiar names leaped from the typescript and came crowding round him. These names threw chains upon him: the other world retreated another stage away. Now the two existences were almost exactly balanced in his mind, one against the other.

Only one man wounded, Adam noted: twelve reinforcements posted; everything seemed to be in good order. . . .

Suddenly he sat straighter in his chair; he read through every name on the list.

'What's this?' he demanded, his finger pointing to the typed roll. 'I don't see Jones's name here.'

'No—he's been posted to the Padre, as Chaplain's helper.'

Adam's gaze was furious on Ramsay's face. 'Who the hell approved that posting?'

'Bazin—he was acting 2 i/c.'

Adam glared at Ramsay, and he swore.

Ramsay's glance remained steady. 'Look, *sir*,' he said—after all he had been a captain when Adam was still a lieutenant—'I'm not responsible for what Major Bazin does. Furthermore, he told me you had specifically asked to have Jones transferred to a safer job.'

'All right,' Adam said, after a moment. 'Sorry.' But there was no apology in his tone. 'Where is he now?'

'Major Bazin? As I said, "D" Company is holding Point 69.'

'No—the Padre! Where's that bloody Padre?'

'Oh.'

Captain Ramsay sat back and looked thoughtful. 'Well, to tell the truth we don't inquire too closely. The C.O. is happy just as long as he doesn't see him around here. . . . But they tell me he spends most of his time driving over the rear areas looking at Wop churches.'

Adam stood up. At that moment he was unquestionably 'B' Company's commander again, looking hard and alert. He was thinking with all his war senses once more. That other existence was dissipated like a morning mist.

'I want a jeep at once,' Adam said. 'I'll call Begg from Tac H.Q. and get up to the Company later today. First, though, I'm going to see Bazin at Point 69.'

'Yes, sir,' said Captain Ramsay.

Adam turned and strode from the room.

18

THE chapel of the Sacrament was on fire with afternoon gold. On the high altar shafts of sunlight lanced the poor breast of Saint Agatha, making her wounds bloom again, like two huge roses.

In this town of Vestali, at the church of Sant' Agata, the search

94

of Padre Philip Doorn was ended. The search was ended: only the act remained, and the act was planned in minute, scrupulous detail. Now, like a gaunt, skulking sentry, the Padre stood posted outside the church door. The concealing folds of a long trench coat cancelled his rank and identity; his upturned collar attempted to do the same for his face. From his vantage point he stared unremittingly at the chapel beyond the nave; his eyes burned with the reflection of sacramental light.

One street removed, parked at the corner with the engine running, was their truck, with Rifleman Jones sitting patiently behind the wheel. Unit markings had been carefully covered with layers of applied mud; it looked no different from a hundred thousand other Allied vehicles in Italy. The front of the truck pointed toward the main highway, only five miles away.

The Padre's hands clenched restlessly in the pockets of his trench coat. There was cold metal in the grasp and command of his fingers: one pocket contained a pistol, the other a canister grenade. His glance kept flickering from the fount of holiness inside the church to the ticking second-hand of his watch.

Time had brought even greater urgency to his task. Back in Ortona advance parties from the relieving Indian units had already arrived; preparations for the move south had started. The Canadian Division was, above all, an assault division: now it was to leave the static Adriatic front and go where assaults were being made. It was to cross the Apennines and enter the line somewhere near a town called Cassino. At this very moment the 2nd Rifles might be heading south; if so, it was the Padre's plan to rejoin them en route.

On the altar he could see the ark that held the Sacrament; beside it was a reliquary, a case of chaste mother-of-pearl, glowing ruby-red now with the reflection of Saint Agatha's wounds. The sexton began to extinguish the candles on the high altar. Censer in hand the priest went slipping through the sacristy door.

The Padre's eyes were on fire. His gaze at the gleaming reliquary was devouring, consuming, as though in glance he celebrated a visual Mass. That reliquary held doom and salvation, life and death—everything. . . . Inside the case was the object marking the end of his search. His glance flicked to the ticking seconds on his wrist. Then his fingers tightened inside his trench-coat pockets. He turned to face the holy chapel of Saint Agatha. He walked into the blaze of sacramental light.

19

IN DAYLIGHT getting to Point 69 was almost as uncomfortable as living there. A muddied foot-path trailed through vineyards and flat tableland, exposed for most of the way to enemy fire and observation. The pedestrian in that wide landscape felt like a naked, mud-bound target.

Adam laboured through the sucking mud, scanning the hump of ground ahead known as Point 69. This was the only place on the Divisional front where the opposing forces were not separated by some physical space or feature. Here, this hump was held jointly by both sides because its sole possession would allow one to outflank positions of the other. It was a turtle-back of land, bisected and neatly partitioned at its ridge. Ten yards below the crest, on each side, and within grenade range, the opposing infantrymen were dug in. A week's duty at Point 69 was equivalent to a month—a year, some said—in one of the other relatively safe positions. On the southern slope of the hump was a smashed stone villa, its white tower still prominent and surprisingly intact. This was 'D' Company's headquarters; and it was on this tower that Adam now marched.

On one shoulder Adam's tommy-gun was slung; on the other a familiar companion had come back to perch. Fear, the vulture, came flopping back to him when he reached Tac H.Q.; and until that moment he had not even noted its absence. While he was away in Bari the obscene bird must merely have been squatting on an overhanging branch, renewing itself perhaps, awaiting his return to descend. Not that its presence caused him special pain: this fear Adam simply accepted as part of the life he had to lead.

Adam plodded steadily across the sodden landscape. Long ago his anger over Jonesy had spent itself. He accepted his return; he had discarded all thought of that other existence, the possibility that had been briefly opened by Bari, and Elena, and the things they said to each other. There was only one difference in his state before and after Bari. Now he was aware of the emptiness inside him; and he knew that not all his competence, nor all his passion of concern for the men of his Company, would ever suffice to fill it.

He had lost his anger about Jonesy; there was really no reason now why he should still go on to search out Bazin. But there also seemed no reason why he should turn back. With the white tower of the villa in his glance Adam plodded on.

20

'Amo,' said Major Bunny Bazin, snapping the bolt of his rifle closed. 'I love.'

He squinted through the peep-sight, steadied the barrel on its sand-bag. 'Amas,' said Major Bazin. 'You love.'

He stopped breathing, took the first pressure, and then he fired. The report echoed loudly inside the small tower room. 'Amat,' said Major Bazin. 'He loves. Christ, we *all* love—but I missed. Pass me up the rum.'

Adam sat on planks laid across the floor joists of the dilapidated tower structure. He felt around on the planks until he found the quart bottle of issue rum, and he handed it up. Major Bazin was installed on a high, uncertain perch. Several layers of sand-bags had been piled on a large wooden table; on top of these a thin mattress; on top of it all, stretched out in firing position, was Major Bazin. The muzzle of his rifle pointed at a broken window frame two feet away. From the floor Adam could see only a blue patch of sky, but from his height presumably Major Bazin could observe enemy positions on the other side of the hump. Binoculars lay on the mattress beside him.

Major Bazin drank with a gurgle of contentment. Then he handed the bottle back, and his long face peered companionably over the edge of the mattress. 'Amabo, amabis, amabit,' he recited. 'We'll love in all the future inflexions too.'

Adam stared gloomily at the square of sky framed in the broken window. Any moment now an A.P. or H.E. shell might come screaming through. 'What the hell are you doing up there?' he demanded.

On the mattress Major Bazin considered the question carefully. 'Tell me,' he asked. 'Do you know any better way of passing the afternoon than to lie at ease sniping the enemy, while conjugating the verb "to love", and drinking the best issue Egyptian rum? Hell, it's the vocation I've been searching for all my life!'

Adam was silent while he tilted up the bottle himself. 'There are safer places than this to drink,' he said, after a moment.

'Yes; there are safer occupations than the one we've chosen too.'

There was nothing Adam could say to that. He leaned back and he calculated the odds of some kind of unpleasantness blowing them out of the tower. Adam was a good enough soldier always to want the available odds on his side. But today he was in a curiously listless mood; it seemed too much effort to stir.

Major Bazin flopped over on his belly and pulled the rifle into his shoulder again. '*Amamus, amatis, amant,*' he recited in a gay voice; and he squeezed off another round.

Adam knew there could be no real targets to fire at. But in a position like this, he realized, one had to snipe—or the enemy would snipe first and make movement impossible, life unbearable. Somebody had to do it; and he guessed Bazin had elected the job himself in order to spare somebody else the dirty work.

'Have a drink,' Adam said. He passed the bottle up again.

Bazin seemed quite content to lie up on his mattress all afternoon. The bottle passed back and forth between them. Adam had done with calculating the odds, found them remarkably poor, and he still sat in his place on the planks. He was feeling almost at peace with himself.

'Have you ever tried to bury a dead horse?' Bazin asked.

'No.'

'Well, I strongly recommend that you don't. It's a revoltingly unpleasant task. That's what my boys are doing down below.'

'I know.'

Adam had seen them at their work, before he climbed the ladder up to this tower room.

'Well—' Major Bazin cupped his long chin in his hands, the rifle lay neglected at his side. 'May I ask what the hell brought *you* here?'

Adam shifted position on the hard planks. 'Nothing,' he said, after a pause. 'Just a social call.'

Then he started to grin. He felt warmed with rum; suddenly it seemed to him the funniest, most fitting thing in the world for the two of them, being what they were, to be occupying this fool exposed little room: drinking rum, even—if Bazin wanted—conjugating Latin verbs.

Adam waved his hand expansively around the broken, ventilated tower room. 'A house-warming visit,' he said with a straight face.

Bazin laughed aloud. Then for a moment the two men shook with contented laughter.

'Of course it was Jones you came about,' said Bazin.

'Yes—but that doesn't matter any more.'

'Not if you understand'—and now Bazin was deadly serious, 'that Jonesy is the one man in the Battalion—perhaps in the whole Army—who can never really be changed by the Padre. If anything, it could work the other way. . . . Also, remember that Doorn can never do anything as final to Jonesy as one of those machine-gunners over the hump can do.'

Adam saw the sense of this. 'Yes,' he agreed.

Again the rum bottle changed hands. From his perch Bazin's horse-like face peered down with an expression of quizzical good will. Adam felt a surge of affection for Bazin; he began to feel with rising elation that he could talk to him about anything.

'Philip Doorn,' he said, 'was my friend, and yours too. But now—what is the damn fool trying to do?'

'He's out searching.'

'For what?'

Bazin closed his eyes for a moment. 'For himself,' he said at last. 'We are all out searching for ourselves.'

Adam looked up at him, uncomprehending.

Bazin peered in Adam's intent face. 'Put it this way,' he said; and his voice held only the faintest trace of habitual self-mockery. 'Each man's life is a voyage of discovery to discover himself.' He stared down at Adam with a sombre look.

Of course, Adam thought: One way or another each one of them *was* out searching for himself. . . .

Adam forgot about Padre Doorn. All at once he burned with eagerness to tell Bazin about Bari and the girl Elena: to discover the meaning concealed in the experience.

But there was a whoosh of sound in the room. A patch of tiles in the roof behind them disappeared, disintegrated: opening another circle of blue in their ceiling.

'Jesus,' said Adam. 'An A.P. What if it had been H.E.?'

'Jesus would be right,' Bazin replied. He balanced the bottle of rum gingerly between his hands.

'A funny thing about A.P.,' Adam said suddenly. 'A funny thing happened to me in the attack back on the Ortona ridge.'

As he said the words he was thinking of Bari and Elena, and he was trying to talk about them too; but he did not know how to begin. He could not come right out and say: 'In Bari there was a girl called Elena.'

Instead, he said: 'It was a pretty confused attack with tanks—*you* remember. By the time we got to that river bed it was an utter bollocks: tanks brewing up, Companies—what was left of them—mixed up together, people running around shouting, trying to regroup, and fire still coming down—'

'Yes, yes. Go on.' Bazin peered from his perch with an air of absorbed interest.

'Well—' Adam forced the word out, and he heard his voice go on.

This was the damnedest thing. He was thinking now of the moment when he followed Elena into her room; but his voice talked, was going on talking about this attack which meant nothing to him.

'Well,' Adam said, 'I had Company Headquarters by a small house in a hay field. The tanks were milling around and every now and then one got hit. Everywhere there were a lot of little haystacks—stooks, one of the men called them; it was the first time I'd heard the word—'

'Stooks,' repeated Bazin, in a tone of relish.

There was so much more between us than the physical act, Adam was thinking: because we made it that way. . . . But how would I ever explain that part to him?

He accepted the bottle of rum from Bazin's hand. 'Those haystacks,' he said, 'those goddamned stooks—that was the funny part. As I ran around trying to find my platoons I kept noticing something wrong about those stooks. Every so often one of them would move, with a slight, almost imperceptible motion. For an instant I wondered—you know how nothing seems too crazy at a time like that—if a German soldier could be hidden inside. But then I got the idea that it looked more like an invisible bayonet being pushed through each stook—'

It was a possibility, Adam thought: another possibility of living that was offered; some kind of force that gave meaning to life. But how could I ever talk about that? His throat pained him.

'Go on,' Bazin commanded.

He was listening with all the rapt interest of a boy who hears a new adventure tale at bedtime.

'Nothing was disarranged in the stooks,' Adam forced himself to say. 'As I said, it looked more like an invisible bayonet poking through.'

'Yes. What *was* it?'

'It took a long time to figure out.' Adam spoke with a kind of spent anger in his voice; he knew now he would never be able to talk about this thing, not even to Bazin.

'I saw it at last when a tank got hit,' Adam said. 'And that's another funny thing—' he was only talking now to stop from thinking—'that tank turret jumped at me through a circle of 360 degrees, until the gun pointed in my face. Well, anyway—I saw then that they were A.P. shells cutting through those stooks— those were the invisible bayonets.'

'How perfect!' Bazin breathed a sigh of deep satisfaction.

'But—' Adam looked up, frowning; as though he had not been understood. 'It only stays in my mind because I think I was the only person in the whole damn battle either to see the stooks move or know why they did.'

'That's what I mean,' Bazin said. 'That's what makes it so perfect. Here—give me a hand.'

He leaped down from the mattress and eased himself onto the planks beside Adam. He put his back to the wall and stretched out his long legs. He placed the bottle of rum on the floor between them.

Outside now afternoon was about to merge with dusk. The patches of sky showing through the tiled roof were darker blue, almost purple. Soon it would be time for stand-to.

Adam spoke in a low, despairing voice. 'That's not what I wanted to say at all.'

'I know you didn't,' Major Bazin replied gently.

Adam turned his head and looked at the other: his friend, his former Company Commander, a man whose sense he may have doubted, but never his wisdom. He looked Bazin in the face.

'Bunny,' he said. 'What's it all about, and where is it going to end?'

For a moment Bazin's long face looked sad, then he smiled. 'Johnny,' he said, 'I don't know where it's going to end because you and I, after all, live each day fairly close to the brink of eternity. . . . Not that that's such a bad thing—' he added quickly. 'In compensation we are granted increased aliveness of our senses. We think and see and feel more keenly—'

Adam regarded him, frowning.

'Like your leave in Bari,' Bazin said. 'You may have lived a whole lifetime there in five days—'

Outside there was the booming of grenades, in quick succession. In another position that would have meant an attack; here, it was only part of the day's work. Both men ignored the sound.

'As to what it's all about—' Bazin's face had become sombre. 'That's obvious, if you dare look at the thing—instead of building up and hiding behind a shield of competence. . . . What it's about, of course, is execution. It started in that Sicilian barn-yard, with your two Italians—big Jim and little Joe, did you call them?— when you stood by and acquiesced in their execution—'

'Acquiesced?' said Adam, in a voice of fury. 'Hell, I *killed* them!'

'No,' Bazin said sharply. 'That part was a mere act of mercy. It was the acquiescing that mattered.'

Adam's look was sullen. 'All right,' he said, after a moment. 'All right. On that basis, you were much more to blame than I was.'

'True,' said Bazin, with no change of tone. 'But then I've already participated in enough of the world's injustices so that one more has little effect. But for you it was the first time; and remember— execution is the ultimate injustice, the ultimate degradation of man. Look what it's done to the Padre, that poor bastard Philip Doorn. . . .'

Adam said nothing. He stared at the square of purple sky showing through the window frame.

'Don't ask me what the answer is,' said Bazin. 'Perhaps it is man's plight to acquiesce. On the other hand, even recognizing execution as the evil may be victory of sorts; struggling against it may be the closest man ever comes to victory.'

Adam said, half speaking to himself: 'You see no end to it?'

'Not for you,' said Bazin.

And suddenly he looked away. In that moment Adam knew that Bazin saw only death in battle for himself; some men seemed to have that knowledge. They sat together on the planks and each man avoided the other's glance.

After a moment Bazin stretched out his hand and gripped Adam's leg. 'Johnny,' he said. 'Maybe you found something in Bari—something stronger than the other thing. Whatever it was, hang on to it—*believe* in it!'

Then Bazin sat up straight and reached for the rum bottle. In that instant he became a different person, bubbling with good spirits; and from experience Adam knew the change to be quite real and genuine. 'Hell,' Bazin declared. 'We've left some rum in the bottle.'

Adam gulped down a burning throatful. Bazin had the bottle at his lips when the head of a perspiring corporal poked through the hole in the floor.

'We got that goddamn horse buried, sir,' the corporal reported.

'Splendid! Then we can come downstairs.'

'And the Sergeant-Major has the Company standing-to.'

'All right, Meikeljohn. Watch you don't break that ladder. I'll be down right away. And warn the chef that Major Adam is staying for dinner—tell him to chill the wine and lay out our very best linen.'

Corporal Meikeljohn grinned rudely. The head disappeared through the hole again.

Both men stood up together. In the uncertain light Adam started to stumble toward the hole where the ladder was.

'Wait,' said Major Bazin.

With the empty rum bottle clutched in one hand he approached the gaping window. He took his wind-up, a round-house swing, and then he let the bottle fly. It soared through the window, up into the darkening sky, tumbling toward the waiting enemy.

'I don't suppose,' Major Bazin observed thoughtfully, 'that it will really hurt them much more than my shooting did.'

21

FROM the south one famous road, a natural corridor, leads to Rome. Once known as the Via Casilina, it is now called Highway

Number Six; and it cleaves boldly, invitingly, between the Apennine massif on the north and the Aurunci range on the south.

It is the classic road to Rome, and at one part of its length it provides the classic position of defence. Successive hordes and generations of invaders have paced this road, in their eyes the lust for Rome as bright as sunflash on their steel, until they came to a halt, always, at the same place: that part of the valley commanded by the immense, dominating Monastery of Monte-Cassino. Here the defenders stretch their defence line across the valley floor, with the Monastery of Monte-Cassino an impregnable anchor. When modern-day generals seek to illustrate the classic defensive position they think first of Monte-Cassino.

At this place Field-Marshal Kesselring, lashed on by the half-crazed adjurations of his Führer, constructed a fortress. The outer bastion, with the Rapido-Gari rivers for moat, was called the Gustav Line. From here defences extended back in depth for five miles—to one last, irrevocable Line, beyond which the road to Rome lay open. It was the Führer's command that this Line was to be held at any cost; if necessary the life of every German soldier in Italy was to be spent in its defence. Field-Marshal Kesselring heard and hastened to obey.

Officers and technicians of the Todt organization came pouring into Italy. With the sweat of thousands of impressed labourers they lavished forth their engineering skill. Forests were felled to establish enfilading fields of fire; excavating machines remodelled the earth. Tons of concrete were poured; steel and reinforced concrete structures took shape. At cunning intervals Panther tank turrets, with their long snout-like guns, were imbedded in concrete emplacements; connecting bunkers were tunnelled deep in the ground. Anti-tank ditches were scientifically sited; and belts of wire were planted everywhere.

Then they laid mines. There was every type of German mine: charted fields of anti-tank Teller mines; in the meadows, 'S' mines and Schu mines. An 'S' mine is a canister of 350 ball-bearings packed round a core of explosive; on contact the canister springs five feet above ground and explodes its charge. A Schu mine is simply a small box of picric acid designed to blow off a man's foot. There were these mines, and more.

The steel and concrete was impervious to bombs or shell fire.

The defenders had only to fall back, man their prepared positions, and then annihilate anyone foolhardy enough to attack. At last, in the spring of 1944, the Todt captains and their labourers departed, their task completed. They had built their Führer an impregnable Line defending Rome. They called their work the Adolf Hitler Line.

It was the kind of defensive position a general dreams about.

And yet: every general knows that the line of defence has never been built which cannot be broken—provided the attacker is strong enough, and willing enough to pay the price. Even the Adolf Hitler Line. . . .

22

THERE was shocked disbelief in Adam's face. He stared at Colonel McNabb. 'Me?' he said. '*Me*—L.O.B.?'

With a khaki handkerchief Colonel McNabb dabbed at his forehead. The sun trickled between oak branches overhead; it was hot in this grove where they held their 'O' Group. 'Yes,' the Colonel said evenly. 'You—six other officers, and twenty N.C.O.s.'

The officers sitting round the oak tree looked down at their map-boards. At another time there might have been jokes about Adam being Left Out of Battle. The L.O.B.s inhabited a never-never land called 'X' Area; they could not be summoned forward until the battle was finished. It was more comfortable in 'X' Area, and certainly a lot safer. . . . But on this particular occasion, when they were the shock troops of the 8th Army, moving closer each day to a place called the Adolf Hitler Line, it was nothing to make jokes about. Especially not with Major John Adam.

Adam's face was red with anger; his glance wildly appealed the sentence.

'No, John.' Colonel McNabb shook his head. 'You're long overdue. I want you in command of "X" Area, and I want the L.O.B.s cleared out tonight.'

Adam continued to look angry but he said nothing. His military good sense told him that the C.O. was right—this was a time the L.O.B.s would be sorely needed. He accepted the necessity but his mind clamoured at once with all the urgencies he must now discuss with Bill Begg, his second-in-command, who would take the Company in.

Colonel McNabb glanced round the circle of faces. 'Well,' he said, 'I think you all know the general picture. There is steady progress all along the front. The Poles have the Monastery ringed off. Out on the left the French are steaming ahead. Those Goums of theirs, apparently, are running riot through the mountains—'

'With knives at night-time,' said Major Bazin in a reflective tone of relish.

'Yes—well, they haven't any tanks, of course; but they have infiltrated their own section of the Line. Tomorrow we cross the Gari ourselves and start firming up toward the Hitler Line.'

Colonel McNabb paused while the officers consulted their maps. Adam was still frowning, intent with his own urgent thoughts.

Major Bazin sat comfortably forward on crossed legs. 'After firming up to the Line, sir—what then?'

The Colonel's face was thoughtful. 'One appreciation from Intelligence says that pressure on both flanks, especially on the left, may make them pull out. In any event, two Armoured Divisions will be right behind us waiting to break through.'

The officers studied the maps and air photographs spread on their knees. A thick ribbon of red ink ran across their defence-overprint maps, indicating the known enemy positions of the Hitler Line. Each officer had studied these overprints for days; they could see no reason why the Germans should pull out, unless the Line was penetrated elsewhere in force. Their own axis of advance was parallel to Highway Number Six, directed toward the thickest part of the Line's defences.

Major Bazin's long face prowled forward from a cloud of cigarette smoke. 'And if they don't pull out, sir?'

Colonel McNabb allowed himself a wintry smile. 'Then a set-piece frontal attack, with trimmings.'

There was silence for several seconds. The Major commanding 'A' Company spoke then. 'Well,' he said, 'the boys have never been more ready.'

Each one of them knew that this, at least, was true. After a tedious winter of living in slit-trenches every man relished the breadth and freedom of movement they had experienced in recent weeks. Also, there was the blossom-tang of spring in the air, the excitement of participating in big events, the glittering prize of Rome lying before them. Soon, even, there might be that long-promised Second Front in North-West Europe; the war seemed moving into a new, climactic phase.

Adam could not sit still as the talk continued; uneasiness throbbed like a pain inside him. The moment the 'O' Group ended he leaped to his feet. He wanted to spend every available minute working over plans and procedures with Captain Bill Begg. Then, of course, he had to move his L.O.B.s back to the place where they would live a suspended, half-real existence: eating, sleeping—and waiting. Waiting, Adam thought, for somebody else to finish the battle. . . .

23

IT WAS two days later at another, and much more important 'O' Group that Brigadier Ian Kildare committed military hara-kiri.

The event occurred in a villa thirty miles behind the front. Inside a domed, white-walled room a group of red-tabbed officers sat and listened while a General talked. Forward in the battle area the troops had forged ahead according to plan—until they reached a point within one half mile of the Adolf Hitler Line. There resistance had become fierce; it was clear the Line was going to be held, and held with all force the defenders possessed. Today's 'O' Group was final briefing for the set-piece attack.

At the front of the room the General talked in a fluent, precise voice, emphasizing his points by gestures, made without turning, to two map-boards set on easels behind him. His voice throbbed with rich power and confidence.

There is something about a set-piece attack which the professional soldier finds irresistibly pleasing. The most minute detail can be provided for, each least item and contingency forecast and dovetailed into a beautifully exact operation order. In this attack Start Lines were to be literally 'taped'; timed barrages and stonks and interdicting fire would fall at the prescribed second; tanks would advance at a fixed density per hundred yards of front. Administration—wire-cutters and bangalore torpedoes must be indented for. Traffic Control—it would be vital to keep clear lanes back to the Advanced Dressing Stations and Casualty Clearing Stations. . . .

Brigadier Kildare's huge body squirmed in his chair as he listened. He made a loud breathing noise through his nostrils.

'Any questions, gentlemen?'

The General paused for a summary moment. His glance ranged round the room until it settled on Brigadier Kildare, who seemed to be muttering aloud to himself.

'Your Brigade delivers the main punch, Kildare,' the General said. 'What do you think?'

Brigadier Kildare stood up. 'I think it's balls,' he declared without hesitation. 'Utter balls!'

A disbelieving silence eddied through the room. Every officer, as though to dissociate himself, looked away from Brigadier Kildare. Those closest shifted their chairs slightly.

The General stood stricken at his map-boards. If the statement had been less insolent, or even delivered with less assurance, he would have known what to do. As it was, he simply blinked in Brigadier Kildare's glowering face. 'I beg your pardon?' the General said.

Brigadier Kildare's immense figure seemed to fill the room.

'I say your plan of attack is balls,' he repeated. 'It violates every elementary principle of war. Instead of exploiting success—over on the left where the Line is already penetrated—you're mounting a frontal attack on a position which cannot be taken by frontal attack.'

The General's face was now white, and grim. The senior General present walked to his side. He looked at Kildare with a terrible, raking glance.

Brigadier Kildare saw this and understood. Already he had said sufficient to destroy his career. Perhaps he was marching toward court-martial; but he could not stop now. He had to go on.

'I recognize,' said Brigadier Kildare, in a firm voice, 'that the left flank is outside the Divisional, even the Corps, boundary. I recognize the administrative problems: poor lateral roads, inadequate supply, formations already mixed up. I recognize all this— but, goddammit these *are* administrative problems! It's no solution to throw away two brigades of infantry simply because it is administratively difficult to mount the attack the right way!'

Brigadier Kildare stood with his fists clenched, breathing heavily. The other officers shifted uneasily in their chairs. The same thought had occurred to all of them, of course; but they were realists. It was too late: their forward units were already engaged with the enemy; it would be a nightmare now to change their groupings. There were times when troops simply had to attack where they were. But each one of them felt uneasy, and not merely because of Kildare's disgraceful outburst.

The silence in the room lengthened until it became painful.

Brigadier Kildare drew in his breath and spoke again, with a kind of measured finality. 'To put my Brigade in against the strongest part of the Line—when the battle can be won elsewhere —is not war; it's bloody execution!'

The briefing General said, in a deadly voice: 'Do you wish to be relieved of your command?'

'*If* that choice exists,' added the senior General beside him.

Brigadier Kildare closed his eyes. He had done what he had to do; now he made a quick appreciation of his personal situation. They would not want to fire him at once because there was no replacement available. Also, they would doubtless want him to retain command because if anyone in the Army could get his Brigade on to the objective Kildare was that man. He had done what he had to do; and he no longer had any power to alter events.

'No, sir,' Brigadier Kildare replied at last. 'I do not wish to be relieved. I wish to take my Brigade in.'

Again silence settled like snow in the white-walled room. The two Generals exchanged a long glance. 'Very well,' the senior General said. 'I will see you alone at the end of this Orders Group.'

The briefing General turned back to his map-boards. Once more the assembled officers gave their attention to the set-piece attack.

24

THE valley floor was sea-green with rich, May grass. In one corner of the meadow, sheltered by poplar copse, Padre Philip Doorn sat at a trestle table. His dark glance touched on the bustling scene, but he seemed quite unaware of the medical supplies heaped on the table before him. He sat motionless at the table, and he smiled.

Messengers hurried in and out of the farm-house where Battalion Headquarters was located. The Medical Officer and his assistants, among whom in theory at least the Padre was numbered, laboured to erect a canvas marquee which would house the R.A.P.

But the Padre saw none of this. At the moment he glanced westward where an Aurunci peak sliced the setting sun in half. Sunset colour spilled into the valley; the Apennines, and the bulking Monastery itself, stood sunset-flushed. Guns all along the front were quiet, as though resting their strength; the evening was calm and clear, so that one waited to hear the toll of chapel bells, the chanting of devotions. But the Padre was unaware of the evening too. One hand patted his inside breast pocket. He was viewing private images projected on the screen of his mind. And as he viewed he smiled.

His cheeks were sunken, his eyes black-ringed and hollow, so that his smile seemed gaunt, without warmth or human recognition for those few who chanced to see it. It was the smile of a man who hugs to himself some inner secret, whose revelation would cause ruin and discomfiture to his fellows. The table before him was stacked with boxes of shell dressings, morphine syrettes, and plasma, but he did not see them. The Padre's glance touched lightly, without ever lingering, on each object in the rose-flushed sunset. And he did nothing more than smile.

Rifleman Jones, the servant, followed his master's example. He lay full length on a nearby stretcher, eyes closed, smoking a cigarette; occupied with nothing more weighty than isolating the call of the evening cicada.

Neither one even tried to comprehend the vast events around them. Every other man in that meadow knew that the rifle companies were in contact with the enemy up ahead; that tonight patrols would go out to cut wire and sweep mines. The men of the rifle companies were already deployed: they would sleep only yards from tomorrow's Start Line. In a spell of fine May weather, this was the clearest evening of all. The front was quiet tonight; but back here there were hours of frenzied preparation ahead. Except for Padre Doorn and his helper every soldier there, from rifleman to colonel, worked with a mounting fever of urgency.

The Padre sat incuriously while the R.A.P. corporal lifted one of the boxes to his shoulder and carried it away. Again—it was now a long-familiar, practised gesture—the Padre's hand went up to pat the inside breast pocket of his tunic. And after this touch his smile seemed wider, as though invigorated or renewed.

Inside that pocket, where it had lain in its wrappings for weeks, was the object which once stood on the altar of the church of Sant' Agata. Inside that pocket was salvation and redemption, and doom and damnation too. Inside that pocket was—

But Padre Doorn was not yet ready to say the word. Tomorrow, he thought: tomorrow. . . .

The Padre's smile glinted whitely. The church of Sant' Agata, he mused: what a long search it had been, and yet in the end how perfectly successful. . . . And poor Saint Agatha—how fresh her bleeding wounds had looked; but how easy the whole affair had been. . . . He regretted now, as indeed he had from the first moment of success, that smoke grenade he had exploded. In the event it had been unnecessary; it was a measure planned to aid their swift flight by making it appear that the church was on fire. . . .

Jonesy flicked his cigarette in the air and the Padre watched its tumbling arc. The meadow was now bathed in crystal-clear light, or so it seemed; in reality it was day merging into night: creating a wine-light of filtered amber. It was a breathless hush-filled moment.

The Padre's glance flashed quickly to the sunset mountain perimeter, but not as though he wished to observe—merely to orient himself before darkness. It was not yet time for him to look in earnest. That was for tomorrow. Tomorrow, for the first time in almost a year, he was going to gaze upon the sky. It would lie revealed before him; and great events would come to pass.

25

AT 0459 hours, somewhere in the rear, an over-eager gunner fired the first round. Seconds later 800 guns were firing at once; the noise shivered, pounded and possessed the world.

The troops had been stirring for an hour already. In pre-dawn darkness they had rolled from their gas-capes into the dew-soaked grass. At the cook trucks there was a mighty breakfast to consume: hot porridge, bacon, slabs of bread and jam, and burning mess-tins of hot tea. Then there was the first cigarette of the day, tasting exquisitely sweet as they trudged through the meadows to their Forming-Up Points. There they spread out, sat down, and waited for the barrage to begin.

In that roaring surf of noise the coming of tanks was soundless. Silently the tanks churned into position among them. Platoon commanders grinned up at troop commanders. Every soldier was grinning, delighted at the torrent of noise made by the guns.

There was comfort in the obliterating weight of steel screaming overhead, and in the steel mass of tanks around them. Now the sun topped the Apennines. The infantrymen hefted their weapons in their hands; they peered through the rolling mist toward the forest and the objective waiting beyond.

At first Captain Bill Begg had been surprised to find so much forest still standing; but he quickly realized that the woods were tank trap: they forced the tanks to follow a pre-determined route, mined and under enemy fire. In front of the Line itself, he knew, the cover had been cleared for more than one hundred yards on the attacking side of the wire.

Captain Begg had the Company deployed beside a track, a kind of wide logging trail, which led through the woods directly to the Line. They were to follow behind 'D' Company; with nobody else on their right flank. Bill Begg did not like the looks of that exposed right flank. It was going to feel naked being overlooked by those mountains; and once beyond the Start Line they would probably come under ground fire from enemy positions on the right.

Everybody liked Captain Bill Begg: he was cheerful, lazy and easy-going, an uncomplicated man who enjoyed life, women, and drink. In his later years, if he survived, he would probably be a satisfied old roué, charged with every possible sin, except that of omission. Bill Begg was a good fellow—but he had never commanded the Company in action before.

Now he looked about him, at the waiting men of 'B' Company. The platoon commanders kept their casual glance on him, alert for visual signals; Sergeant-Major Mitchell leaned in unperturbed dignity against a tank. Bill Begg felt genuine surprise that Mitchell, Sergeant DiCicco, Lieutenant Venner, and all these others seemed quite content to have him as their commander. Perhaps, Begg thought, this is just the way Adam has made them. In any event, they were not the least concerned. Whereas *he* . . . Bill Begg longed to be any other place; to him it was sheer irony that Adam would rather be here in his stead. . . .

Still with his sense of surprise Begg looked in the faces of the men nearby: he found there nothing but readiness for whatever lay ahead. Some were newly-arrived reinforcements, but most were Adam's veterans; many of the men had been with the Company since Sicily. Begg looked at these men objectively; and he was able to perceive them the way the British staff officers who planned this attack must have visualized them: lean, hard, stripped for action. These soldiers knew exactly what to do at any given moment of battle; they had pride in their competence; each individual knew himself part of a superbly trained whole. They deserved the title of shock troops, assault troops. In this meadow were four rifle companies of assault troops, ready, waiting. . . .

In the final minute the artillery fire thickened with a last, desperate outpouring. At 0559 hours Captain Bill Begg raised his hand above his head. Everywhere his soldiers came to their feet; half turned, his platoon commanders stared at his upraised hand. Lips moving, Captain Begg was counting aloud, and then his hand started down. At 0600 hours the first wave of attackers crossed the Start Line.

26

CAPTAIN Bill Begg was running. Heart pounding, lungs bursting, he ran with all his being. In the forest there was a woodpecker succession of hollow knocks as bullets struck the tree trunks. Tart sweat from under his helmet splashed in Captain Begg's eyes.

Wherever his bobbing glance went Begg saw men falling—sliced down by shell fragments, bowled over by machine-gun slugs. Every few yards a tank seemed to be hit; dazed troopers bailed out into the stream of machine-gun fire. The German artillery D.F. was merciless; but the worst part was the blast of small-arms fire from the right flank where they were nakedly exposed to view.

Begg had known an instant of panic when he realized he could not possibly exercise control over his running, stumbling men. But then he knew that it must be the same everywhere; the most anyone could do was get forward, closer to the Line, as quickly as possible.

Now he saw the end of forest, ahead was meadow blazing in sunshine, a glimpse of wire, and an ugly tank turret peering from concrete. There were men of 'D' Company in front—out in the open meadow, running for the wire. For an instant he caught sight of Major Bazin's bobbing figure.

At the edge of the wood was a fold of covered ground. Begg threw himself down and signalled those behind to do the same.

The frontal fire alone, Begg thought, might have been surmountable; it was the fire from the flank that was murdering them. . . . He lay panting for breath as he peered around.

To the left he saw a wireless aerial in a ditch alongside the main track. There, only ten yards away, was Colonel McNabb kneeling in the ditch, microphone in hand. Begg went running over.

The signaller lay dead by the set. Colonel McNabb was bleeding from small perforations in his face; a fold of his scalp dangled over one eye.

'*Smoke!*' Colonel McNabb roared into his microphone. 'I've got to have smoke to cover the right flank. Smoke—for Christ's sake—*smoke!*' He was not in the least aware of his wounds or of Begg's presence—only of the microphone that he held in his hand.

Yes, Begg thought: smoke would help, but it really wouldn't change things. . . .

He glanced to the front again. There were tanks out in the meadow, but none seemed to be moving; most were burning. He saw the figure of an occasional lone infantryman bob forward in the grass. He stood up then and he walked back, with no appearance of haste, to his former position. Mitchell and the others were lying there, waiting.

Bill Begg was experiencing an excruciating pain of sadness, a moment of desolation. He knew that he could not come through today alive. He was saying good-bye to his twenty-five happy years, and whatever else might have followed; he was saying good-bye to all the girls he might have bedded, the bottles he might have emptied. He knew he could not possibly do his job and still survive. And that was the whole point: Adam was not here today—this *was* his job. . . .

Captain Begg cupped his hands and put his head back.

'All right, "B" Company,' he bellowed. 'Let's get through that goddamned wire!'

Captain Begg plunged ahead into the meadow. There must have been a lot of men lying at the edge of the wood waiting his signal

because a ragged wave of infantry got up and came charging out
behind him.

27

LITTLE Frazer ran with a quick, chopping step, head up, rifle
held across his chest, ready in an instant to sprint ahead or go to
ground. Each motion was controlled. He moved over the field
expertly: if there had been such a profession as crossing a steel-
swept, mine-exploding field, Frazer would be its master professional. He hummed to himself as he ran; his darting glance at the
same time located the chief originating points of fire and
calculated the distance to each available piece of cover.

Now, Frazer decided . . .

He had been aiming for a bomb crater ten yards in front of the
wire. He jumped, landed squarely in the crater, and pulled his
head down to rest for a moment while regaining his breath.

He became aware that he had a companion. A soldier stood
peering foolishly over the lip of the crater: a reinforcement called
Russo, who was trembling and lathered like a race horse. His
eyes were wide, his nostrils flaring. His denim tunic was drenched
with sweat; and Frazer saw the heaving ribs, the heart pumping
violently underneath. Russo's gaze was fixed, with dreadful
fascination, on the source of destruction ahead.

'Hail, Mary, full of Grace,' said Russo. He stared blankly to
the front, his hands pit-propping the earth of the crater.

Jesus, Frazer thought, what a guinea to be stuck with at a time
like this. . . .

He reached up and pulled hard on Russo's web belt. 'Why don't
you learn how to relax, sport?' said Frazer; and Russo plopped
to the bottom of the crater beside him.

Then Frazer stood up himself to take sights over the edge. He
had picked the way through the wire—a place several yards to
the right where a tank had crashed over before. The most dangerous machine-gun was one firing from the tank turret immediately
ahead. Frazer clocked it, estimating the moment the belt would
have to be changed.

He slapped Russo's cheek with one hand. 'Hey,' he said. 'It's
time to git a-going.'

'Holy Mary, Mother of God,' replied Russo.

His eyes were glassy; but he stood up obediently and tensed himself, ready to leap.

'Come on!' cried Frazer. His voice was as gay as pouring wine.

Together the two men hurdled the lip of the crater and went charging toward the gap in the wire. In the lee of the burning tank Frazer pulled Russo down to the ground beside him, hard.

Frazer did not hear whatever Russo was muttering now. On the ground, six feet away, he looked into the dead face of Simpson. Simpson, the Bren gunner: Simpson, his closest friend: old Sim he had gone on leave with to Bari.

'Jesus Christ,' said Frazer. That, and no more.

He crawled over to the body. His hands went out searching, gently stroking Simpson's dead limbs. Then he stopped; he lay with his head on the earth for several seconds. But almost at once his head came up; his glance darted round the battlefield. He began to empty the Bren magazines from Simpson's pouches and stuff them into his own. He left his rifle lying on the ground. He picked up Simpson's Bren gun, and he went crawling quickly back to Russo.

Frazer's face was white. 'We're going again,' he told Russo. 'You ready?'

Russo made no reply. His gaze was still fastened to whatever vision of Armageddon he perceived to his front. But Frazer saw that he understood.

Hundreds of smoke shells were now dropping from the sky, and this time as they ran they were enfolded part of the way in comfortable white clouds.

Plop, plop, and they fell together into a crater only ten yards away from the tank turret. The body of someone dead felt yielding under Frazer's boots.

'Hail, Mary, full of Grace,' Russo recited at once. He was trembling now more than ever.

Frazer ignored this; he sat down on the corpse and cocked his head. The machine-gun in the tank turret was a cracking whip over their heads; when the big gun fired their crater shook with concussion. Frazer pulled out his cigarettes, lighted one, and sucked tobacco smoke deep into his lungs.

There's no hurry, he thought: the next part has to be done very carefully. If only it could be Simpson with him now, instead of this guinea Russo. He and Sim together with a bottle of steam or cognac would take the Line by themselves. . . . Or, he suddenly wondered, *would* they?

Finding Simpson dead had cut Frazer loose from his familiar anchors. He felt giddy and light-headed. He became aware of his utter loneliness up here; he had never felt like this before.

He gazed at the muttering Russo. He grinned in a friendly way, and he tried to place a cigarette in his companion's hand, but Russo let it fall in a pool of blood at his boot. Russo's teeth were chattering but he went on speaking, in an unending monotone. 'Hail, Mary, full of Grace,' he said; and a second later, 'Holy Mary, Mother of God.' There were one or two other phrases which Frazer could not make out.

Russo's utter self-absorption made Frazer feel lonelier than ever. He listened to Russo's voice, and he began to delve deep into his own memory. 'Hey, Russo,' he cried in triumph, across the few feet of crater. 'Listen to this one: "Matthew, Mark, Luke, and John—bless the bed that I lie on—" '

There was no response from Russo. He went on with his mumbling.

Frazer frowned, puzzling his words out slowly. 'If I should die before I wake,' he said. Then he stopped. Suddenly his head went back and he shook and he roared with laughter. 'Oh, Christ,' Frazer said aloud, wiping the tears from his eyes. 'If only old Sim could be up here now. . . .'

He cocked his head again. Up ahead was the unmistakable bark of a Bren gun. One of the guys had got up there; it was time to be going.

'All right, Russo, sport,' he said, all businesslike. 'Just stay with me. We're going in behind that tank turret. Get it?'

Again he slapped Russo lightly on the cheek. Obediently Russo stood up and tensed himself against the side of the crater.

An unexpected gun cut in on them as they ran. Frazer almost tripped as Russo's body went tumbling at his feet; he saw the burst of machine-gun stitching running up his side. Frazer weaved and spurted toward a ditch.

Poor Russo, he thought as he ran. Scared shitless, but he still kept on going. Poor Russo, he thought: poor Russo, full of Grace, poor Russo full of holes. . . . He jumped and landed with a jarring crash in the ditch.

A Mark 4 tank came rolling toward him. He had caught glimpses of them earlier this morning: they roamed up and down behind the concrete emplacements as mobile pill-boxes.

Frazer jammed the folded bipod of his Bren into the earth, muzzle just peeping clear of the ditch. He watched the tank, and from the corner of his eyes he watched two figures kneeling on the concrete ramp leading into the tank turret emplacement. His right hand on the trigger guard also held a grenade.

The tank slewed in his direction and stopped. The hatch opened and the head of a German officer appeared. The officer wore black *Panzer* coveralls. He was young, fair-haired, and smiling. One hand negligently waved a pistol. '*Kommen Sie her,*' the officer ordered.

Only in that moment did Frazer realize he himself was not the object of this command. Farther along the ditch was another khaki-clad figure. Slowly this Canadian soldier stood up—he was a man from another Company—and he let his rifle drop reluctantly from his hands. He stood in the ditch, looking angry and helpless, covered by the tank and the officer's pistol.

Frazer steadied the muzzle, and pressed the trigger. He fired a burst long enough to slice the top of the officer's head off. The black-clad body slumped at the centre and fell heavily across the hatch. In the same instant Frazer was darting forward on hands and knees dragging his Bren gun behind him. He leaped for the level ground and swung himself up underneath the tank. He knew that tank wasn't going anywhere in a hurry with its dead commander still hanging from the hatch. He aimed his Bren gun back at the point where he had lain a moment before.

Seconds later the two figures he had glimpsed at the emplacement came darting forward in a crouch, Schmeissers pointing at the place Frazer had fired from. Frazer let them walk squarely into his sights, then he pressed the trigger. The two German soldiers went crashing down together.

From his place underneath the tank Frazer peered toward the concrete ramp of the emplacement. Now, he thought: if I can only get over there and roll some grenades down. . . .

Frazer was on the objective, and he was fighting. Frazer might be the only man in the Company still alive on the objective, but one man, at least, was there; and therefore 'B' Company was on the objective, and fighting.

28

THE Brigadier's jeep got to a point just beyond the Start Line where a knocked-out tank blocked the way. The three men in the jeep looked at the obstruction silently.

'We'll walk from here,' Brigadier Kildare declared, starting to dismount. 'At least, Fergus and I will. Hunter—you take the jeep back to the Rifles' farm-house. You can call that Advanced Brigade H.Q.—anyway, get some kind of communication with Division.'

Major Hunter sat behind the wheel of the jeep and made no move. As always the Brigadier wore his Balmoral cap; the silver Hart Rampant winked bravely in the sunlight. His hulking figure filled the roadway. Hunter hated this man's guts, or so he had always thought. At the moment he felt differently. His thin face expressed his worry.

'Shouldn't you wear a helmet, sir?' Hunter ventured.

There was no reply.

'Sir,' Hunter persisted slowly. 'Can you really accomplish anything by going up there?'

On the track Brigadier Kildare was busy getting his cigar properly alight. 'Probably not, Hunter,' he said, between puffs. 'Probably not.'

He looked in Hunter's face; he appeared genuinely surprised at what he saw. 'Look,' the Brigadier explained then. 'No one in the rear can influence the battle today. It's going to be decided on the ground, and I want to be where that decision is made.'

'Sir,' Hunter said suddenly. 'Let me come too.'

The Brigadier looked at him steadily. After a moment he walked back to the jeep. He clapped a huge hand on Hunter's shoulder. 'We're going to need a good man on the set today, Hunter. But thanks anyway.'

'Good luck, sir,' Hunter said soberly. He put the jeep in reverse.

He received an airy wave of the hand in reply. Already the Brigadier and Fergus had fallen into step, and were marching together along the forest trail.

They had gone twenty paces before the Brigadier discovered
that he carried no weapon, not even his pistol which he had left
in the jeep. He glanced quickly at Fergus who plodded dourly at
his side. Fergus marched with his bagpipes tucked under one arm
—and nothing else.

The Brigadier stopped. He picked up a stout length of ash which
had been cut by shell fire from one of the trees. Thoughfully he
hefted his stick in his hands. 'Fergus,' he said, 'I'm thinking ye
might find a rifle more useful than yon pipes today.'

Fergus stood bandy-legged on the track. He scowled and said
nothing.

'Leave the pipes there, man.' The Brigadier gestured toward
the ditch.

Fergus's black eyes glittered. 'The pipes stay with me,' he
declared in a tone of hot defiance.

The Brigadier detached a lazy plume of smoke from his cigar.
He was enjoying this exchange. Both men were actors. They had
created a rare character role between them: that of laird and gillie;
and now Brigadier Kildare wanted to see if Fergus would play his
part to the end.

They had acted their roles for a long time. More than this, there
was a secret they shared between them: an immense, supreme
joke. It was a secret which Brigadier Kildare had uncovered when
he plucked the dour Fergus out of his British Holding Unit. Others
only knew that Fergus came from the Glasgow slums; that he was
an ill-tempered little man, with no redeeming qualities. They did
not know about the joke. Normally the Brigadier had only to
think of the joke to be put in good humour for the rest of the day.
It was the explanation for Fergus's preferential status, his eleva-
tion to the rank of corporal, and all the other privileges nobody
could understand. It was a joke they shared between them, but
could never express. The joke was that Fergus's real name
happened to be Cohen.

And now the Brigadier looked in Fergus-Cohen's angry face.
He looked at the bow-legged, ill-visaged little man, and he
thought: this man is only what he is, only where he is, because of
me. . . . The Brigadier felt an unexpected stirring of compunction.

'Fergus,' he said. 'You don't *have* to come with me. This is not
really your job. You can turn back if you wish.'

Fergus made a noise in his throat. He walked over to the ditch. He picked up a dead soldier's rifle and bandolier of ammunition and he slung both on his right shoulder. The pipes he tucked under his left arm again. He returned to stand glowering up at Brigadier Kildare.

'Sorr—' said Fergus, rolling his 'r's' outrageously. 'Dinna ye be sich an unco bluidy fool!'

The cigar dropped from Brigadier Kildare's mouth and fell to the track. He shook with an immensity of laughter. 'Oh, perfect!' he roared, slapping his thighs. 'Fergus, man—you're absolutely perfect!'

When he stopped laughing at last Fergus handed him back his cigar. The two men allowed themselves a brief regard of understanding; then they turned about. Together they resumed their march along the forest track. Now Fergus carried his pipes, and a rifle too. The length of ash stick fitted like a shepherd's crook in the Brigadier's hand; he wielded it with the authority of a drum-major's baton.

In the forest clearing the Brigadier came upon Colonel McNabb's dead body lying on top of his smashed wireless set. He knelt in the ditch for a moment, then his glance swept to the open field ahead with its carpet of dead soldiers. Burned-out tanks stood in the field as markers of forward progress. Along the edge of the wood a few soldiers lay spread in firing position, their weapons pointing toward the enemy. At this moment there was a lull of silence along the front.

Back at Division, the Brigadier knew, battle-maps had been marked to show two companies of the Rifles on the objective; and two companies of the Royals similarly forward on the left. But this information was based on the first sit-reps before all the wireless sets had been knocked out. *He* knew differently; he dreaded confirming the fact that the edge of the woods here marked the real limit of advance. His third battalion, the Scots, lay in reserve a few hundred yards back in the woods. The important decision left to him now was whether or not to commit them to the attack.

In the ditch he sat with his chin cupped between his hands. From the group at the edge of the wood a soldier rose and came doubling over, rifle in hand. He was a stocky, powerful-looking man, at this moment bloodied and dirty. 'Sergeant-Major Mitchell, sir,' he reported.

The Brigadier regarded him steadily. 'All right, Mitchell,' he said. 'What's the situation? Where are the forward companies?'

Mitchell knelt at the ditch; he did not reply at once. 'There aren't any, sir,' he said then, with a slow pain of reluctance.

The Brigadier's glance stayed on his face. Another officer would doubtless have disputed the statement. The Brigadier merely said: 'You're sure?'

'I've been up and through the Line myself, sir. Captain Begg is dead up there. He told me to bring back as many men as I could. I've got eight men from "B" Company, a few from the others. There are no officers left. As far as I know I'm now commanding the 2nd Rifles.'

Mitchell spoke with pain and effort; until now he had not accepted the fact that his beloved Battalion had been wiped out.

The Brigadier said nothing. His glance strayed back to the open field. 'Well,' he said, after a moment. 'All right, Mitchell—you've done your job well. . . .'

But he did not go on with whatever else he was going to say; his voice trailed away. He was suffering the same grief for the men of his Brigade that Mitchell felt for his Company and his Battalion.

The Brigadier sat on in the ditch. Now he saw the whole picture, and it was what he expected. This insane attack could have had no other outcome. By now the break-through on the left might be complete; if that was so the enemy would have abandoned this sector of the Line in any event. The thought made him feel worse.

But now—should he order the Scots in? It was possible, remotely possible, that another battalion assault might do it. It went against every fibre of his being to withdraw from this attack, leaving the field strewn with his hundreds of dead bodies. And yet —perhaps the one last important service he could perform was to save the lives of those who remained. He could simply order the Scots to firm up to this present position here. . . .

In the ditch behind him Fergus came to his feet.

Brigadier Kildare looked over his shoulder and he saw the first files of Scots infantry advancing toward him through the woods. They came on steadily, holding good section formation despite the trees and the broken ground. They were big, strong, powerful men, their faces serious, marching with their weapons at the ready. Brigadier Kildare stared at them blankly. Their Colonel must have decided to wait no longer; of his own accord he was moving his battalion to the attack. The Brigadier stood up; he was the only person in the world who could stop them now.

Fergus was out of the ditch. There was a wild glint in his eyes, one of his boots was tapping the ground. He put the reed of the pipes to his mouth, and a thin screech split the air. In a moment the first savage, vengeful notes of a Highland lament came keening out, powerful and ear-splitting.

The marching soldiers looked about in amazement; their pace quickened.

The Brigadier moved away from the ditch. He stood leaning on his shepherd's crook, his eyes stony, and he let the leading files march by him; he made no move to stop them. All along the front the guns were silent, almost as though they cocked their barrels to hear the furious wail of pipes. The wild music seemed to fill and overflow the whole battlefield of the Adolf Hitler Line.

The Brigadier let the leading platoons pass by. Then there came the flapping aerial marking a Company Headquarters group. Brigadier Kildare moved with long strides. He marched to the side of the startled Company Commander, fell into step, and moved forward with him. He marched forward leaning on his stick. Still piping furiously Fergus wheeled and followed in the steps of his Brigadier.

29

JONESY heard the whistling screech and started to fall in the same instant. The Padre, unheeding, continued to stride down the centre of the track.

'Look out, sir!' Jonesy had time to call; then there was a crash.

Luckily the shell landed squarely in the ditch; there the explosion spent itself.

The Padre cast his glance round for his lagging disciple. 'Come,' he ordered severely. 'Let us not delay.' He turned and stalked forward like a stern, avenging prophet.

Jonesy ran to catch up. His rifle banged on his helmet which in turn bobbed askew on his blond head; his guileless face palpitated with alarm. For one of the very few times in his life Jonesy knew it was *his* task to look after somebody else. This dour master of his knew everything in the world; everything, that is, except war. Whereas Rifleman Jones was an infantryman. And a man who has attended the School of Shooting-and-being-shot-at, no matter how low his I.Q., has acquired certain reflexes which the non-graduate lacks, to the possible detriment of his survival.

Jonesy pulled nervously at his rifle sling. The cannonading up ahead was the heaviest he had ever heard. He tried to match the long steps. He marched close beside the Padre's gaunt, striding figure.

Long ago Padre Doorn had banished the secret smile from his face. Instead he wore the dedicated, indrawn look of a priest telling his beads, which indeed he was doing.

'*Ubi crux est martyr ibi,*' the Padre declared in a firm ringing tone.

His glance flashed sternly, in challenge, at the shell-stripped, bleeding trees of the forest. When they raised no comment he repeated the words in a slightly less emphatic register of triumph. The trees bowed before him like admiring acolytes.

As he strode on his hand went with a miser's reverence to touch the object inside his breast pocket. This was the object which had been granted him in the Chapel of the Sacrament of the Church of Sant' Agata; on the altar, at the feet of the wounded saint. In his pocket it lay swaddled by The Title and The Testament: proof indisputable, probably the only such in Italy, or in the world. . . .

Chosroes, King of the Persians, the Padre recited to himself— it was a familiar, private liturgy—stole it from Jerusalem. Until the avenging Emperor Heraclius came to slay him, it was kept enthroned always at his right hand, because Chosroes knew the significance of what he possessed—it was much more than mere wood, more than mere representation. . . . Then for centuries it had performed miracles: given sight to the blind, life to the dead, cleansed lepers, routed demons. The object was the Son of God himself.

Because that was the whole glory and magnificence. It was not merely a relic of Christ suffering, it *was* Christ: our crucified Lord

124

in person—*ubi crux est martyr ibi.* . . . All this was attested, in writ now swaddling the object.

Inside the Padre's pocket, wrapped in its parchment, was a piece of the True Cross.

This vision had long ago crowded reason from Padre Doorn's mind. He was insane; only temporarily perhaps, but at this moment in time, insane. He marched toward the battlefield to hold parley with the Father, and he carried the Son of God in his pocket.

The two men drew near to the final clearing in the woods. Impatiently the Padre moved aside to allow two stretcher-bearers to pass by on the track. He spared no glance for their burden; his mind was engaged with far graver matters. But Jonesy looked at the huge lump of body, the chalk-white face, the eyes gone-away-somewhere. Jonesy stared; he came to attention; and he saluted.

Those eyes returned for an instant to regard him.

'See that?'

From his litter Brigadier Kildare spoke in the faintest but proudest of voices. 'A damn fine soldier! Your name is Jones. I remember you well from Sicily.'

Then the Brigadier fainted. His bearers hurried their pace.

The Padre, oblivious, strode forward, and halted at the ditch where Colonel McNabb's dead body lay. Since the Brigadier first came here other corpses had been added; now many of the bodies wore the word 'Scots' emblazoned at their shoulders.

Padre Doorn gazed about with a judicious eye, appraisingly, as though to determine whether or not this setting would be fit for his purpose. His glance was majestic. He peered toward the open field beyond the woods, toward the Adolf Hitler Line.

The occasional black air-burst broke like thunderclap in the sky above, but the Padre paid no heed.

Then, for a moment, his glance touched on Colonel McNabb's sightless face. The Padre frowned slightly, and shook his head as though to clear the frown away. He moved forward a step and his boot struck the dead-weight limbs of Corporal Fowler. He looked in Fowler's unseeing eyes and his frown became deeper.

Now he looked about him anew, his prophet's face puzzled. He saw the bodies nearby, the carpet of dead soldiers strewn in the meadow. In the meadow the carpet was so thick in places that bodies, of necessity, lay on top of one another.

In his first glance the Padre had supposed these soldiers on the ground were performing some kind of military duty, or sleeping perhaps; but now he saw and he understood. A shaft of pain pierced his face.

About him, in every compass of his glance, he recognized the faces of friends—those he had known in England, on shipboard, in Sicily. These were the young crusaders he had once admired and marched with; and now they lay dead everywhere around him.

The Padre was seized by an emotion he had not known for months. He felt pity; his soul began to ache and grieve with compassion. This human feeling forced his mind to voyage outside itself; for a moment it jostled his insanity aside; and he saw the plight and the end of plight of those he had once called friends.

An air-burst smashed blackly overhead. The Padre saw a young soldier kneeling at the edge of the wood; he saw the boy's back begin to shake, his neck quiver, with a wild uncontrollable trembling.

The Padre's mouth opened. 'No,' he cried, in a loud and terrible voice. 'No—there must be no more execution!' And he began to beat his right hand upon his breast.

Sergeant-Major Mitchell stood at his elbow. 'Take it easy, Padre,' his distant-weary voice was saying. 'Come on now; just take it easy. . . .'

The Padre's right hand worked violently into his inside pocket; pieces of parchment and paper fluttered to the ground; his hand emerged with an object in its grasp. He broke loose from Mitchell; and he went charging headlong for the open meadow.

Out on the track, half-way to the wire, the Padre halted. He planted his feet wide apart, he threw his head back. His gaze went searchingly, imperious, to the sky. He stared full at the flawless blue heaven. With his right hand he thrust out the object at extended length from his body.

This was the time. This was the time he had been awaiting. He held the True Cross in his right hand—such was his insanity, he believed he held the Son of God in his hand—and he gazed and waited. This was the way he had planned it. He waited to open parley.

From the woods Sergeant-Major Mitchell expected to see him shot down any second. But the gaunt figure stayed erect, stark and threatening. Perhaps the enemy did not yet observe him; perhaps the gunners were sated with killing—one more life, debit or credit, could make no difference now.

The Padre stood waiting, his gaze fixed on the sky, the True Cross thrust demandingly at heaven. The Padre stared unremittingly at the sky, waiting for the parley to open—and nothing happened. Nothing except air-burst.

All that happened was a black explosion above him. It did him no harm, but it must have seemed that this was the answer he awaited. These air-bursts were the idle droppings from a negligent war-baron's pocket; and there was to be nothing else.

The Padre's right hand dropped, his gaze came to the horizontal, then below. The piece of the True Cross fell to the dirt at his feet. A moment later the Padre himself sagged to the ground. From the woods Mitchell saw his gaunt back heaving and shaking. Padre Doorn lay among the dead soldiers on the track, weeping.

Mitchell and Jones went out in a rush together. Mitchell threw the long body across his shoulders and started to double back at once. Jonesy hesitated; he was searching, peering down at the ground. Then he picked up an object from the track, stuffed it in his pocket, and started to run. A belated machine-gun traced dirt arabesques at his feet as he went sprinting back to the shelter of the woods.

30

AT SEVEN o'clock in the evening Major John Adam climbed from his carrier and stood on the battlefield. Since early morning he had stayed at rear Brigade H.Q., seizing on each meagre wireless report, pleading with anyone who would listen for permission to take his L.O.B.s forward. At last he had won grudging consent to advance as far as 'F' Echelon, and that was enough: Adam drove his carrier force right through.

His gaze swept to the ground at once. He walked up and down the forest clearing and he looked in the dead faces of his men. Adam moved without stopping; he wore a tight frown of concentration.

He walked beyond the trees, and into the meadow. Nobody fired at him. In reality, of course, the battle was over. The Line on the left was broken, and even here the enemy was starting to thin out; during the night they would evacuate completely. In the meantime they did not fire at small parties searching for wounded.

Adam walked as far as the wire. There, like a pointing arrow on the track, was Lieutenant Venner's body. A few paces forward Sergeant DiCicco lay, his striving fingers within inches of the wire. Strewing the ground around them were the bodies of other 'B' Company men. After a moment Adam turned about. He walked back to the woods.

In the clearing he sat with his back to a tree trunk and let Mitchell tell about it. He heard of his own Company's attacks, of Brigadier Kildare's charge at the head of the Scots—that impossible charge which came within an inch of succeeding, until they were overrun by tanks. Fergus, the piper, was killed. Then the crazed Padre appeared. . . .

Adam sat without moving and listened. He knew he should be going about reinvigorating the men who remained, trying to recreate some semblance of military order, but he could not stir. No effort—now, or ever again—would seem worth the trouble. He glanced idly at two men lying by their Bren gun, smoking cigarettes. Why, he thought with surprise: it's Krasnick and Ewart, a whole Bren team intact.

Next he saw Rifleman Jones walk past, and that seemed perfectly natural. He had forgotten that Jonesy had ever been away from the Company. He was reminded of something. 'Jonesy,' he called. 'My pack in the carrier. There's a bottle of Scotch. Bring it over, please.'

Mitchell drank deeply. Adam motioned to some of the men nearby and the bottle passed from mouth to mouth. He did not drink himself. He thought: Here is their Company Commander arrived at last, and all he can give them is a drink of Scotch— when it was his own self that they needed.

He glanced through stripped branches of the trees. The meadow was now golden with evening sunlight. The air was still; he fancied a call of German voices in the distance.

If he *had* been here, of course, he would be lying out in that field himself. The attack could have had no other result. Bill Begg and some of the others, he knew, were lying dead on the objective.

He could have done no more than poor Bill did—and no less. . . .

And what now? Reinforcements would come forward; it would be his job to rebuild his unit all over again. But no matter how hard he worked—even if, miraculously, he created a duplicate of what had been destroyed today—there might some day be another Line like this awaiting, stronger than any care or solicitude or planning could ever be; and then that Company too would cease to exist. At least, Adam thought: that time I would be with them, I would finish doing my job. Perhaps, he thought, the only end in life is to be functional: to do one's job is as much as a man can ever do. . . .

But he was only thinking thus to hold the other thing at bay. Soon, there was going to be a terrible, cumulative weight of grief to be suffered. For the men lying dead in the field were not merely soldiers—they were his friends; each one a human being he had loved; and he did not know if he would find life supportable without them.

From the right flank there was a sudden clatter of machine-gun fire. Stolid Krasnick poked his Bren gun in the direction of the sound; the other men slipped down to cover.

Adam stood up. But as he walked forward the sound spluttered out. The evening calm descended again. The sun was a glowing ball of gold above the meadow of dead bodies.

In the field, parallel with the woods, a limping figure came lurching into view. Bedraggled, bloodied, begrimed. . . . Hopping on one leg, using a rifle for a crutch; no helmet, tunic torn in shreds. It was Major Bunny Bazin. Bunny Bazin returning from the objective, where he had spent the day.

He hopped into the shelter of the woods, rested a moment against a tree, and looked about him. The first person he saw was Adam. He forced himself erect; he created a little smile on his lips. 'Ah,' Major Bazin breathed. With an air of gravest, gentlest courtesy he extended his right hand. 'Dr. Livingstone, I presume. . . .'

But his face was too unaccustomed to smiling; the attempt failed and slipped away. Muscles in his throat worked; his eyes blinked.

Adam seized his hand before it could fall. He placed one arm round his friend's shoulders. 'Bunny,' he said; that one word. Then the two men clung tight to one another.

BOOK THREE / *And More*

1

IT WAS late August. Adam and Rifleman Jones were driving south. Adam held the wheel of the plunging jeep. The wind and the sun were kind on his face: he looked young, carefree even. It was the first time he had looked or felt this way all summer.

By the roadside ahead there was a sudden, startling splash of green. It was a pond of water; an oasis of emerald green: vivid, magic green—hachured dark in the glare of yellow sun. Willow trees bowed down to touch the water. It was a picture-book illustration of a place fit to cast spells of enchantment.

Adam slowed, and braked the jeep to a stop.

'Lunch time,' he announced. He left Jonesy to unpack and hurried to the edge of the pond.

Adam knelt and looked at his green reflection. Willow branches tapped his face; he felt refreshed. This summer he had spent in a state of shut-away torpor. Only today had he felt expectation again stir inside him—he had ceased to hibernate and come alive.

After the Hitler Line the Division had been moved into the mountains for an extended rest period; the survivors were granted liberal leave to visit the exciting new cities of Rome and Naples. Adam himself had only gone away for two days—and then only as far as Bari. On his return he withdrew utterly to himself, seeming indifferent even to the training of his new Company. But now at last he was going on real five-days' leave. He was on his way to visit Bunny Bazin.

The cause, which had brought Adam alive again, was a letter from Bunny Bazin. Now Adam sat beside the pond and he drew the well-creased letter from his pocket. He unfolded it and started to read the familiar words.

'This place is purest Kafka,' Bazin had written. 'To myself I call it *Der Strafekolonie,* and I recognize, of course, that I am the principal prisoner; the difference being that mine is an indeterminate sentence while my charges serve only twenty-eight days.... I have at last, you see, found my vocation in life: I am Commandant of a Field Punishment Camp. I have a Sergeant descended from Captain Bligh, and an Adjutant straight out of Stendahl.'

There was just enough in this vein to whet Adam's curiosity. The mere thought of his friend Bunny Bazin so grotesquely misemployed was enough to bring him fully alive again. For a moment Adam glanced up to see Jonesy busily opening a tin of Spam. He went on with his reading.

'As befits the Keeper,' Bazin wrote, 'I live in comfort. We inhabit a castle, which in more recent years has served as a tobacco store-house. It is half-way up a mountain and has a real portcullis and a keep. There is an unlimited supply of Benevento gin, and in the evening when my charges are tucked away I sit on my private battlement and drink against a backdrop of passably-painted Apennines.

'My constant visitor—and this will surprise you—is none other than Philip Doorn, our late and lately-crazed Padre. Now he has found his sanity, although I sometimes doubt that he will ever find anything else. He stares at me with gaunt, wounded eyes and I tell him to have another drink—and that's one reason why I want you here: I need help in working over that Benevento gin. Anyway, I tell Doorn that if he must be tormented he has come to the right place, because here it is our trade, our profession and calling. This *Strafekolonie,* I tell him, is a minor beach-head of Hell established on earth; but of course the poor bugger himself has been straightway to Hell's headquarters and back.... Seriously, though, Philip and I are friends again; after all—with you—we share something in common. He lives, in theory, at the nearby Convalescent Depot; and apparently the hierarchy of Padres believe he only suffered exhaustion on the Hitler Line. He is still a chaplain in good standing—if there ever was such a thing....

'It will also interest you to know that the Area Commander is none other than Brigadier Ian Kildare, recovered from his wounds, and now apparently the darling of all Canada since the newspapers told of his gallant charge to the bagpipes. There's been nothing like it since Balaclava or the Relief of Lucknow—he's to get another D.S.O., and the most heart-warming part of all is that the big brass doesn't dare fire him—they're stuck with Kildare for ever. And, oh, there's so much more to tell you. . . .'

Adam was smiling when he looked up to see how Jonesy was progressing with lunch. Some slabs of Spam lay abandoned in a mess-tin, and Jonesy trailed his fingers over the glass surface of the pond with a child's dreamy absorption.

Adam sighed. He had made Jonesy his batman simply so he would have him close at hand to look after; but what, he wondered suddenly, would happen to an innocent like this in the world Bazin wrote about? What would happen to *Jonesy* in a Field Punishment Camp?

'Jonesy,' Adam said, in a gentle voice, 'eat some Spam. We won't bother with tea. Just bring that bottle of cognac from the jeep.'

Jonesy went trotting toward the jeep. Adam rolled on to his side and picked up the letter again.

'Each evening,' Bazin's words continued, 'we sit out on the battlement and drink gin in the wine-light. I crack jokes and the Padre makes feeble response. The mountains hunch up their shoulders like make-believe volcanoes, and that creates a nice air of doom at the banquet.

'Also, there is a Countess who owns our castle-tobacco factory and a *palazzo* on top of the mountain. She is deliciously decadent and *fin-de-siècle;* we have become quite intimate friends. She has a niece, here temporarily, whom I have reserved for you. She is a sad demented little beauty, and I know you will love her at once. The niece's name is Antonia, Toni for short.'

The letter went on for six more pages. And under all the bantering self-mockery Adam could feel Bazin's affection leap from the pages like a solid force. This letter had brought him awake and alive again. Now it was pulling him irresistibly, with Jonesy, along the road south, speeding toward Bunny Bazin's penal colony.

Without looking Adam took the bottle from Jonesy's hand and drank. He leafed through the rest of the letter quickly. There was one part in particular which he found disturbing.

'As you may know,' Bunny Bazin wrote, 'they are giving me a D.S.O. for my contribution to the total absurdity of the Hitler

Line. This would serve admirably to advance my professional career—if I happened to have one. For a brief while it seemed to me I was escaping my destiny by coming to this place. But I am not, of course. When the times comes I shall simply punch the Brigadier in the nose, or set my inmates at large, or do something sufficiently disgraceful to get sent back to "D" Company, where I belong. I'll be there in time for the appointed rendezvous. The awful part is, though, that for a moment I was really tempted by an utterly obscene proposal. I want to tell you all about it—so come, and come quickly. . . .'

Adam stood up. He tucked the letter into his tunic pocket.

He started toward the jeep. 'Let's go,' he said, grinning at the uncomprehending Jones. 'If we hurry up we may be just in time to drink a decadent slug of gin in the wine-light.'

2

THERE was the squat little castle, nestled half-way up the hillside, and it had a real portcullis and keep. Inside the grating stood a glowering Sergeant, holding a quarterstaff at arm's length across his thighs. It was seven o'clock in the evening and Adam felt weak with hunger, light-headed with the cognac he had consumed en route.

'Open up, Sergeant,' he called. 'I've come to see Major Bazin.'

There was a long pause, then a clanking of iron and the jeep drove through. The Sergeant was a big man. He made a perfunctory bus driver's salute and continued to glower. 'The Major's gone for the evening,' he said shortly, his tone suggesting that this unwelcome visitor should follow suit. Adam climbed stiffly from the jeep.

A soldier came scurrying round a corner, weighted down with a bucket in each hand. He seemed close to the limit of exhaustion but the instant he caught sight of Adam and the jeep he spun himself round and jumped to quivering attention with his nose pressed flat to the stone wall. Some unclean liquid in the buckets slopped over on to his legs. Jonesy stared with amazement; impulsively he started forward.

'Hey you—get the hell back!' the Sergeant roared.

Jonesy stopped. Adam turned; coldly his glance raked the

Sergeant up and down. He gestured to the soldier at the wall. 'What is that?' he demanded.

'One of the prisoners.'

'I can guess that much, Sergeant.' Adam's voice was as cold as his icy-blue glance. 'I want to know what he's doing against that wall.'

The Sergeant had shuffled to a partial position of attention. 'Prisoners are not allowed to look an officer in the face. They must stand against the wall.'

'Tell him to put the buckets down,' said Adam, in a softly vicious tone.

'Yes—sir.'

When the Sergeant returned Adam's glance was colder still. He did not like this Sergeant, and he did not like this place. In his letter Bazin could joke about it—perhaps because he had to; but once you were there there was nothing the least amusing about a Field Punishment Camp. Most of the prisoners came from field units, and whatever they had done to merit their sentences one could not forget that they had first come to this alien country as volunteers. They were here to receive a little planned brutality, be toughened physically, humiliated, and sent back to their units with the certain knowledge that nothing would ever be worth the risk of being returned here again. It took a special breed of N.C.O. to accomplish the purpose of this place, the kind Adam would never have allowed in his own Company—and this Sergeant before him now was a prime example.

'Sergeant,' Adam ordered, 'show my batman to Major Bazin's quarters. I shall stay the night.' Then he added, as though the Camp's cruelty was already seeping into him: 'And hold your entire staff in readiness for possible inspection later.'

The Sergeant's eyes narrowed; he looked at Adam appraisingly, as though to test the strength of the officer who issued such orders. He had noted the Rifles' shoulder flash, and the ribbons—both these were impressive. His own position he knew to be precarious: he had been here since Ortona; if he was ever sent back to his unit some of his former graduates would undoubtedly try to murder him. Major Bazin, with his relaxed severity, he regarded as a weakling, but he was absent so frequently it made little difference; and Lieutenant Benny did what he was told. But this hard-looking officer now. . . . The talk of inspection might mean he was preparing to take over as Commandant; but more important than anything, the Sergeant could recognize steel in an officer's being when he saw it.

The Sergeant brought himself to a total position of attention. 'Yes, sir,' he said. 'Right away, sir. And I'll send you Lieutenant de Rougemont. He's in charge while the Major's away.'

Adam turned his back. 'Do that,' he said indifferently.

He walked toward a flight of stone steps leading to the crenellated wall above. Somewhere up near the highest battlement, he knew, Bunny Bazin had his own quarters.

The apartment, when he found it, was spacious. French doors opened on an enclosed battlement which seemed to nestle among the surrounding Apennines, isolated, detached from the rest of the castle and its burden of silent, suffering humanity.

While Jonesy struggled to set up his safari bed Adam sat down at a table and looked at the empty bottle of cognac. Already he had sloughed off the gloom of this place; it was simply not as strong as his good spirits, his bright anticipation in the day. And now he wanted a drink.

Without warning the door was flung open. A floridly handsome young man, breathless, excited, burst into the room. He wore a pre-war cavalry tunic, with breeches, riding-boots and spurs. One guessed that his appearance would usually be dapper but at the moment something like fish flakes caked the sides of his mouth; obviously he had come straight from the dinner table. His black eyes glittered.

'Major Adam, sir,' the young man said in a rush. 'This is indeed an honour. Major Bazin has told me so much about you. Permit me—I am Lieutenant Bernard de Rougemont, 24th Lancers, and Camp Adjutant—entirely at your service.'

The Lieutenant bowed from the waist and tried to make his voice bow in unison.

Adam stared and said nothing. The 24th Lancers were an Armoured Car unit; he knew they could not muster a pair of spurs in the whole regiment. This must be the Stendahl character Bazin had mentioned.

'Sir—' de Rougemont immediately rattled on. 'I am most desirous to return to Canada. It is an affair, you see, of preventing my fiancée from marrying another man—a sheer bounder, I might add. Major Bazin has promised, and I thought perhaps if you would write a letter to the Commanding General also. . . . Well, the word of two such gentlemen. . . .'

Again his voice and his body bowed low together.

Adam concealed his astonishment. This was the place, he supposed, to encounter a curiosity like this. 'Where's Bazin?' he demanded.

'But, of course, sir. How silly of me—I quite forgot. It is the Countess's birthday tonight. There is a party up at the *palazzo*. It will be my pleasure to escort you when you are quite prepared.'

De Rougemont laughed. He made his voice tinkle up and down a scale of laughter.

Adam said nothing.

'Are you comfortable now, sir? Anything—'

Adam cut him short. 'Yes—what have you got to drink?'

'Gin, sir. Lots of Benevento gin.'

'What else?' Adam's glance was stern on the Lieutenant's face.

De Rougemont hesitated. He looked unhappily at Adam's severe expression. 'Well,' he said reluctantly, 'as it happens there is a little Scotch in my personal supply—'

'Good!' said Adam at once. He allowed his face a wintry glimpse of smile. 'Bring it on.'

'Yes, sir.'

Spurs clanking, de Rougemont turned and walked from the room. He exited with considerably less enthusiasm than he had entered.

When he returned both officers sat at the table. Adam drank the Scotch while the anxious glance of Lieutenant de Rougemont regarded the falling level of liquor in the bottle.

Adam had never felt better. The Scotch was as warming as the sunset glow on the battlements outside. He was alive again, in love with the world; and after a little he was even planning what he might do to help Lieutenant Benny here. . . . For Adam this was a moment of suspended time, enchanted time, after which anything would be possible; a time charged with wonder and expectation. He poured himself another drink to maintain the bliss of the moment.

'Sir,' de Rougemont persisted, eye still on the bottle, 'are you ready to leave yet?'

'All right.' Adam stood up at last, and he beamed affectionately at the anxious Lieutenant. 'How about Jonesy—has he got a place to sleep?'

'Yes, sir.'

'Good. Then lead on, my splendid Adjutant.'

Prudently Adam allowed Lieutenant de Rougemont to drive the jeep. They swirled through the portcullis in a cloud of dust. As they departed the Sergeant stood at rigid attention and saluted like a guardsman.

3

A DRIVEWAY of sick cypresses wound through a garden of weeds dotted with umbrella pines. Mauve shadows moved on the *palazzo* walls. This near side was rose-red with sunset, like brave rouge applied to impossibly faded cheeks. The whole setting was quite suitably *fin-de-siècle*.

And Adam was quite suitably, happily, drunk. While de Rougemont went ahead to park the jeep he stepped off the driveway and stopped at an abandoned patch of roses. He looked at the forlorn, bedraggled blooms, and he picked out one meriting special concern. He felt moved to speak aloud, with genuine sympathy: 'O, rose, thou art sick—'

Behind him a voice added: 'The invisible worm—'

Adam turned. He saw an oval, Madonna-like face, a girl in an evening gown, holding a wineglass in one hand. '. . . that flies in the night,' her voice went on.

He looked in her dark eyes, they looked at one another; their voices blended in unison. 'Has found out thy bed of crimson joy——' And then they both stopped.

'Have a drink,' the girl said. She looked up in his eyes and offered her wineglass.

They stood looking at each other. Both had spoken and acted exactly the way they felt, and for that reason they had created between them a rare moment of communion which could, of course, be shattered any instant.

Adam took the glass from her hand. Why, she is beautiful, he saw then: small, delicately detailed features, crowned by a glory of dark hair. . . . She had a rosebud of a mouth, which at this moment he wanted to crush more than he wanted anything in the world. He stepped closer and looked down at her.

'Who are you?' she asked, not moving away in the least.

Adam bubbled with interior laughter. He said: 'Madam, I'm Adam.'

She laughed and clapped her small hands in delight. 'Forward and backward,' she said, 'but mostly forward. Bunny has told me all about you. Come along.'

She took his arm and started down a path leading away from the *palazzo*. There was a bench among the rose briars; at one end a silver tray held a newly-opened bottle of *spumante*. They sat down.

'It was getting tiresome inside,' the girl said, nodding toward the *palazzo*. 'Bunny and Tante are on the subject of British landscape painters. Philip is gloomier than ever. And some officer whose name I didn't catch has passed out on the terrace—'

'You're the niece,' Adam said. 'You're Antonia, Toni for short. Bunny says you are a sad demented little beauty.'

She said nothing.

'*Why* are you sad and demented?' Adam persisted, hoping to force her gaze up, and because he wanted to know.

'Of .course,' he went on, when she remained silent, 'Bunny is only interested in things that *are* sad and demented. And by some awful coincidence everything around him becomes in fact—just that. . . .'

'Oh,' she said, 'be quiet. Drink your wine and talk to me about roses.'

For that moment Adam wished he was completely sober; that way, he knew, he would love her all the more. . . .

He drained his glass. The *spumante* felt like rising bubbles inside him. He was wildly anxious to please this girl and he tried to think of some of the things men have devised to say about roses, but nothing came to his mind. Instead he filled with a gentle melancholy: a slow ecstasy of mood keener than any pleasure. Then he did remember one line, a throbbing line, and he spoke it aloud—'I said to the rose: the brief night goes in babble and revel and wine. . . .'

He leaned over and kissed her. She stayed quiescent in his

138

arms; for a moment she stirred as though wishing to respond and then deciding not to. She did not pull away; she allowed her rosebud mouth to be possessed—but there was a kind of aching hurt in their kiss. As he held her Adam thought of another line, which he did not speak this time for fear of losing her lips—'When both our mouths went wandering in one way, and aching sorely, met among the leaves. . . .'

She pulled away from him and stood up. Oddly, he sensed that she was close to tears. 'Let's go inside,' she said.

'No, Toni—' Merely saying her name was pleasure. 'Please stay.'

She sat down. They sat together in the dusk and looked at one another. They both knew that Bunny Bazin had planned for them to meet: in this, or some other way; but long ago that fact had lost its importance. The only importance was their two selves, and what might come of their meeting.

Then they talked: they told about each other. Toni's voice became gay and lilting, as though to outstrip and keep at bay talk of more urgent things. She was staying with her aunt, she said, for a few days before they went to their villa at Positano. Normally she lived in Rome. Her mother was American—from Philadelphia. Yes, she spoke several other languages too. . . .

She told him all this, and more; but it was not what Adam wanted to hear. Why is she sad and demented? he wanted to know: because that surely is the thing that binds us together. . . . As he listened Adam felt immensely gentle and protective. He only waited for her words to stop and then he was going to kiss her again.

From the direction of the *palazzo* there was an explosion and a flash of flame. Adam leaped to his feet; for an instant he had almost dropped to the ground in instinctive reaction.

But Toni stood laughing up at him. 'It's only Bunny,' she explained. 'He's arranged some fireworks for Tante's birthday. Come on!'

She seized his hand and led him darting along the path through the tangled gardens.

Breathless, they rounded a corner and saw a group of people outlined on the terrace. Above them was strung a line of army hurricane lamps, gaily wrapped in coloured paper to lend the illusion of Chinese lanterns. The garden below the terrace was dotted with pieces of eroded statuary; in peace time probably there would have been peacocks to strut among them.

At the moment the whole scene was suffused in clouds of infernal red smoke. Coloured smoke pots, Adam thought with amazement: the kind used to signal aircraft. The explosions were caused by bakelite grenades which Bunny Bazin was still tossing from the terrace. Then a Very flare went looping into the sky.

Oh, Bunny, Adam thought with a wild surge of affection—who else could ever have arranged a fireworks display like this. . . .

Toni still clung to his arm while Adam put his head back and cupped his hands. 'Major Bazin,' he shouted. 'What's your axis of advance?'

Up on the terrace there were wild moments of tumult. Bazin flung both arms round Adam and pounded his back; he seemed to be singing. Then Adam shook hands with Philip Doorn. In the light of the hurricane lamps the two former friends looked at one another: it was a curious, suspended look; then their glance suddenly erased all that had happened since Sicily. There were several other officers Adam did not know; then he was presented to the Countess.

Once she had been an undoubted beauty. Her neck and arms were bare, revealing a swan-like expanse of white flesh; her dark hair was arranged in two graceful buns. There was a dramatic, somewhat wild and disarranged look about her. She welcomed Adam warmly.

'Antonia, dear,' the Countess said. 'Allow me to present Major Adam.'

Bazin was watching with an air of proprietary delight. 'Dear lady,' he said, and thoughtfully he stroked one of her bare arms.

'I am acquainted with your niece,' Adam said, bowing. 'In fact, we are going to be married.'

Toni laughed easily. 'John is somewhat drunk.'

Adam thrilled to the sound of his name on Toni's lips. Bazin, who had been listening eagerly, suddenly frowned and looked serious.

'The whole world is drunk,' Bazin declared earnestly. 'Drunk, that is, in non-alcoholic terms; and therefore the only way to meet the world sober is to get drunk in alcoholic terms.'

But he stopped, in some small confusion, perhaps, at finding his remark less profound in expression than it had seemed in concept. He busied himself loading another cartridge into the Very pistol in his hand.

Lieutenant Benny de Rougemont, still in jangling spurs, bustled about with a tray of filled wineglasses. The drawing-room off the terrace flickered in candlelight; shadows moved on the paintings and panelled walls. Someone—a butler or major-domo, in crimson livery and a flowing mane of white hair—sat at the piano playing a lively mazurka.

'Your shot, dear lady,' said Bazin, handing the pistol to the Countess with a flourish.

'Nobody's hit Neptune yet! ' one of the officers called in a vexed tone; and Adam realized they were shooting Very flares at the statues in the garden.

Casually Bazin rolled another bakelite grenade off the balustrade. The explosion boomed at the same instant the Countess pressed the trigger. The pistol leaped in her hand.

'Missed,' Bazin said sadly.

Stone Neptune held up his trident and seemed to jeer at the group on the terrace. The Countess's shot went ricocheting through the umbrella pines like an Army Corps of enraged fire-flies.

But the Countess was not in the least daunted. She returned the pistol to Bazin's hand. 'Dear friend,' she said, 'I love your fireworks.' For a moment Adam thought she was going to add: 'And I love you, too.' She was undoubtedly quite giddy with wine. In the darkness Adam put his arm round Toni's shoulder; unresisted his hand cupped her small breast.

Beside Bazin at the balustrade Padre Doorn seemed to be declining the honour of the next shot. For an instant his head was caught in the green light of a hurricane lamp, and Adam was shocked to see how wasted his features were. Perhaps Bunny observed the same thing because at once he set down the Very pistol and lifted his wineglass. 'A toast to the Rifles,' he called gaily, 'and especially to the three of us reunited here tonight!'

The toast was taken solemnly. Adam had to release Toni to put his own glass to his lips, and she clinked her glass to his. She stood close beside him. Whenever his hand touched her bare flesh now each one trembled involuntarily.

One of the officers at the balustrade started to throw grenades into the garden in quick succession. 'Here's a three-gun salute for you, Bunny!' he cried; and everyone clapped his hands.

More guests seemed to be arriving. The Countess moved toward the drawing-room to greet them. Now the piano was tinkling out a waltz.

Adam again had his hand on Toni's shoulder; for a moment he felt her shiver deliciously. Bazin sat pensively on the balustrade. 'In life, of course,' said Bazin, 'it is always a problem of what to do after the fireworks. . . .'

He started to follow after the Countess, but he halted and turned. He took his wind-up, a round-house swing, and then he hurled the Very pistol into the darkness. 'I don't suppose,' Major Bazin observed thoughtfully, 'that it will really hurt Neptune much more than my shooting did.'

He glanced quickly toward Adam to see if the remark had been caught; it had been, of course, and for several seconds the two men smiled comfortably in the darkness. Then Bazin turned and followed the Countess into the drawing-room. Adam and Toni walked together along the terrace. After a few moments their figures merged with the velvet softness of the night.

4

SUNLIGHT prickled on Adam's eyelids and brought him awake. The day was only begun but already a light film of sweat covered his body. He lay motionless in his safari bed while his mind ventured forth to position himself in relation to this new day of living.

First, he had a hang-over: the pulsing throb in his temples made that fact explicit. But—this was a good hang-over, without regret: filled instead with warm, golden images.

Second—and this was at once of supreme, overriding importance—he was going to see Toni again, later today. Adam opened his eyes and stretched luxuriously. He was ready to greet the new day.

He looked through the opened windows. Above the battlements the sky was pure blue; a breeze eddied in to ripple over his naked body. There was a sound of voices shouting orders in a distant part of the castle. And closer at hand there were other voices, engaged in low, whispered conference.

Adam shifted his glance. Sitting on a bed at the far end of the room were Jonesy and the Padre, deep in urgent conversation. Their voices were an indistinguishable murmur; he could not pick out the words. But after a moment Jonesy passed an object into the Padre's hand and stood up, a radiance of joy and relief flooding his face. Jonesy marched from the room with a quick, bounding step.

'Morning, Padre.' Adam swung his legs over the side of the bed and grinned at the other.

The Padre wore clean khaki-drill. In the morning light his face appeared younger, less gaunt and haggard. He smiled back at Adam; each man was genuinely glad to see the other.

'Bunny's gone to Volpone for the day,' the Padre said. 'Some sort of conference with the big brass.'

'Oh. You don't happen to have a bottle of beer, do you?'

'No,' Padre Doorn replied, smiling. 'Anyway, last night you said you were going to try Bazin's swimming-pool this morning. Remember? It's the mountain flume outside the castle gates. The colder the better, you said. Jonesy is waiting to show you the way.'

Adam grimaced, then he laughed. 'All right,' he said. 'I don't suppose it can kill me.'

He stood up. 'By the way, what were you and Jonesy in such weighty deliberation about?'

The Padre no longer smiled. He paced up and down the stone floor, hands clasped behind his back. 'Oh,' he said, 'we talked about a lot of things.'

'But he gave you something.'

'Yes.'

The Padre stood at the doorway, staring out over the battlements.

Adam walked to the table in the centre of the room, sat down in a wicker chair, and lighted a cigarette. 'Come on, Philip,' he said to the Padre's back. 'Come clean.'

The Padre swung himself round. 'All right,' he said, in a tone that was unexpectedly fierce. 'If you must know—he gave me back the piece of the True Cross which he picked up on the Hitler Line. He was saving it for me, very anxiously, very carefully. . . . And there it is!'

He tossed a small object toward Adam, a jagged splinter of

wood, which dropped on the table top, rocking slightly before it came to rest.

Adam stared at the object, disbelieving. 'Padre,' he said, aghast. 'The True Cross. . . .'

The Padre's tone was short. 'You knew about it, didn't you?'

'Yes,' said Adam, after a moment. 'I knew.'

He stared, fascinated, at the piece of wood. With the utmost respect he picked it up between his fingers. Suddenly he leaned over; he brought the object up to his eyes to examine it more closely.

'Philip,' he burst out, 'This is no ancient relic. It's an ordinary piece of very modern wood. In fact, it looks to me like a piece of broken rifle stock!'

The Padre stared out over the battlements. He choked a little as he spoke.

'Of course,' he said. 'That's all it is. Just a stray piece of wood that Jonesy picked up—nothing else.'

Adam leaned back in his chair. 'Philip,' he said softly. 'Then where is the real piece—the real piece of the True Cross?'

The Padre spoke over his shoulder. 'Ground into dust on the Hitler Line—I suppose.'

Adam sat back and looked thoughtful for several seconds. Suddenly he started to chuckle, then the chuckle became laughter. He sat back in his wicker chair and he howled with laughter. Tears streamed down his cheeks.

The Padre turned about and watched him. Mixed pain and anger worked on his face.

Adam saw this; he forced himself to stop laughing. 'Sorry,' he got out, while he dabbed at his eyes. 'But it is so damn funny. Don't you think it is—at all?'

'*Funny?*' the Padre said, in a low, cornered voice. 'No, I'll never see anything funny about it—at all.'

Adam's chair clattered back, he came to his feet. 'Oh, Philip,' he said, with a breathless compassion in his voice. 'I didn't mean it that way. . . . After all, Bazin and I are caught up in this thing, too. . . . And that part's over with now, done with—'

But now Padre Doorn had produced a smile on his face. 'Never mind, Johnny,' he said. 'Never mind. Go and have your swim. I'll look for a bottle of beer while you're gone.'

For another moment the two men looked at one another. Then Adam turned and busied himself searching for a towel.

The water racing down the mountain flume was paralysingly cold; and for an instant Adam felt that his heart had stopped. But when he came out, shaking the rainbow splash from his body, he was fresh and invigorated. He drank in huge draughts of the new, golden day. The thought that he was going to see Toni again tonight remained with him like another cold shock of exhilaration.

He and the Padre had breakfast in Bazin's room. While they ate Adam plied the Padre with questions, anxious to uncover the least detail about the Countess, her *palazzo*, her way of life, and, of course, her niece. . . . The Padre answered quite willingly. Toni, he said, knowing where the real interest lay, was a fine girl. She looked after her aunt; she was able, kind. . . .

Adam nodded. 'Tell me,' he asked. 'Why does Bunny hay she is sad and demented?'

Padre Doorn shrugged. 'That's Bunny's way of putting it. After all, her husband was a lieutenant in the Italian Submarine Service, and has been missing, presumed dead, for several years. Her two-year-old son died suddenly a few months ago—killed almost overnight by some disease. She is lonely, lost, uprooted. That's what Bunny means, and that's probably enough. . . .'

Adam let his coffee go cold. These were things she had not yet told him herself. Yes, he thought, that would certainly be enough. . . . The son, of course, would be the worst part. He remained silent during the rest of breakfast.

5

LATER that afternoon they drank gin on Bazin's private battlement while awaiting his return. Adam sat at ease in a chair, but his glance kept constant touch with the watch on his wrist. He was calculating to a nicety the amount of time remaining before he could start the ten-minute drive by jeep to the Countess's *palazzo*.

There was a clatter inside the apartment, a door banged, and a moment later Bazin came striding on to the battlement. His face was a long, forbidding scowl. He tossed his cap and belt on a chair and went straight to the gin bottle.

'First a drink,' he said. 'Then I've got news.'

The other two watched while he tossed off a neat drink.

'What's the news, Bunny?' the Padre asked. 'Somebody get annoyed about the fireworks last night?'

Bazin opened and closed his mouth. His glance went to Adam. He looked at him seriously, consideringly. 'Well,' he said, 'before my big news I've a minor piece of intelligence to impart. Johnny, do you remember I wrote you that a certain obscene proposal had been put to me?'

Adam nodded. He sat forward with interest.

'Well, it was repeated today—by the Major-General, Administration, himself. By the way, don't blame Kildare about this—his reaction was much the same as mine——'

'Oh, get on with it,' Adam commanded.

'Well, it seems the Major-General wants to promote me to Lieutenant-Colonel—'

'Good!' cried Adam and the Padre in one voice.

'To take command of the Base Detention Camp,' Bazin added sombrely.

'Good God!' Adam said.

All three men sat in silence.

'You see,' Bazin went on then, in a voice devoid of expression, 'being Permanent Force, about to have a D.S.O., and with my penal colony experience here, I would be the ideal choice. Then there's my career to be considered. The General said, and I quote: "Bazin—when the war's over you'll revert to lieutenant, or captain at best. But if you get this Detention Camp experience—man, you won't even have to stay in the Army! You'd be a natural for prison work—start probably as Warden somewhere, then with luck, and if you keep your nose clean, you might some day end up as Commissioner of Penitentiaries!" '

Bazin stopped. He ignored the stricken looks of his companions. Very precisely he poured himself another drink. 'I had thought,' he observed, 'that my appointment here was the supreme indignity. But now—I'm to be Commissioner of Penitentiaries. *Jesus!*'

'What did you say?' Adam asked quickly.

A smile began to form at the corners of Bazin's mouth; his long jaw relaxed. 'I was discourteous,' he said.

Adam and the Padre both groaned aloud. What Bazin deemed discourtesy a Major-General would undoubtedly consider court-martial action.

'It was nothing really rude,' Bazin added. 'I merely said to him: "General, you can take your goddamned Penitentiaries, and you can—" '

'What did *he* say?' Adam demanded, in an agony of impatience.

Bazin frowned. 'Well, at that point, unfortunately, Kildare stepped in and somewhat blunted the force of my advice. Anyway, the upshot is—' Bazin's face cleared and he grinned engagingly, 'I'm to be relieved of my command here as soon as a replacement can be found.'

Adam and the Padre exchanged a glance of quick relief.

'Yes,' Bazin went on. Now he looked directly in Adam's face. 'The action became necessary, really, because—and this is my big news—they've started to move up north.'

Adam placed his glass down on the table beside him.

'The whole Division's on its way north,' Bazin said. 'Once in the staging areas units will be on eight hours' notice for battle.'

Both Bazin and Padre Doorn were watching Adam closely. Knowing him so well, they wondered if he would order his jeep at once and start back to find his Company while it was still moving north in convoy.

'Here we go again,' Bazin added inconsequentially.

His two friends watched Adam and wondered what he would do.

Adam frowned and regarded his watch again. 'Well,' he said, 'I've still got three days of leave left. And I'm due up at the *palazzo* in exactly twenty-six minutes.'

Bazin and the Padre looked at each other, startled. Then Bazin put his head back and laughed. The Padre joined in. Their voices rang with mixed pleasure and relief.

'Good boy!' cried Bazin. 'It's time for another drink.'

The three of them stood up. They stood close together while Bazin poured the drinks. This was a moment they would always remember. In the wine-light they stood on Bazin's private battlement and touched their glasses together.

6

IT WAS a week later.

Two miles inland from the Adriatic the day was grey and sullen. Low, overhanging clouds threatened to spill their rain loads at any moment.

'B' Company was advancing: trying to force the enemy from a tactically important ridge. The task would become progressively more difficult: the ridge lay at right-angles to the axis of advance; at the far end there would be violent resistance.

Adam trudged along, his mind as slow and reluctant as his boots in the clinging mud. This reverse slope of the ridge was matted with vineyards, thick with tangled cover. They moved on a dirt track: one platoon up, with a troop of tanks in support. Behind Adam the leading tank churned through a revolving sea of mud.

Sergeant-Major Mitchell's face was an ugly scowl. Twice already today he had given orders that his Company Commander should have issued. No one else, not even the platoon commanders, knew it yet, but Adam was only along for the walk today. He did not even pretend interest in what was happening. It was Mitchell who really controlled the Company's advance.

Adam's body plodded on, but his mind had voyaged away elsewhere so that this present business of moving along a ridge had no reality for him. That other existence was the real one.

From ahead, near the forward platoon, came the lashing of machine-guns: Brens and Spandaus firing together; grenades boomed; there were single rifle shots, the shouting of voices.

Adam stopped and cocked his head, as though surprised.

Beside him Mitchell was shouting in his ear. 'Tank up, blast 'em out with H.E. Then push ahead as fast as possible!'

For a moment Adam stared blankly in Mitchell's angry face. Beyond him the tank commander, a young lieutenant impressed with Adam's ribbons and reputation, leaned his head from the hatch, awaiting orders.

'All right.' Adam made a gesture with his hand and the tank went churning ahead. Mitchell seized his elbow; they followed behind at a lumbering trot.

From the ground Adam watched the tank fire H.E. shells into a hedge of vineyard trellises one hundred yards away. Then its

Besa expertly raked the whole length of hedge. For a moment pieces of German uniform seemed to float up and hang suspended in the air.

A detached, professional part of Adam's mind told him: 'This thing's a cinch. Unless they have tanks of their own, or anti-tank guns, and until we hit mines, we can go on doing this all day long. . . .'

But it took Sergeant-Major Mitchell, cursing in his ear, to get the advance under way again. Adam resumed his plodding pace without a glance for the dead bodies sprawled behind the hedge.

His mind had journeyed away, of course, to Toni. He was reliving the three days they had spent together; thinking of how their two selves had come groping together, of what they found in each other, and how much more there remained to discover.

And with thought of Toni, oddly, there had come vision of that other girl, the one he had known in Bari, called Elena. When he went back to find her after the Hitler Line she had gone away— but none of that mattered now. What did matter was that she was the girl to whom he said, *'Ti amo.'* In a disbelieving, halting voice he had said, *'Io ti amo,'* because she needed to hear it, and when it was said he had achieved something, too; for the first time he caught glimpse of another possibility of living. A possibility which seemed the reverse—indeed, a conflicting, opposing force—to this daily necessity of killing and being killed.

A mist of rain touched lightly, freshly, on Adam's face. Oh, he thought suddenly: Toni—my Toni. . . . He felt drunk, he almost staggered with the force of tenderness which overwhelmed him. He walked on, feeling bruised and physically weak.

This new force had removed meaning and necessity from his other life. Today he was not aware of himself as the commander of 'B' Company, but only as one soldier of many, plodding along this ridge because his circumstances had brought him here.

There were noises up ahead again, louder and more intense this time. The tank went clanging past; again Mitchell took his arm and they doubled along behind. When the tank stopped Adam dropped to one knee and lifted his binoculars.

Two hundred yards ahead was a large stone farm-house, seen from here in profile. Beneath the angled roof were two small windows, with a larger one below. For an instant, as Adam watched, the side of the house assumed the outlines of a human face: two eyes and a mouth, with the roof for ridiculous cap. For that instant it seemed like a living face—and a face which would have to be smashed because there were Germans firing from each of its features.

The tank commander awaited his signal, and Adam nodded. Before the first H.E. round went off he held his glasses back on the target.

Adam's body stiffened; he stared, appalled. For a full second at the big lower window he had seen a real face, the face and figure of a woman. A woman—and something else?—but then the 75-mm. shell scored a direct hit. When the rubble dust cleared there was nothing to see but smashed, gaping window. The gun went on firing, pumping round after round into the side of the house. The lineaments which Adam had first glimpsed were destroyed, or, if one still looked for a face, twisted in grotesque and wanton lines.

The well-drilled point platoon needed no orders. They were up and doubling forward by sections. The tank hosed a steady spray of Besa fire round the base of the building.

Adam was up and running too, Mitchell pounding beside him. That face—it must have been imagination, simply a moment's aberration. . . . He tried to force himself back to reality.

The fire from inside the house was silenced. The lead platoon kept going; they ran past the house and deployed in fire position facing their front. The following platoons swerved left and right from the track. The Company was so well drilled that it needed only Adam's presence, not necessarily his orders, to effect the right purpose.

Breathless, Adam and Mitchell halted in front of the farm-house. The tank, with swivelling gun, bulked like a bully-sentinel behind them.

They went to their knees and peered over the ground. Here the track dwindled to a foot-path and arched out of sight round a bend. Tanks could no longer follow that route; they would have to switch their axis of advance toward the crest of the ridge.

Adam stood up to speak to the tank commander. The other two tanks now squatted silently behind the first. The lieutenant listened and nodded his head. He spoke into his microphone; the engine roared and the tank started to lumber up the slope of the hill.

Then, from close by the house, there came a wail. It was a human voice, a woman's voice, raised in a cry of agony. Every head turned. The woman appeared and in the first look Adam recognised the face he had glimpsed at the window. She came struggling uphill toward the track they stood on. Her face was cut; her shapeless dress torn and grey with rubble dust; tears scarred her cheeks. Despite all this she was young; at another time she might have been called pretty.

The soldiers stepped off the path to make way for her. She peered about her as though sightless; her mouth hung open, and the unremitting wail continued.

Adam could not bear this. 'Mitch,' he said, turning away, 'see what you can do.'

Mitchell went to take her arm and lead her back to the house. Adam swung his glance back to the advancing tank. In that instant there was a loud, black explosion.

'She's hit!' a soldier cried.

'Just a mine,' Adam answered automatically.

One track was ripped from the tank. The lieutenant jumped from the turret and waved his hand vigorously above his head. The engines of the other two tanks roared; they started forward, line ahead, to try a lower route along the ridge.

' "B" Company!' Adam bellowed, with the full power of his lungs. 'Prepare to advance.'

It was too dangerous to wait here. They stood in the bottom of a saucer; any moment the enemy might appear along the rim. They had to get moving.

Then Mitchell was back beside him. He looked sick and angry.

'They were standing at a window,' Mitchell said. 'One shell killed her husband and her baby at once. There are also a lot of dead Germans inside the house. I think the shock has driven her crazy—she's afraid to be left alone there.'

Mitchell's face was black, working with anger. He was remembering that other time, back before Ortona, when the Italian farmer's son was killed, and the old man threw the word *'Morte!'* into their tortured ears until the sound became unbearable.

Mitchell's lips moved. Christ, his face seemed to be saying: this sort of thing isn't war—it's something a million times worse. . . .

Then, behind him, the woman came stumbling back toward the path again. The file of soldiers was already moving; the men held their weapons at the ready; they moved in silence except for the creak of their equipment. When she reached the path they turned their glance away from the wailing woman, although her hands stretched out to pluck at the sleeves of each one of them. As they passed her each man was sweating; some swore aloud.

Adam moved then, against the stream of his advancing men.

He placed his hands under the woman's arms and he drew her away from the path. He stood looking down in her eyes.

She was aware of him: he saw that much; her terror-crazed eyes pleaded on his face. This was up to him now, this was his job, but he did not know how to begin. In this moment he could not even remember one word of Italian.

Then he did recollect one phrase from the soldier's guide-book they had once been issued: *'Non abbiate paura—noi siamo amici'* —'Don't be afraid—we are friends.' His mouth opened, but his voice only got as far as *'Non abbiate—'* and he stopped. We kill her husband and her baby, he thought, and then I tell her: 'Don't be afraid—we are friends. . . .'

Adam's body trembled. He did not hear the second explosion which announced that another tank had blown its track. Two paces away his soldiers marched by and each man held his gaze averted.

If she follows us, Adam thought desperately, there's every chance she will be killed by the Germans round the bend. . . . How can I make her stay here, what can I say that will penetrate?

Adam was looking over the woman's shoulder, seeing the smashed hulk of her house. For an instant, while he hesitated, his mind created an image of another home: a red-brick house set in a green Canadian suburb. He peopled and populated this house with those he had loved in his former life. There were a mother and a father; a girl—was it Toni she looked like?—and then enemy tanks came and smashed the house, killing all inside except one, and that one came out on a path, plucking at the sleeves of the soldiers who had done this thing, and they marched by and would not look at her.

Adam groaned.

152

In the sky above the ridge a D.F. signal, three yellow Very flares, exploded. Adam did not see them.

He leaned forward and drew her closer. He stared in those stricken eyes. 'Listen to me,' Adam said fiercely. '*Ti amo.*' He said it slowly and distinctly. '*Io ti amo.*'

Something happened in her eyes; there was some response or acknowlegdement. Her body went limp, she stopped crying. She was submissive when he picked her up in his arms. He ran with her toward a gaping black hole in the side of the house. There, in the darkness, she allowed him to place her in a chair. She sat in the chair and she began to whimper, quietly to herself; that noise made it plain at least that she consented to stay. Adam stumbled for a moment in the darkness. At last he turned and ran toward a break of daylight in the wall. And then he was back on the path he had left only moments before.

In those few seconds the scene had changed. The advance was stopped. There was a loud lashing of machine-guns. His men were racing to take up position along the rim of the saucer. Mitchell stood on the path, with cupped hands, bellowing orders.

Adam became as alert, as battle-wary as he had ever been. He surveyed and appreciated the situation in a glance. It was a counter-attack, coming any minute. And any minute they would be mortared.

'Twelve Platoon—' Adam shouted.

Men from this last platoon were just leaving the foot-path to double toward the crest of the ridge. 'Get inside the house and man the windows,' Adam roared. Their lieutenant heard and at once he had his men turned about, racing for the farm-house.

Now Mitchell knelt at Adam's side, tense and eager. 'Mitch—' Adam ordered. 'Go and pull Ten and Eleven Platoons back from the crest. They're to stay ten yards *below*—got it?'

Mitchell nodded. He was grinning slightly as he doubled away.

Adam stayed where he was and considered. Even with their tracks gone the tanks could act as pill-boxes; their guns and machine-guns would sweep the perimeter of the crest and slaughter whatever appeared over it. In fact, they would *let* the enemy come. . . . This was an excellent defensive position—once it was properly established as such.

He found the tank commander and gave him quick orders.

Then the first mortar bombs came pelting down, unheard until the instant of explosion. Adam saw that Ten Platoon was poorly disposed; there was better cover only yards away. He started to run toward them.

Adam did not hear the explosion which hit him. For a giddy instant he felt himself floating in the air; then the force which had picked him up dropped him back on the ground again, hard. It was the end of the battle for Major Adam.

7

THE war went on, but its end could not be long delayed. Such, at least, was the comfortable conclusion of those who were separated from war's blast furnace by a cooling spread of ocean. Such was the conclusion of those who did not have to stoke its daily fires.

In every capital of the Allied World Civil Servants plucked neatly-ribboned files from pigeon-holes. These were the blueprints from which the shape of the brave post-war world would be fashioned. It was only a matter of some necessary details being attended to by the military before these plans could be implemented. And the very first set of blueprints concerned the soldiers themselves. Nations were grateful: they wished to reward their soldiers and speed their return to civilian life. This set of plans bore the file-title of 'Rehabilitation'.

In the city of Ottawa there were conferences, reports, and abstracts—all to be read, discussed, and legislated. And when this task was done the Civil Servants regarded one another with pride and satisfaction. The end is close, they decided: let our boys know at once. In 1944, therefore, couriers were despatched to take the good news to the fighting men.

There was only one trouble: the fighting men were still fighting. In Italy the Canadians had broken through the Gothic Line, but the dream of debouching on to the Lombardy plains, of swift break-through and envelopment, was dissipated by reality. The advance went against the grain of the country; there was an unending series of rivers to cross, each one defended as though it was the Rhine itself. These soldiers knew that at each river the Germans would be waiting—with their tanks and guns and mortars. Even the least perceptive infantryman knew that many among them were still to die. To them there was no end of the war in sight.

These were the soldiers to whom the Rehabilitation couriers of Canada were speeding.

8

VILLAS—painted vivid pink, blue, and orange, in an abandoned slap-dash of colour—crowded gaily together on the Adriatic beach. Here there were thirty miles of firm, shimmering sand. In times of peace the place would have swarmed with family holidayers, but now the summer villas served to billet foreign troops— Canadians who had been withdrawn from the line for ten days of rest. The 2nd Rifles had arrived last night; they were still settling in.

Sergeant-Major Mitchell's once brilliantly polished boots were filmed with dust. He was ploughing through the sand, going from one villa to the next, visiting each platoon in turn. He had some orders to deliver about a Battalion parade.

On the terraces of the villa and on the beach itself the men of the Company had nothing more urgent to do than to sprawl in the sun and let their breakfasts digest. Most had removed their shirts and lay stretched on the sand; some merely sat and watched with pleasure as sunlight touched the white flesh of their bodies.

Mitchell paused at the sea-wall to light a cigarette. He observed two soldiers sitting with their backs to a villa wall, staring blankly at the beckoning fingers of sea on the shore-line. One of them was big, one small; they sat together without interest—like travellers in a railway station forced to share the only space available.

Without even seeing their faces Mitchell knew at once that they were Krasnick and Ewart, Numbers One and Two on the Bren gun, and—this came to him with surprise—probably the only Bren team in the Battalion which had remained intact since Sicily. In fact, he realized, they were the only two originals still with Ten Platoon. There were Jonesy and himself at Company Headquarters; Major Adam in hospital; Krasnick and Ewart; and that was it.

Mitchell studied the oddly assorted pair: Krasnick the farmer, stolid and dumb, but reliable, and a good Bren gunner. Shifty little fox-faced Ewart, always figuring the percentages, working out what was in it for himself. And yet—Krasnick was a good soldier; even Ewart had always done his job. Both men had always done whatever they were called upon to do.

Mitchell kept looking at the two, and then—it was the last thing he would have expected—a feeling very like affection stirred inside him. After all, he had marched alongside these two ever since Sicily; they were linked by many shared experiences.

Mitchell stood up. He trudged across the sand to the terrace where the two men sat and he stood looking down at them.

Both men returned his look incuriously—certainly not with any affection, Mitchell thought wryly. They looked at him with resigned expectancy, as they would at any company sergeant-major, awaiting the inevitable command. Krasnick and Ewart would never believe that Sergeant-Major Mitchell had stopped merely to pass the time of day with them.

'Krasnick,' Mitchell said then. 'How'd you like to be promoted lance-corporal?'

Krasnick's stare remained blank and uncomprehending.

Ewart did not often laugh, but this once he had something which really amused him. Ewart put his head back and hooted. Tears streamed down his cheeks, his thin body shook.

Krasnick's moon-like face only appeared blanker, more puzzled.

Mitchell looked at them, and after a moment he sighed. 'All right,' he said. 'Forget it. But did you guys ever stop to think that you're the only two left from the old Ten Platoon?'

Mitchell turned and walked away, pulling a piece of paper from his tunic pocket.

The sound of Ewart's laughter petered out. From the corner of his eye Mitchell saw the two men turn to stare at one another, in the usual silence, but with curiosity now too, as though after years of familiarity each looked to discover something new about the other.

Mitchell planted his boots on the terrace and cupped his hands. Now he was all Company Sergeant-Major. 'Maitland!' he roared.

Within seconds the Platoon Sergeant's head appeared at the window.

'Twenty minutes to parade by platoons outside your billets,' Mitchell ordered. 'Web belts and caps. We're parading to hear a

lecture on something called—' he looked down to read from the
piece of paper in his hand—' "Rehabilitation". . . .'

His shout was heard the length of the beach. Already men were
standing up, putting on their shirts and brushing sand from
themselves.

9

'FELLOWS...'

The man on the platform plumped the word into the air and held
it there invitingly, like a fruit. Before him, sitting cross-legged on
the sawdust floor of a riding academy, the men of the 2nd Rifles
were arrayed in battalion strength. The man's mouth, showing an
expanse of white teeth and gold inlays, hung open as though to
tether the word in place. A moment before he had come bounc-
ing on to the platform with quick, energetic steps. He wore officer's
uniform, but without rank badges or unit markings. He was bald
and plump; even his face looked bald, as though it was merely an
extension of the glistening dome above. The soldiers stared at this
person who had come to address them. They had never seen his
like before.

'Fellows—'

The fruit was retrieved, then suspended again temptingly in the
air. The man's grin was white and gold glitter.

On a folding chair Major Bazin sat and surveyed this oddity
through half-closed eyes Not that he was really curious; it was
just that he was trying to decide where he had seen this style of
opening before. Of course, Bazin realized then: He is playing
Bob Hope; and he's so sure his patter will panic the audience that
he's prolonging his first moment on stage. The Liaison Officer
from Corps who accompanied him, completely upstaged, cleared
his throat at the rear of the platform.

'Fellows, I've got news for you—big news. But first—' the voice
paused on a gay, uplifted note—'let's see if your Colonel here will
give us all permission to light up a fag?'

It took Bazin some seconds to realize he was the 'Colonel' re-
ferred to. Colonel Bond, the new C.O., was visiting at Division
today; the 2 i/c was occupied with paper work; hence, in fact,
Bazin was the senior officer present. And now this buffoon on the
platform had addressed a request to him, and was waiting.

Well, Bazin decided, why not? Smoking could not make this affair any more ridiculous than it was. Without standing, without even looking, he semaphored one hand above his head, and the men, knowing their Major Bazin, took this to mean 'permission granted'. Cigarette packages appeared; little puffs of flame popped on the academy floor.

The man on the platform puffed at his own cigarette. 'All right,' he said, after a moment. 'All right, men, here's the big news: the folks back home are proud of you—right proud of every one of you.'

With a showman's timing he paused, and peered confidingly round the hall. 'Believe me, fellows, the folks are really sincere. But as we used to say in the war that *I* was in—"Thanks don't buy no whisky!" " '

He paused again, awaiting the inevitable ripple of laughter. In fact, there was a mumbling, communal noise of sorts. Each man muttered and stared at his neighbour. What the hell was this guinea talking about?

Now the voice dropped to a deeper, solemn register. 'We know you boys are going to finish things off in Italy p.d.q.—and then you'll be coming home. When you do, you'll find that your country has established the most generous, most comprehensive Rehabilitation programme in the world. Every aspect of your return to civilian life is accounted for. You're guaranteed your old job back, if you want it. If you want to go to university—the Government will pay the cost. Some of you may want to learn a trade—fine, the Government will pay. Or you may want to buy a farm, or a small business. . . . There are lots of provisions like this, and in a moment I'll go over them in detail, clause by clause. But first, fellows, let me mention the little matter of gratuities. I mean the amount of cash that you'll receive at discharge—' The man laughed comfortably. 'I'm sure you'll be interested in that.'

Now there was vibrant silence in the riding academy. The men stared at the man on the platform, enraptured. At last they understood what he was talking about. Their pulses quickened, their breath came faster. Their thoughts had raced back to Canada. Some of the men were thinking thoughts they had not dared to think until now.

'For each six months of service,' the man enunciated, 'you will receive a cash grant of one week's pay and allowances, plus 25 cents for each day of overseas service. Now, some of you have been overseas 4½ years—that means you'll get about $400.' He laughed, and rubbed his hands together. 'That's 400 smackeroos in your pockets, men.'

A murmur of sound rolled through the academy; each man said something aloud to his neighbour.

'Look fellows—' The voice at the same time persuaded and confided. 'If you have pencil and paper handy bring them out and let's do some figuring. Let's figure out how much each one of you will have in his pocket on Discharge Day. Then we'll get on with the other Rehabilitation plans.'

He stood waiting. In an instant pencil stubs appeared and were held poised over cigarette packs and scraps of paper. This promised to be the best game the men had ever played: figuring out how much money their grateful country was going to pay them.

'O.K., fellows—that's fine. Now, take this example first: 4 years overseas equals 1460 days, divided by 4, equals $365. To that, add—'

The voice surged on, gay, full-bodied, brimming over with promise and expectation. Pencils worked at a feverish pace. From the floor of the hall came a ceaseless murmur of voices as men jotted down sums and chattered the results aloud. Throughout the hubbub the presiding voice sounded strong and clear.

Bazin was appalled. He shifted his chair and regarded the sea of bent heads as the men worked their laborious arithmetic. Directly before him, squatting in the sawdust, were the men of 'B' Company, the men he had once commanded. He saw big Krasnick and little Ewart bending over their fisted pencil stubs in absorption; Jonesy laughing aloud with contagious excitement. Beyond them were the men of his own Company, every man in gay, holiday mood as he worked out his sums. His glance touched on every face in the hall; and it was the same everywhere. These were Christmas morning faces, looking at the tree. . . . But there was Sergeant-Major Mitchell looking grim: with folded arms he glared at the man on the platform.

Yes, Bazin thought with a choke of anger, and it won't be long before the rest of them see it that way too. . . . It is only cruel and stupid to fill a man's mind with visions of the promised land—if that man is going to die before he gets there, before the journey even begins. And there was no doubt at all that a lot of men in this hall were going to die—at the next river crossing, or the one after that, or the one after that. Only now they would go into these actions thinking of how valuable their lives had become, of how much the future held, and how much they had to lose. . . . Some men would die, trying to be careful.

Again Bazin looked round the mass of rapt faces, and he was swept away by an emotion of enraged tenderness. He felt a fierce, protective ache for all these men.

Bazin stood up and beckoned to one of the company commanders. The two officers stood below the platform and spoke in low tones. Above them the voice of the man on the platform had assumed the singsong lilt of a salesman, or a revivalist making his pitch: it spumed forth a ceaseless torrent of good will.

Bazin clambered up on the platform. The man stopped and stared with surprise. He had only half finished; he had much more to tell the boys. His enamelled mouth opened to protest. Bazin turned his back.

'I want to say,' Bazin announced, facing the audience, 'that we are all grateful to the speaker who has come all the way from Canada to address us. The things he has said will undoubtedly be of interest at some future date. In the meantime, however, I don't need to remind you that there's still a war on, and we are in it. The parade is dismissed. Company Commanders, please carry on.'

What a hell of a thing to do, Bazin thought morosely: like saying there is no Santa Claus; and anyway the damage is already done. . . . The troops had fallen in now; 'A' Company was beginning to march through the doorway.

Bazin turned, prepared for words with the man on the platform. To make it worse he had lost his anger now; he realized this man, after all, had only been carrying out what he considered an important duty. Bazin tried to fit a placating smile on his face.

The troops marched out of the riding academy with a swing in their step. They had been transported to another world; there was a light in their eyes as though they were regarding far-away, long-unconsidered things. From tunic pockets pencil stubs and little bits of paper still protruded.

10

KRASNICK sat alone on the beach and had a vision. It was all the more vivid and real because for him this was an unknown experience. In his life there had been no time for day-dreams; nor was his mind endowed for sorties of the imagination.

Krasnick saw himself one sun-filled morning standing at the corner of Portage and Main. He wore a new blue suit—sober and neat; sturdy black boots; and a grey fedora with a feather in the hat-band. He had just come from the lawyer's office, and inside his pocket was the deed to the quarter sections of land he had purchased. In the same pocket were crinkling bank-notes, drawn from a limitless account with an institution called the Bank of Gratuities. And now he paused a moment in the heart of Winnipeg before returning to his golden, waving acres of wheat. Perhaps on his way home he would stop in at the farm implement store to consult catalogues and prices. . . .

Krasnick wriggled his buttocks more comfortably into the sand. Only yards away the blue Adriatic licked toward his boots. The sun was a blazing presence; its heat forced him to close his eyes. In some dim way, perhaps, he was musing that this was the same sun which crossed the ocean to ripen the stands of grain in Manitoba fields. . . .

But he was not at all drowsy. Senses alert, Krasnick stood on his own rich land, a solid, powerful figure. In one instant he designed and constructed a house, then peopled it with a wife and a family of strong boys. In the evenings neighbours came to seek his advice on how to increase their yield of bushels per acre. With grave, unvarying courtesy Krasnick told them. There was no doubt at all that he was a man of substance—the mainstay of his community, a solid, respected figure.

He was quite unaware of the irony, if such it was, that this vision was the exact reverse of what he had known in his own life. His father had been a sad, harassed failure, beaten by drought and depression, who sent his son to work on neighbouring farms at the age of ten. That same year his mother died in the one-room prairie shack they inhabited. But for the moment Krasnick did not remember any of this.

He rolled on one side and from a pocket Krasnick pulled out the piece of paper on which he had scrawled his laborious sums. He stared at the totals, the results of his Grade Five arithmetic, and he felt breathless with joy, heady with happiness. Krasnick stared at the figures and he experienced a state of ecstasy—this by a man whose greatest felicity until now had been the mere absence of physical discomfort.

Krasnick raised his head with the furtive care of a sniper; his glance went swivelling over the whole perimeter of beach and villas. Slyly then his hand snaked inside his battle-dress, until it met flesh, and at last made contact with the belt fitted snugly at his waist. There his fingers pinched the belt with loving care, ensuring by touch that each compartment held the correct number of 1,000-lire notes. Krasnick had saved almost every lira he had ever been paid; his one extravagance was this money-belt which he had purchased on his last leave. And in due course these lire would be converted into good Canadian dollars to swell the total of his riches. The existence of that money-belt was Krasnick's most closely guarded secret.

He was content with the fit and feel of his belt. He rebuttoned his shirt and pockets, stood up, brushed the sand from his clothing, and started to walk back toward Ten Platoon's villa. On Krasnick's face a small smile formed. This was an expression he would use sparingly; but he judged it the fitting look for a man of substance to display at times.

At the villa as soon as Ewart observed this smile, by a kind of reflex action, a scowl possessed his own face; it stamped an even meaner cast on his ferret-sharp features. He sensed at once that Krasnick was keeping something from him, some secret that made him superior, and that thought was unbearable to Ewart. That smile on Krasnick's big, foolish face infuriated Ewart. His black eyes glittered.

With his quick intelligence, his ability to calculate the odds of any situation, Ewart too had been profoundly impressed by the talk about gratuities; to the last penny he had calculated the amount that would be coming to him. And this gave him the clue to Krasnick's smile.

He knew Krasnick so well that he understood and was able to see Krasnick's vision. After the war it was quite likely that Krasnick *would* become a successful farmer, a solid, respected figure. Ewart knew his man, and he had to concede this very real possibility. In contrast he knew that he himself, no matter how much money he acquired, would always be the sort of man that policemen looked at closely on the streets. He would never command respect in the way that Krasnick might.

To Ewart the thought was unendurable. Always, Krasnick could have crushed him physically; and now he felt himself losing the ascendancy of his superior mental powers. He could not bear the thought that Krasnick might be considered the better man of the two.

From that moment Ewart took to following Krasnick wherever he went; he watched his least motion with hawk-like vigilance. Behind that smile, Ewart had decided, there must be some real, physical secret, something that Krasnick concealed on his person, and he determined to discover what it was at any cost.

Craftily Ewart even arranged his trips to the latrine to coincide with Krasnick's. At night they slept on the same stone floor but Krasnick never fully undressed, and Ewart could only guess at what might be concealed under the blankets. The big man even gave up taking his daily swim with the rest of the platoon; and hence there was never opportunity to search his clothes. It became quite clear that Krasnick *did* have a secret concealed on his body, and it remained intact. To make things worse, Krasnick pretended to be unaware, contemptuously unaware, of Ewart's ceaseless watch. But both men knew, and as long as the secret stayed hidden Krasnick remained the superior of the two. Ewart began to hate him.

Thus the calm blue Adriatic days slipped by. In the northern sky each day guns rumbled with a beckoning sound, reminding the soldiers that soon they would be called back to their accustomed places.

On the ninth day Ewart was sent on a work party to Battalion Headquarters while Krasnick, off duty, remained behind. When Ewart marched away with the others he kept one eye cocked over his shoulder. By means of a 100-lire note he had arranged to be replaced in the party en route; he planned to return and mount special guard on Krasnick's movements. Today might well be the last opportunity of uncovering the secret before they returned to the front.

After half an hour of watching Ewart was rewarded. Krasnick

came lumbering out of the villa, looked carefully about him, and then strode quickly along the beach. He was heading for a small beach-house, painted in bright diagonal stripes of green.

Ewart sucked in his breath. Krasnick was seeking solitude, all right. That particular beach-house had concrete walls, four feet thick. It was a disguised pill-box, a dummy, once planted by the Germans among the innocent summer homes. In place of windows it had weapon apertures.

Ewart had never used more skilful field craft in advancing to a position. In the harsh sunlight he held his breath and peered through the concrete slot. After a moment, once his eyes were accustomed to the gloom inside, he made out Krasnick's bulky figure wriggling into a state of undress. Then he saw Krasnick holding a belt in his hands; he was opening up little pockets in the belt and withdrawing squares of folded money. *This* was Krasnick's secret then—a loaded money-belt! The excitement was too much; Ewart could not repress the sob in his throat, and Krasnick heard him. For an instant the big man stood stock still in the gloom, nostrils flaring, body as taut as an animal at bay. Then, with a sudden rush, holding his belt and clothes in both hands, Krasnick went charging toward the entrance of the bunker.

Ewart slammed the heavy steel door in his face. Even so, Krasnick emerged in time to see Ewart's figure racing across the sand toward the nearest cover. And after that each man knew that the other knew.

At once Ewart began to form designs on the money-belt, but so, apparently, did Krasnick. That evening Ewart suffered the final frustration of watching Krasnick march into the Paymaster's office; he knew then that the contents of the money-belt had been deposited for ever beyond his reach.

Neither man had ever spoken an unnecessary word to the other, and now neither one mentioned the affair of the belt. Still, in billets there were lengthy pauses when they looked at each other—warily, with a kind of calculating surmise. And Krasnick had stopped smiling.

Ewart, who noticed everything, observed that Krasnick had now cut down on the number of cigarettes he smoked. Smoking was the one indulgence Krasnick allowed himself; formerly he had always smoked one package a day. But now he limited himself to three cigarettes a day, one after each meal. And to Ewart this was further evidence of the miser's new hoarding. He knew that Krasnick's pack bulged with cigarettes; the metal box in his battle-dress pocket was always full.

Ewart adopted the habit, several times a day, of asking Krasnick for a cigarette. It was what most men did after all; those well stocked were expected to keep their companions supplied; but it was curious on Ewart's part since it was well known that neither man had ever given or offered the other anything at all. At such requests Krasnick simply acted as though he had not heard. The expression on his moon-like face remained unaltered. He said nothing; and he continued to smoke his own three cigarettes per day.

On the tenth day, when the men of Ten Platoon stood arrayed in full battle-order outside their billets, waiting for the troop transports to arrive, Ewart again sang out his request.

'Hey, Krasnick, old pal,' he called. 'You got a smoke to spare?'

Krasnick stayed motionless, his Bren gun across his shoulders. He looked to his front and said nothing. One or two of the men regarded him curiously. And Ewart snickered aloud.

11

EVERY man in Ten Platoon was running. It was 0700 hours of a bright, dew-fresh morning; they had just crossed the crest of the ridge which was their Start Line. Now they sprinted down the forward slope of a broad sweeping valley.

At another time, in other circumstances, this would have been a pleasing outlook. To the right was the Adriatic, with the blue and white town of Rimini sparkling on the coast; farther still in the distance the misty towers of Ravenna. The valley was dotted with lush gardens and fruit trees; farm-houses and villas formed interrupting splashes of white upon the green. In the bed of the valley was a stream, and this was their objective.

Ewart stayed a step behind Krasnick's lumbering form, his glance fixed on the centre of that thick, red neck. His mind was occupied with one single, absorbing subject: cigarettes. Would Krasnick break down and smoke more than three today? On a tough day like this there might well be chances to pilfer or cajole some from him. . . .

Black explosions blossomed on the slope as they ran; all around was the lash of machine-guns, the flat crack of rifle shots. For this moment no man worried about the source of enemy fire; he simply ran at full speed to make as fleeting a target of himself as possible. Soon they would go to ground, pinpoint the enemy positions, and call their tanks forward to blast them out. The men of 'B' Company had done this often enough before; for all of them it was another day's job of work. Before the first ten yards were covered men were already being hit, and spinning or dropping to the ground.

Ewart kept his glance fixed on the red, bobbing neck two yards in front. All the times they had done this kind of thing, he thought with disgust, and Krasnick had never even been nicked. Why did they bother shooting at him? They could never hit that big, dumb ox. . . .

But in the same instant they *did* hit him. Krasnick's body faltered; his powerful legs drove him ahead a few feet, then he crashed to the ground. The toes of his boots scuffed at the earth, his muscles still working instinctively to drive him forward. Ewart fell to the ground beside him because his place was with the Bren gun of his section.

'Jesus,' said Krasnick, with hurt and surprise in his voice.

That was his last distinguishable word; after that from his throat there came a bubbling sound instead of a voice.

The two men lay behind scrubby bush, cover of a sort. Ewart peered at Krasnick's heaving body, he heard the throaty gurgle which came from his mouth, and he thought: he must have taken a burst of slugs in the belly. And almost at once the thought came to him, with a surge of fierce elation: Why, the big slob's helpless; I can reach into his pockets and take his cigarettes any time that I want to—

But—this was one hell of an exposed spot to be lying in. Ewart lifted his head and surveyed the battle. He heard the bark of Bren guns, the boom of grenades: that meant men had gone to ground and were fighting their way forward. He glanced over his shoulder and saw their three tanks brewing up, only yards beyond the Start Line. Fifteen yards to the front was a house; men were moving and firing from a kind of open-end garden shed. One of them was Corporal Mason, his section commander, and that was where *he* should be. But Krasnick was lying here making noises, and he was lying on top of their Bren gun.

Ewart put his mouth up against Krasnick's ear. 'Hey, listen, stupid—you hear me?'

The gurgle in Krasnick's throat stopped for a moment.

'All right.' Ewart seized Krasnick's wrist between his hands. 'We got only a couple of yards to go. Keep your right arm around my shoulder, hang on to that Bren, and get those legs of yours working. I'll give the word. Now—you got that?'

Krasnick made another noise in his throat which might have signified assent.

'All right, you dumb son of a bitch—let's go!'

Ewart brought the words out in a voice of fury. Then, at once, he was pushing upward; he took most of Krasnick's weight and started to drive forward. For his size Ewart possessed exceptional strength. Krasnick came up with difficulty; his face was strained and working; his mouth hung open and bubbled with saliva; but he got his legs going under him, and as though bound together the two men lurched down the slope, partly impelled by their own momentum. A belated machine-gun did nothing worse than kick some dirt into their faces.

Some men came running from the garden shed. Two of them grabbed Krasnick and took his Bren gun; then they lifted him inside where they laid him down gently on the dirt floor. In the lee of the house another man looked at Ewart with curious respect. 'Say,' he remarked. 'That was nice going, boy.'

Ewart said nothing. He was trembling slightly. He walked into the shed, sat down in a corner, and pulled his tin of cigarettes from his pocket. He had the match lighted before he remembered that he was going to help himself to Krasnick's supply. But, hell, he thought: that can wait. He smoked his cigarette and he stared across the shed at the heaving, tormented body. Krasnick was gasping for air, a bubbling sound of pain passed through his lips. One of the men knelt beside him, doing what he could to ease the agony. Ewart blew smoke from his lungs; his eyes glittered blackly at Krasnick, with a fixed unwavering stare.

There was a lull in the firing.

Sergeant-Major Mitchell poked his head into the shed. 'Stay

put,' he told Corporal Mason. 'We've lost our tanks, and the Major's working out a new plan.'

Mason was a smart young N.C.O. who had been with the Company since Ortona. He stood with his hands on his hips, looking at Mitchell, and doubtless both men were thinking the same thing: this is not the way our Major Adam would have done it. . . . We had them disorganized, on the run; *he* would have got us down to the stream bed without the goddam tanks. Now it will be tougher when we do push; they'll have had time to get themselves organized all over again. . . .

Mitchell's head disappeared, and Mason moved outside to join him. By now most of the other men had drifted away.

Krasnick's fingers were clawing at the earth. His back arched. He made a loud, liquid, suffocating noise.

Ewart got to his feet. A fresh cigarette dangled from one corner of his mouth. He moved over and knelt on the ground at Krasnick's side. He pressed the big head over so that one cheek lay flat against the ground; the throaty, spluttering noise became easier. Then he unbuttoned and rolled up the sleeve on Krasnick's right arm. He was still doing something to the arm when Sergeant-Major Mitchell came into the shed and stood looking down.

Ewart spared him a quick glance. 'Two half grains,' he said, indicating the morphine syrettes which lay beside him. 'That ought to hold him until the R.A.P. guys get up.'

Mitchell made no reply. He looked down at Krasnick, an expression of pain and anger on his face. 'The best damn Bren gunner in the Battalion,' he said, in a low voice.

'Yeah.'

Ewart did not argue this verdict. The cigarette angled from one corner of his mouth to the other.

Mitchell spoke again, in the same quiet tone. 'But it makes no difference about the R.A.P. He's had it.'

Ewart's ferret face seemed to sneer. 'You can't kill a big dumb ox like that,' he said, with flat finality.

Mitchell shrugged; he looked at the watch on his wrist.

'Now, look—' Ewart sounded angry. 'This guy's tough—see?'

Mitchell regarded him levelly. 'Ewart,' he said. 'You're the last man left from the old Ten Platoon. That was a good job you did—bringing him in.' He started to turn away.

168

Ewart reached for his arm. 'It's like I told you,' he insisted. 'The guy's too tough to be killed that easy.' His black eyes burned on Mitchell's face.

Mitchell stood still. 'Sure,' he said. 'And you're tough, and I'm tough too, but nobody's as tough as a burst of slugs in the belly.' He turned again to leave. 'We got maybe twenty minutes here. Here's another couple of syrettes if you need them.'

He handed Ewart a packet and walked out of the garden shed. He left Ewart alone with Krasnick.

Ewart sat down again. He peered closely in Krasnick's face. 'Hey,' he said. 'Hey, Krasnick, you feel all right?'

Krasnick could not speak, but his eyes were vocal enough. His eyes looked at Ewart and they said: No, I feel awful sick. . . .

Ewart guessed that the morphine had not yet taken effect. He moved to the opposite side and shot the other two syrettes into Krasnick's arm. Next he looked at Krasnick's chest and abdomen and he saw why no one had bothered to apply a shell-dressing, or even cut the blood-soaked uniform away. There was no use at all in looking there.

He untied Krasnick's blanket and gas-cape, and slid the small pack under his head with the folded blanket on top. That way Krasnick could rest partly on his side, and the liquid, bubbling breathing became easier. Ewart resumed his place at Krasnick's head.

The two men were silent.

Unthinking, Ewart had his tin out again, a fresh cigarette in his mouth. He paused with the lighted match in his hand. 'Krasnick,' he said. 'You want a smoke?'

No, Krasnick's eyes said: No. . . . And they closed for a second.

'Listen, you big dope,' said Ewart, with a sudden flare of anger. 'You can't go and die on me now—or like Mitchell said, I'll be the only one left from the old Platoon—'

But Krasnick's eyes said nothing. The morphine had now journeyed to his nerve endings and his pain was a tired, ebbing sea. Krasnick was dying, but he was dying now in relative peace. In his mind he had recreated his vision again: he was viewing his house and his golden acres of wheat, but it was all slipping away fast, and he watched it go without sorrow because it was more than he should ever have hoped for anyway. He heard the rushing

169

wail of a prairie wind. A film covered his eyes, then the film covered up the vision too; and he could no longer see.

Ewart saw the look, saw how far away Krasnick had gone.

'Listen, you dumb bastard,' he said urgently. 'You're going to be all right. The R.A.P. guys will plug you up fine.'

With effort Krasnick's eyes came open again.

Ewart's body was trembling; he tasted salt sweat on his lips. In this last moment he knew for sure that Krasnick was dying, and only now was he discovering the full anguish of the event. He and Krasnick had lived together for three years. They had seldom spoken, but then there had seldom been need; they were able to converse without words. Krasnick was the only man in the Army —in the whole damned *world*—who knew him. He was the only man to whom Ewart's own death would have made the least difference, the only one even who would notice he was gone. With Krasnick himself gone there would not be a single person left to give a damn about Ewart. In the few remaining minutes of Krasnick's life Ewart discovered that the man who was dying had been his friend, and perhaps the only friend he would ever have.

There was a shout from outside the shed. 'Hey, Ewart—hurry up, and bring that Bren gun with you.'

Ewart did not move. He cleared his throat because it was sore.

Ewart sweated, but at last he got the word out; it was especially difficult because he had never used Krasnick's given name before. 'Walter,' he said, 'is there anything I can do back home? I could get out to Manitoba easy—see your folks, anything like that. . . .'

Ewart stopped; his throat was too sore to go on.

Krasnick's eyes found his face. No, the eyes said: none of that matters. And in the moment that followed they might have been adding: just like you, there's no one to care a damn anyway. . . .

'Ewart!' It was Corporal Mason's voice, raised in an angry roar.

'Walter—you'll want some cigarettes. I'm going to leave some right by your hand here, and some matches—'

Eagerly now Ewart was tumbling cigarettes from his tin box. He made them into little heaps which he piled around Krasnick's head, anywhere he might be able to reach.

'I gotta go,' Ewart said then.

Krasnick's eyes looked at him and they didn't say yes, they

didn't say no about the cigarettes; they simply waited for him to go, and then they would close.

But still Ewart hung back. At this moment he would have done anything for Krasnick. In fact, of course, he had done the most that a man could do, and although this thought would never occur to him, the most that a man can do is everything. In one hand he held the Bren gun which he and Krasnick had carried between them so many laborious miles. Ewart stayed there, kneeling at Krasnick's side.

Then Mitchell was standing at the entrance of the garden shed. 'Come on,' Mitchell said in a low voice. 'It's time to go.'

Mitchell's glance dropped for a moment and said good-bye to Krasnick. He walked over and he took Ewart's arm. 'Come on,' he said again. 'There's no more time.'

Ewart stooped for a last moment. He moved one of his heaps so that the cigarettes lay within inches of Krasnick's face. Then he stood up. He did not look back again as he followed Mitchell out of the garden shed. Ewart went back to the battle quite unaware that he carried no cigarettes in his pocket.

12

BY THE end of that day the talk of gratuities and Rehabilitation had faded to nothingness in each man's mind. The infantrymen who answered the next roll-call could see no end of the war in sight.

13

FOR Major John Adam, on the other side of Italy, the war itself had faded to nothingness. Wearing swimming trunks he lay stretched on the hot sands of the beach at Positano. Here there was no autumn of forced river crossings; instead it was perpetual summer. A rim of mountains, with hunched, blue shoulders, stood as an isolating barrier between the beach and the world of war on the other side.

In theory Adam was still on strength of the Convalescent Depot fifty miles beyond the mountains. The Medical Officer had told him he was fit to return to duty, but to rest and take his time in doing so. Now he lay on the hot sands, body and mind filled with a vast content. In a moment Toni would come walking down from their villa. In a moment Toni would come to join him.

The sunlight was white, brilliant, all pervasive. Adam had his head cradled on one arm, eyes almost closed, pretending to be asleep. Actually he had chosen this position so that Toni would have to approach in his direct line of sight. Then he saw her: descending a flight of stone steps, walking past the wine-shop with its coloured umbrellas, on to the beach itself, and coming ever closer to the place where he lay. To Adam it was a joy, almost like physical touch, to see Toni walk. Under her beach robe was a glimpse of blue bathing-suit, the same colour as the sky. Then it was another thrill—always new and unexpected—to see the light in her eyes, her radiance, when she caught sight of him and quickened her pace.

'Hi.'

Toni knelt down on the sand. She dropped her towel on his supposedly-sleeping body.

He rolled sideways on one elbow, simply so that their bodies would touch for a casual moment.

'Hi,' he said. He grinned, and busied himself lighting two cigarettes.

'Swim now?' she asked.

'No,' he said. 'Nothing now. Nothing at all now.'

Toni sighed with contentment; she settled down on the sand beside him. Each knew, of course, that soon they would swim, they would stroll along the beach, and probably paddle in one of the little kayaks. Every instant of this and every day was budgeted for and filled to the brim. They would lunch in the wine-shop; then a long, golden afternoon stretched ahead. With growing, breathless excitement they would return to the villa, the aunt's villa which they had quite to themselves. This was siesta time, but for them it would more likely be a wild, tempestuous afternoon of love-making. That evening they might stop at the cabaret on the hillside, where wine and music flowed, where they were known to all as lovers, and violins and tinkling wineglasses would tell them they were fortune's darlings.

Every minute was accounted for because they could not escape the underlying urgency of time. The mountains shut the war out, but it still existed. And often, perhaps because of this unexpressed urgency, they pretended to have nothing at all to do, that time was a trifle—as it might be for any casual, peace-time vacationers.

Adam blew smoke from his cigarette. 'We'll do nothing at all today,' he repeated firmly. 'Except lie here in the sun and get hotter and hotter.'

'Fine,' Toni said lazily. 'And tomorrow—'

Adam sat up straight with excitement. 'Tomorrow! Did you speak to that boatman?'

'Yes—he's going to take us; we'll spend the whole day on Capri.'

Adam let his breath out. He flicked his cigarette toward a diving sea-gull. 'Capri,' he said, 'and with you. . . .'

He jumped to his feet and stretched down his hands. 'Come on —let's have that swim.'

That day, and that night, were like those that had already slipped by, fused into the one continuing, unending experience. Late that night in their huge room which overlooked the sea they lay in bed together. Moonlight was a white flood. From the cabaret a hundred yards down the slope came the faint sound of violins and an accordion. They sat up in bed and watched the little toy-like world outside perched on the hillside. It seemed to exist only to please them, as their private possession.

For the moment they had assuaged their thirst and their ache for each other. On the table was a decanter of cognac. Adam reached over and placed a glass in Toni's hand. She was peering down at the cabaret, with its Chinese lanterns gently asway in the night breeze.

'All we need now,' said Toni, with dreamy recollection, 'is Bunny setting off some fireworks. . . .'

Adam laughed, but after a moment he fell silent. He had tried to shut out thought of Bunny, and all the others. Where were they now—were they in action somewhere? And how were the men of his Company? These questions were disturbing; they nagged at him. Adam set his glass down, got out of bed, and padded on bare feet across the tiled floor. He stood at the window staring out at the night.

'What do you see?' Toni asked, from her soft heap of pillows.

'Moonlight,' said Adam.

But he saw more than that. By turning his head he could pick out the North Star, brightest in a gaudy heaven, and he was remembering how first in a night attack he always looked for the North

Star, and next he estimated the power of the moon—its capacity to shield or reveal, to help or hinder his military purpose.

This is damn foolishness, he told himself angrily; but he continued to stand there, naked in the moonlight. If he wanted to he could stay here for weeks—the Medical Officer had told him so. After that—and he had given much thought to the matter recently —with his record he could easily wangle some kind of base or staff appointment. The point was that he never did have to go back to the battle, to that other existence three hundred miles to the north. He could end it by simply forgetting; and he could spend the rest of the war in some place like Positano, with Toni always beside him. Anyway, he had already reached this decision; and what the hell use was it thinking of Bunny, or the Company, or North Stars and night attacks?

Adam walked back to the bed. He poured cognac into his glass and sat down.

Toni's fingers touched, in a light tracing pattern, along his back. 'Your wounds, my dearest—they do not hurt?'

'Hell, no.'

She was so tender, so solicitous; and Adam was only ashamed of these so-called wounds. Christ, a few pieces of mortar bomb in the rump. . . .

He reached round with his hand. 'Give me your glass,' he said. 'I'll fill it up.'

'First, tell me that you love me,' Toni demanded. Her fingers made a tingling tracery on his back.

Adam spoke at once, what he believed, without thinking. 'Toni,' he said. 'I love you. *Ti amo.*'

Adam drank his cognac and he thought: how many times have we said those words to each other? Always knowing it to be true, and at the same time impossible. The fault lay in the underlying urgency of time that they never talked about. There were moments when each knew this present world they inhabited was unreal and unsubstantial—and yet, perhaps that very realization only gave them a sharper vision of what love could be, and brought them as close together as any two humans groping in their own solitudes could ever come.

Hell, Adam thought then: why get so bloody complex about it: why not enjoy the present moment? He started to turn. He was going to take Toni in his arms and he was going to say *'Ti amo'* again. But he paused. As though against his will he recalled the other two women to whom he had said those words: the girl in Bari called Elena, then the sobbing young peasant woman on the ridge who was afraid to be left alone with her dead. He had said *'Ti amo'* to them both because they needed something and it was all he had to give. And he thought, as he had before, perhaps the attempt to love, when there is need, is a force in its own right—the antithesis of war, and killing, and execution. It is that other possibility of living I have been searching for. It is the justification of my decision to leave the war and stay with Toni.

To hell with it all, Adam decided, and then he did turn. He stopped Toni's tracing hand and he touched her body. *'Ti amo.'* he told her. *'Ti amo, and Ti amo, and Ti amo. . . .'*

They kissed; it was a long lingering kiss, without desire as yet; but that came as they lay in each other's arms, quietly, without stirring, and Toni's body began to tremble.

Again they made love; and at the end Adam's disquiet was gone. He was utterly happy in the present moment.

He stirred his limbs with drowsy pleasure. There was one last expectation he had to confirm in his mind. 'It's Capri tomorrow?' he asked.

'Yes. All day—and just the two of us.'

Adam sighed. 'Then I'll have to get up early, and go to that Officers' Hotel where I'm supposed to be staying. I need some clothes. Also, I suppose it's only fair to check in once a week. . . .' His voice trailed off.

Toni's reply was a contented murmur. An instant later they were gloriously asleep in each other's arms.

14

ADAM climbed the perpendicular streets of Positano. The morning was dew-fresh, the sun already a friendly warmth. No one stirred in the narrow streets; the only sound was the cawing of gulls, the hollow echo of his own footsteps on the cobble-stones. It was half an hour's climb to the Officers' Hotel perched at the top of the hill, but Adam's step was jaunty. He felt like singing.

This was the start of what might be the happiest day of his life. He had left Toni asleep in their huge bed, breathing softly like a child, but coming closer to the joy of her awaking. By now she would be showering, or getting dressed; perhaps packing the wicker-work basket she had purchased specially for their trip to Capri today.

Adam looked about him, regarding the closed door of each sleeping house with affection. There was a rakish, raffish, almost perpetually hung-over air about this town—as though it would always awaken with the muskiness, the slight limb-heaviness of too much wine and too much love. Adam was tempted to shout, to startle the sleeping streets awake. Wake up, wake up, he wanted to call: wake up, and enjoy the day. . . .

He wore bush-shirt and shorts. In deference to his call at the hotel today he had slipped rank badges on his shoulder straps, but usually he followed the fashion of Positano and did not even go that far in formality. The habitués of the wine-shops and the cabaret, natives and Britishers alike, accepted him as one of their own. Once he had even overheard two Italian girls refer to him as 'molto gentile' . . . It was plain there was a place in this idyllic life reserved for Adam, and he meant to claim it. He had reached that firm decision last night. And now he walked the streets of Positano wanting to sing a rollicking good morning carol.

There was no one at the hotel desk so Adam went directly to the room which he had not seen since he checked in from the Convalescent Depot a week before. He rummaged through his kit, packed the few clothes he wanted in a haversack, and walked back to the desk. There was still nobody there, no messages in his slot, and he was on the point of leaving when he heard his name called.

'Major Adam, sir—' It was the lieutenant who acted as hotel manager. 'Major Adam—there's someone to see you.'

Adam stopped. He looked at the lieutenant with surprise. Nobody in the Army, except that Medical Officer, even knew he was here.

'For me?' he said. 'Are you sure?'

'Yes, sir. He says he's your Company Sergeant-Major. Mitchell is his name.'

For an instant the sun was blotted out; there was an expanding tightness in Adam's chest. 'Where is he?'

'He only arrived two hours ago. I think he's still sleeping.'

'All right. Would you wake him at once please? I'd like to see him as soon as possible.'

The lieutenant went bustling away. Adam sat down to wait in the lobby's only armchair.

15

SERGEANT-MAJOR Mitchell did not look like a man who had gone short of sleep. His eyes were clear, cheeks fresh from the razor; boots polished, battle-dress snugly fitting his broad form —in every respect he looked the competent man that he was.

When he paused in the doorway Adam had a moment to observe him before he was seen himself. In his first glimpse of that rugged face he felt a surge of affection. An instant later Mitchell caught sight of him and strode forward.

Adam stood up. There was only recognition on Mitchell's face, no more—and they had not seen each other since the action on the ridge when he was wounded. Mitchell's face meant grave news, serious news—undoubtedly an attempt to recall Adam to that other world; and he had already decided not to return. At this moment Toni would be waiting, the boatman ready to take them off to Capri, and *that* had become his world. Adam steeled himself.

They shook hands, and for the first moment neither man found anything to say. Adam looked at Mitchell's stark battle-dress and became conscious of his own casual beach attire. He decided to play the role of idle holidayer to the limit.

'It's good to see you, Mitch,' he said. 'But the hell of it is that in just a few minutes I'm off on a trip to the Isle of Capri.'

Mitchell could not repress his start of surprise and Adam felt ashamed. Quickly he pulled out his cigarettes. 'Have one,' he said. Then: 'How did you ever find me down here?'

Mitchell held the cigarette between his fingers. 'It took two days,' he said. 'From Hospital to Convalescent Depot to here. And I'm sorry, *sir*—' this stiffly—'to break in on you like this—'

'Hell, Mitch.' Adam dropped the conversational tone at once. 'Don't ever apologize to me. I know it must be important. Let's have it.'

Mitchell drew a deep breath. 'It's Jones,' he said.

Adam almost laughed with the force of his relief. Jonesy was always in some kind of trouble—maybe this was only a trifling affair after all. . . .

'He's in Rome,' Mitchell went on. 'Under arrest—'

'On what charge?' Adam demanded quickly.

'Murder.'

Adam stared disbelievingly in Mitchell's face. 'Mitch,' he said slowly. 'You're not joking?'

Mitchell shook his head grimly. 'Only wish I was. He's being tried right now by General Court Martial. Major Bazin and Padre Doorn are both in Rome—they sent me to tell you. By now the Court may have awarded sentence. Major Bazin said to tell you they were rushing it through.'

Adam's glance went sweeping round the tiny hotel lobby. 'Look,' he said, after a moment. 'We'd better go up to my room.' He turned and led the way to a narrow staircase.

There were two straight-backed chairs in the room; from the window could be seen a spreading vista of villas, beach, and sea. It was a famous, memorable view. They sat down; but neither man glanced toward the window.

'All right,' said Adam. 'Let's have it.'

'Everything—from the beginning?'

Adam glanced at the watch on his wrist; and for an instant his gaze did stray to the window. 'No,' he said. 'Keep it short. Just as much as I need to know.'

Again Mitchell could not keep his surprise from showing. 'All right,' he said then. 'Most of this is hearsay, of course, because I only arrived in Rome after it all happened. Jonesy was on five days' leave. Incidentally, that's the way things are going up north now—in action for two weeks, then we're pulled out for a week's rest, with lots of leave——'

Adam's voice was a groan. 'Mitch,' he said. 'For Christ's sake, get on with it!'

Mitchell flushed, then he resumed speaking in a rapid tone. 'Toward the end of his leave Jonesy met Frazer on the street. Frazer was wearing civilian clothing. They were delighted to see each other, of course, and Frazer took Jonesy along to buy him a drink——'

'Frazer?' Adam interrupted. '*Our* Frazer?'

'Yes. That's another long story, but I'll try to keep it short. After the Hitler Line, apparently, Frazer went A.W.L. from hospital in Caserta, got drunk and piled up a lot of charges. That wouldn't have been too bad by itself, but he skipped again—in a stolen sergeant's uniform, and this time he was tagged as a deserter. Then he must have figured he'd have to sit out the rest of the war in Detention Camp and he went the whole way. He joined up with that gang of deserter-gangsters operating out of Rome and Naples. You know—deserters from every Army, some Italians, even a few Germans they say; they specialize in black markets, dope, murder, anything—the worst kind of scum and cut-throats——'

'I know about them,' said Adam. 'But *Frazer*. . . .'

'Hell,' Mitchell said. 'Back home Frazer would have finished in penitentiary, unless he was lucky. You can't feel sorry for a man like Frazer. He was just what he was.'

'Maybe,' Adam said softly. 'But you've got to respect him too.'

'I did that,' Mitchell said. 'Anyway, he's dead now.'

Adam no longer looked at his watch. He leaned forward in his seat; he opened his mouth to speak.

'I'll tell it,' Mitchell said quickly. 'And I won't take too long. Jonesy and Frazer got drunk of course. Frazer took him back to the gang's hide-out where the binge continued. Jonesy probably thought it was a gay, exciting kind of place—he simply wouldn't understand what it really was, or what was going on there. . . .'

'Of course.'

Now Adam's mind was wholly engrossed with Jonesy and his plight; he was suffering it in every detail.

'By then,' Mitchell's voice went on, 'Jonesy had overstayed his leave two days. Anyway, the U.S. Military Police closed in—and this is the important part—they raided the house where the gang was hiding out. There was a lot of gun play, several of the gang were killed, a few escaped, and two were taken prisoner—Jonesy and a G.I. deserter.'

Adam's face looked as though he would argue. 'All right,' he said. 'But why *murder*?'

'A U.S. Military Policeman was killed,' Mitchell said. 'Frazer, Jones, and a couple of others tried a break-out through the back. Someone had shoved a Colt .45 in Jonesy's hand, he came running out trying to cock the action and two rounds actually went off.

179

Not that he hit anyone—it was one of the others who killed the M.P. As for Frazer, apparently he was getting away himself when he saw Jonesy standing aimlessly in the alley. He ran back to get him and got shot down in the process. Jonesy was the only prisoner taken from the back of the house.'

Mitchell paused then. His voice sounded bitter. 'Well, that's it. That's probably as much as you need to know.'

Adam was standing up. He paced up and down the room, his face a tight frown. 'Yes,' he said. 'Technically, Jones is guilty of murder—even if he didn't fire a shot. But surely it's easy to prove that he simply isn't— responsible. And, in point of fact, he didn't hurt anybody. He didn't even know where he was, or what he was doing——'

'Major Bazin's been all over that,' said Mitchell in a weary tone. He shifted his seat; for the first time he showed signs of his sleepless night. 'Physically, Jones's Pulhems Profile is Number One across the board; his medical record is clear. As for competence—well, he's served as an infantry soldier ever since Sicily. Also, he was A.W.L. at the time, and he'd been living with the gangsters. . . .'

'But we can produce a hundred witnesses to show that he's *not* really competent, not responsible——'

'We have. Anyway, Major Bazin says it's a matter of politics now. They have to make an example of the gangsters, and they have to punish the death of that American M.P. One of the U.S. Provost officers is boasting they'll have their own man shot within the week. Major Bazin says the Court has to find Jonesy guilty.'

'God damn it—they can't! ' Adam lashed the words out.

All at once he stopped pacing and he stood looking down at Mitchell sitting in his chair. He looked at him for several seconds, then he spoke in a low, intense voice. 'What do you expect me to do?'

There was the least shrug of Mitchell's big shoulders. 'Look, sir,' he said, slowly and evenly, 'I don't expect you to do anything—' any 'goddamned' thing his tone might be adding—'Major Bazin, the Padre, and I—we just wanted you to know.'

The two men looked at each other. In that small room a host of unexpressed assumptions swirled between them. These two were as close as any two men could ever be. Their relationship was so close, in fact, that either one without thinking would have given his life to save the other. In return for this each man owed the other a certain immediate response. And at the moment Mitchell felt betrayed because Adam was not responding the way both men knew that he should.

To the Canadian Army, as such, Rifleman Jones was no more than an expendable six-figure number. But at one point in every army, as in any human organization, there must be one person to whom the number emerges as an individual, and who will to greater or lesser extent accept responsibility for him. In the case of Jones it was quite unmistakable that the one person above all others who had to accept this responsibility was Major John Adam, his Company Commander, his former Platoon Commander: the man, in fact, who had ordered all others under his command to 'look after' Jones or answer to himself. Both men in that small hotel room knew all this very well, and they knew why Mitchell had come here and what he expected; but it was nothing they could ever have discussed.

For a long time Adam stood staring out of the window.

'All right,' he said at last. 'All right, Mitch. Look—why don't you go downstairs, find that lieutenant, and scrounge a bottle somewhere? I'll wait for you here.'

His tone told Mitchell not to hurry about it, that he wanted to be alone. When Mitchell closed the door Adam pulled his chair to the window and sat down.

Adam's glance passed over the raffish, perpendicular town of Positano, and settled on the beach beyond, where somewhere a boatman was waiting. In that moment the world of Positano began to slip away from him—in the same way, perhaps, although he could not know about this, that the dying Krasnick had watched his Manitoba farm slip forever from his grasp. But Adam's only feeling was surprise to find that his decision was already reached, and had been reached in fact from the moment Jonesy's plight was made explicit. He had expected to sit here and wrestle through to a decision. Perhaps, he saw now, being what he was, the question was never in doubt. Jonesy, and whatever he entailed, was his job; and while he lived he had to do his job; there was really no choice or free will about it. . . .

Then his mind was suddenly flooded with images of Toni. She would be standing on the steps of their villa, throwing eager glances up the narrow street, looking for his return. She would be wearing her white sun-dress, holding in her hands the wicker-work basket she had bought specially for this occasion—their whole day on Capri. Adam suffered a thrust of pain and helplessness. For himself he no longer cared; that dream of another possibility of existence never really applied to him. It was only Toni who mattered now: Toni, and how to spare her as much pain as he possibly could.

Adam stood up and busied himself with the triviality of taking out clothes from a suit-case. That wicker-work basket, he thought: he could not bear to look at it; or worse still, to look in her eyes. . . . Could he simply go, and leave her a note? What was the way of least hurt and loneliness? Adam stooped over; he began to lace his boots.

Hell, Adam decided, the only way is the true way. I've got to go and tell her what happened, and say that the war must end some day, that I may come back, and if so there will be that other possibility of living to take out and examine and start all over again.

Adam finished lacing his boots. That's all, he thought: that's all I can do; that's the least and the most that I can do.

When Mitchell returned, carrying a bottle in one hand, Adam was fully dressed, uniformed again as a Major of the 2nd Rifles. His battle-dress was bright with flashes, and the ribbons on his chest; he wore web belt, holster and pistol. He held his cap in his hand.

Mitchell was careful not to remark the change in attire. 'Gin,' he said, plunking the bottle on the table. 'It was all I could find.'

'How did you get down here?' Adam asked.

'In Major Bazin's jeep. It's parked outside.'

'How long will it take to Rome? I'll have to stop in Salerno and put a call through to the Convalescent Depot.'

Mitchell considered. 'Allowing two hours there, we'll make it easy before dark. Six or seven o'clock.'

'Well, you sit down and work on that gin, if you like. I have some—business to attend to. I'll take the jeep and be back here in half an hour.'

'O.K., sir.'

Adam squared his cap and walked toward the door. His boots

made a loud clump on the wooden floor. Mitchell pulled his chair closer to the window. He sat down to enjoy the famous outlook over the town of Positano.

16

IN BRIGHT afternoon sunlight the jeep bowled along Highway Number Six, swiftly clicking off the miles to Rome. Mitchell drove. Adam sat with folded arms, looking stern and brooding.

The stop in Salerno had taken two hours, but finally Adam got through to his accommodating Medical Officer. It seemed there was another Rest Camp in Rome itself, and the M.O. would arrange today to have Adam struck off strength and posted to the Camp in Rome.

Even before they got to Salerno Mitchell had filled Adam in on the other particulars of Jones's arrest and trial. One matter he had almost forgotten.

'Major Bazin said this was the most important,' Mitchell explained. 'He thinks the Court can do nothing but find Jonesy guilty, but the person who can alter or quash their sentence before he passes it to C.M.H.Q. in London is the confirming officer.'

'And who is the confirming officer?'

'The Major-General, Administration.'

'I know him,' said Adam gloomily, 'a dull Ordnance General called—'

'No,' Mitchell said. 'No, *sir*. It's a newly promoted, newly appointed Major-General called Ian Kildare!'

Both men took their glance from the road; for a moment they stared at each other. There was shocked incredulity in Adam's face. 'My God,' he said after a moment. 'I wonder if he will remember Jonesy as that "damn fine soldier" who challenged him at the castle back in Sicily?'

As the jeep raced through the Italian countryside both men allowed themselves to laugh together for several seconds. But then the sound petered out, and Adam sat silent and stern again.

In mid-afternoon they came to the devastated town of Cassino. They drove through the cleared rubble piles slowly, without speaking. They passed through what had once been the village of Aquino, the northern hinge of the Hitler Line. They looked about them at the meadows and the pock marks of ground they had once agonized over; and their faces stayed sombre.

On the open highway Mitchell gunned the accelerator and the jeep shot forward. Eighty miles ahead lay Rome. Adam sat sternly at Mitchell's side; once again he looked the competent, purposeful officer. He was filled now with the same firm resolve, the burning sense of purpose he had known the last time they passed this way.

BOOK FOUR / *The Last*

1

THE last time the three of them had met together was on the battlement of Bazin's castle, when they drank Benevento gin in the wine-light, and cracked jokes, and wondered how and where they would meet again. Never, remotely, had they envisaged circumstances such as these: sitting in a Rome hotel room at dusk, arguing with sick urgency what they could do to save Jonesy's life.

Outside it was velvet dusk; they had shuttered the windows, but still some of Rome's carnival spirit seeped through. There were muffled street noises, distant catches of song and music. Outside was night-rustling Rome, wanton, beckoning; but inside they did not hear the siren call; their minds were closed to everything except Jonesy and his plight.

Hands nervously clenching behind his back Bazin paced up and down the floor of the small room. Adam and Padre Doorn sat on opposite sides of a table. The Padre's fingers drummed a tattoo on the table-top. Both of them watched Bazin's pacing figure.

Adam still did not perceive the situation bared to its essence; he had arrived only an hour before; he had not worried at it the way the others had.

'Look,' Adam said, his glance going from one to the other. 'He's been found guilty and sentenced to death, but you say you expected that—that the Court could do nothing else. But you also say that no death sentence has been confirmed before, no Canadian soldier has ever been executed. And Jonesy had all that character evidence to support him—'

He leaned back in his chair and drew in his breath. 'I ask because I want to know. Why should Jonesy be the first to be executed?'

Bazin stopped his pacing. He looked at Adam; and the Padre looked at Adam. The Padre's glance was burning; his black eyes gaunt and impassioned. At least, Adam thought, this thing about Jonesy has brought him alive again: he has not looked like this since that day on the Hitler Line. . . .

Bazin's voice, acid, bitter, broke into the thought. 'First,' Bazin stated, 'he is a scapegoat. The gangsters have been caught: an example must be made—' He paused; when he spoke again he made a face. *'Pour encourager les autres. . . .'*

'John—' In turn, the Padre's voice sounded outraged and tormented. 'It's infamous—but that American policeman was killed—'

'And therefore,' said Bazin, taking up the account, 'he must be revenged. The Americans say they will have their "boy"—a young thug named Zacco—shot within the week. And it would endanger good relations if our "boy" received less than equal punishment.'

For a moment the room was heavy with silence. The two others continued to stare at Adam.

'Look,' Adam said; he placed both hands flat on the table. 'I still can't believe that once they know about Jonesy, once they understand what a helpless innocent he is—'

'All right,' Bazin broke in harshly. 'We paraded an army of witnesses to describe the real Jones; we showed how harmless he was, how someone always had to look after him; that it was absurd to think of him as a gangster—and the Court had to believe some of it, at least. But through all this there was one unanswerable question in their minds: why tell these things only *now*—when Jones is on trial for murder? If he was the way we described him, then he should have been fired from his unit long ago; he could not possibly have served as an infantry soldier. No—' Bazin concluded sombrely, 'the facts only serve to disprove our defence.'

Adam closed his eyes. He heard the persistent hoot of an automobile horn outside. In the silence, while his two friends stared at him, he became aware of the vast, teeming city which surrounded them, And he thought: somewhere out there Jonesy is locked up, under sentence of death.

He opened his eyes. 'Where *is* Jonesy?' Adam demanded.

The Padre answered. 'He's in a British prison, along the Tiber, about two miles north of here. We've both seen him several times.'

'Yes,' said Bazin, with a mirthless laugh. 'It's a Canadian princi-
pality carved out of British and American territory. They've sent
up a staff from the Reinforcement Depot at Avellino—about
thirty men in all: guards, cooks, drivers, and so on. It's a little war
establishment of its own—all this, mind you, at the peak of the
reinforcement crisis. If it was somebody else it would even be
amusing.'

'Jonesy has asked to see you,' the Padre said. 'He seems happy.
The men there have grown fond of him; they're doing everything
to make him comfortable—'

'Except for that son of a bitch Armstrong!' Bazin burst out.
'He's the Assistant Provost Marshal. He goes around saying that
he's going to show the Yanks and Limeys how to stage a really
efficient execution.'

Adam merely filed this fact in his mind. 'Well,' he said then,
'what *can* be done?'

Bazin and Padre Doorn exchanged a glance. Bazin was still
standing at the shuttered window. He moved closer and looked
at Adam.

'We think there's only one chance,' Bazin said slowly. 'That's
the confirming authority, to wit, Major-General Ian Kildare. The
Court's proceedings are now in his hands.'

'But remember,' the Padre added, 'because it is a death sentence
he is only the first confirming authority. From him it goes back
to C.M.H.Q. in London, and then probably to the Cabinet in
Ottawa. But Bunny is right—Kildare's the only man who can stop
it now.'

Bazin spoke again. 'He has the power to withhold confirmation,
or to do various other things—if he wants to, of course.'

'And that is where I come in?' Adam asked.

'Yes,' said both men at once. They looked at him expectantly.

Adam knew what they were thinking. He had been Brigadier
Kildare's favourite Company Commander, object of an affection
dating back to their first encounter at the castle in Sicily. Kildare
considered him his most capable officer: the ideal fighting man
who could always be relied upon to execute his Brigadier's fighting
orders. There was even that time, Adam remembered, back in
Ortona when the Brigadier urged him to bring any problems

directly to him. Even—he recalled this with a start of surprise, and glanced quickly at the Padre—the time when Philip Doorn's own career had been placed in his hands; when he refused to order him fired. . . . Yes, their peculiar Brigadier had taken a peculiar fancy to Adam; he occupied a special place in Kildare's esteem. Adam knew this, and he also knew that he would take advantage of the fact to the limit, for everything it was worth.

'All right,' said Adam in a tone of decision. 'When can I see him?'

Bazin still peered down at him; a smile touched his long jaw. It so happens,' he said, 'that I know his "A and Q" man—a Colonel who was in my class at R.M.C.—and I called him this afternoon. He says that Kildare can't possibly sign anything, or do anything tonight, because he's going to be very occupied with a certain Italian lady. And you have an appointment to see him tomorrow morning. Nick—that's my old classmate—had to cancel a lot of appointments to do it, but now the General's engagement pad reads: first appointment 10:00 hours, on urgent military business, Major John Adam, D.S.O., M.C., the 2nd Rifles.'

The three men looked in one another's eyes and their glances grew brighter. Suddenly each one felt hopeful. If the affair could only be reduced to a conversation between these two old fighting friends, then surely Adam would be able to explain the truth about Jones, make Kildare see that an innocent like Jonesy simply could not be held accountable.

'Let's all have a drink,' said Bazin. He moved from the window and busied himself with a bottle of Scotch and glasses.

They drank; the liquor warmed them; and it began to seem almost like Bazin's battlement in the wine-light again. Each one began to feel that this impossible, unbearable situation was shortly going to be put right.

Adam said: 'I suppose I'd better check into that Convalescent Camp and make myself legal.' He turned to Bazin. 'Bunny, may I still borrow your jeep?'

'Of course. Mitchell is standing by to act as your driver.'

A few moments later Adam emerged from the hotel and stepped into the Roman night. Bright stars glittered overhead. The sky was a velvet canopy; it seemed within touching distance.

2

THE same star-bright sky, the same enveloping night, lay spread like a tent over the city of Rome. It covered the northern outskirts too: where along the banks of the Tiber, set in a pine forest, was the building which housed Rifleman Jones as prisoner.

Once this place had been used by the Fascists as a combined barracks-prison; but now the British had converted it to their own efficient use. At each barbed-wire barrier a red-capped M.P. stood sentry duty.

Everywhere was the constant, pervading scent of pine trees. Between the buildings one walked on a carpet of sweet-smelling needles and cones. To the Canadian soldiers this forest might have seemed reminiscent of home, except that the stand of pines was too deliberate, too consciously cultivated. Each tree had a tailored look; one felt that each one was numbered on a plan somewhere.

The Canadian contingent occupied a small, wooden-frame building which stood by itself, ringed by a semicircle of pines. At its entrance stood a helmeted sentry. Inside was a central guard-room with cells radiating out on three sides. One of these was occupied by Rifleman Jones; the others served as living-quarters for the staff which had been assembled to maintain him here.

Despite the functional sentry outside, the atmosphere inside the guard-room was warm and relaxed. The windows were open to the night breeze; under bare light bulbs men sat in their shirt-sleeves playing cards. Mess-tins and mugs were filled with coffee. In one corner a man sat with an accordion on his knees, head cocked, squeezing out tentative chords, as though he were just learning how to play. Other men sat on the floor reading magazines, or simply smoking and staring at the ceiling.

At a table in the centre of the room a Sergeant with massive, hairy forearms dealt cards in a game of five-card stud. The table was stacked with match-sticks representing five-lire notes. Behind the Sergeant, leaning forward, and watching with an air of rapt interest, was a fair-haired, good-looking young soldier with a flashing grin. This was the prisoner, Rifleman Jones.

Occasionally the Sergeant turned to glance at him indulgently. 'Jonesy,' he declared now, in a voice heavy with disgust. 'If you want to learn this game go sit behind somebody else—I can't draw a goddamned card tonight!'

The other players smiled. Jonesy put his head back and laughed his delight out loud.

As he played the Sergeant kept one eye on his watch. He did not expect Major Armstrong to lurch in until some time after midnight, and in any event he had a warning system set up with the sentry on the main gate. By the time Armstrong made his usual drunken appearance Jonesy would be safely in bed; the other men sleeping or at assigned posts. The only good thing about that bastard Armstrong, the Sergeant reflected sombrely, was that he was seldom here to bother his small command.

Small command? the Sergeant wondered, as he dealt cards. Actually, he was worried by the size of this detachment: it totalled thirty-one, all ranks—many more than were needed to perform this piddling duty. And nearly all of them were infantrymen, drawn from Avellino; men who had been wounded mostly, awaiting posting to their units, but all men from the field, as was the prisoner himself.

The Sergeant had a black foreboding, which he had not yet communicated to the others. There were too many of them set down here in Rome, leading this suspended, aimless existence, at a time when men were desperately needed at the front. The only logical deduction was that in due course a firing-squad would be formed from their number—with himself as Sergeant. And ever since he reached this conclusion his mind had been busy devising ways of avoiding the duty. He had done his share of killing; he was damned if he'd have any part in this boy's execution.

Also, he was struck by the sour incongruity of the thing. Up north men were being killed every day; there life was regarded as precious; every effort was made to preserve each life—but back here this band of soldiers was assembled for the sole purpose of killing one of their number. Like all the others he could not help feeling this was wrong, in some basic, indefinable way. As for the boy himself, well, it was obvious to anyone that he had never quite grown up, but he was likable and certainly harmless. Even that bastard Armstrong must find it difficult to pretend that Jonesy was the dangerous criminal he liked to make out. . . .

The big Sergeant grunted and leaned forward. 'Pair of queens, back to back. Beat 'em!'

His face was a vast beam as he raked in the pile of match-sticks, his first pot of the night. Behind him Jonesy clapped his hands with pleasure.

'More coffee on the stove!' one of the men sang out.

Becoming bolder the soldier with the accordion essayed a whole tune, and it was recognizable. Outside, the night rubbed in velvet softness against the clapboard of their building. Inside, the men were warm and contented.

3

A SOARING flight of steps, flanked by stone lions, led at last through fluted columns; then into a vast, echoing hall, through corridors and archways opulent with marble. Sentries, then a Captain, courteous to inquire his business: a marble bench in a smaller ante-chamber, and at last Colonel Nick Newgate, the 'A and Q' man himself. 'Adam? Yes. Good morning. The General will see you in a minute. Please sit down.'

A Sergeant, owl-like and white with indoor pallor, presided at a desk dividing the room. Opposite Adam, on a matching bench of marble, sat a red-tabbed Colonel, primly erect, briefcase balanced on one knee. He had a carefully composed face. He wore light, hand-fashioned shoes, and fresh-ironed service dress befitting Cockspur Street; he looked as though he had just stepped from the London plane. His eyes scrutinized Adam as he sat down, registered him with distaste, and passed on.

Adam flushed. Just for the hell of it he lolled in the most slouching attitude the marble would permit. He pulled out his cigarettes, lighted one, and blew billowing clouds of smoke. The match he dropped negligently on the floor.

'Major Adam, please.'

It was the Captain, and hovering behind him Nick Newgate. The Colonel on the bench pricked up his ears; his eyes narrowed; his mouth became a protesting slash of anger. But at once Colonel Newgate was trying to smooth things over. 'This officer bears important despatches from the front,' he explained improbably. 'The General is sorry, but—' His voice was still talking in soothing tones as Adam crossed the threshold of the door which the Captain held open.

It might have been *Il Duce*'s innermost receiving-room that he stood in. But Adam was used to marbled splendour by now, and

191

he did not blink. Then, at once, from a desk acres wide, General Kildare's immense form came bearing down on him.

'Adam—you old son of a bitch!'

The General was shaking Adam's hand, and pounding his back. Then he steered him into an upholstered arm-chair beside the huge desk.

General Kildare sat down. He leaned forward, his moon-face abeam, radiating affability. 'Have a cigar,' he said, thrusting his case across the desk.

Adam declined; he studied the man opposite him. Since his wounds on the Hitler Line Kildare had lost weight. His figure was still hulking, but the cheek and jowls were less fleshy; if anything, however, this only increased the impression of virile power.

The General set the conversational tone: it was the affable talk of two old fighting friends. Kildare leaned back and pulled at his cigar as though there could not possibly be anything more important than this on his day's agenda. His attitude said plainly that red-tabbed visitors from London could sit on their asses all day long—while he and Adam talked about the things that really mattered. Adam observed and could not take his glance away from the single bulky file which occupied the General's in-basket.

At last there was a moment's lull of silence. Adam drew in his breath. 'Sir,' he said. 'About Jones—'

'Ah, yes.' The General's glance flicked to the file on his desk. 'Jones. A sad case. He was in your Company, wasn't he?'

From the way he said it Adam saw that General Kildare had known this fact all along.

'You speak as his Company Commander, of course. . . . That's laudable, Adam; but as I say, it's a sad case—especially so for me because I knew the boy. You will remember I met him at your castle in Sicily; and then on the Hitler Line he was the last person I recall seeing. Must say—on both occasions he impressed me as being a damn fine soldier. All the greater pity. . . .' The General shook his head dolefully.

Inwardly Adam groaned. 'Sir,' he said desperately, 'Jones is *not* a "damn fine soldier". He has the mind of a twelve-year-old boy; he has never grown up; he's—'

'Yes,' the General said. 'I know.'

Adam felt his mouth drop open with surprise. He had expected to argue, maybe plead about this vital point.

'I've spoken to Rowntree,' Kildare went on evenly. 'Brigadier Rowntree, President of the Court Martial, and I can tell you in confidence that the Court reached the same conclusion. Probably Jones should never even have been in the Army, but the fact remains that he was, he got himself into this situation, and must accept the consequences. The Court could make no recommendation of mercy: and I must confirm their finding.'

Adam tasted anger in his mouth, but he forced his feelings under control. 'Sir,' he got out. 'You have the power to withhold confirmation.'

Again the General was shaking his head. 'On two grounds only. That the proceedings were illegal, or that substantial injustice was done to the accused. Neither of these apply. I'm sorry, Adam— bloody sorry—but sometimes circumstances simply have to be accepted.'

Adam's anger leaped beyond his control. 'Especially when those circumstances include strong pressure from the U.S. Army!'

Plumes of cigar smoke eddied round General Kildare's massive jowls. He regarded Adam levelly, with no sign of rancour. No one else could have spoken to him this way; perhaps that was one reason why he respected Adam. 'You can't ignore political considerations,' he said mildly.

'And since when have *you* become a politician!'

Even as he said it, Adam knew he had gone too far; no one spoke like that to Ian Kildare.

But the General still revealed no change of expression. He continued to peer in Adam's face. 'That's a good question,' he said. 'I became a politician, I suppose, the day I accepted this present appointment. Adam, maybe you don't quite understand my position: I'm only Ottawa's office boy. The newspapers made me a bit of a hero after the Hitler Line—for the wrong reasons, of course—but anyway, this appointment was to please the folks back home. The field commanders and the C.M.H.Q. boys hate my guts—I'm only in Italy on borrowed time; and soon enough they'll have me back in Canada as General Officer Commanding Cadet Corps, or something worse. As *you* know, all I ever wanted to do was fight a war, but they won't let me. . . . Anyway, as long as I am in Italy I'm going to give them the best goddamned rear administration they ever had. That's what I mean, Adam, when I say that sometimes one must accept one's circumstances.'

It was a long speech for Ian Kildare; and one of the very rare times he had ever felt need to explain himself. Adam's glance dropped; he felt abashed. The two men sat on in silence.

'I'm sorry,' Adam said, after a moment. 'I didn't mean what I said, of course.'

And Adam was discovering that he really did not. In the midst of all his aching, burning concern for Jonesy, he still found time to accord his respect to the man opposite him. The silence lengthened.

'Tell me,' the General ordered abruptly, 'how much does this mean to you? The matter of Jones's life, I mean.'

Adam looked at General Kildare. He did not reply at once. He was searching inside himself to discover just how much it did mean. 'I feel responsible for Jonesy,' he said slowly. 'If I had been looking after him properly this would never have happened. I feel as though I am to blame—' Adam stopped and sat there frowning.

Carefully General Kildare placed his cigar in an ash-tray, never taking his glance from Adam's face. 'All right,' he declared. 'I can't withhold confirmation, but I can, and bloody well *will*, commute the sentence—to penal servitude, or imprisonment, or whatever the Act allows me. Anyway, his life will be saved, and in point of fact he's bound to get a remission at the end of the war.'

Adam's face felt on fire; his body went limp. Superficially, this thing seemed so easy; yet he well appreciated the magnitude of what had just been accomplished. Kildare had made this decision against his personal interest, and against all the canons of his military judgment.

'Mind you—' the General's voice went on. 'This will make the Americans mad, and the C.M.H.Q. buggers may raise a stink. But once my commutation is entered on the proceedings it can't possibly be overruled.' He slapped one hand on the thick file in his basket. 'And we'll get it duly entered this morning.'

He pressed a buzzer. Colonel Newgate entered the room, received instructions, and departed with the file under his arm.

General Kildare turned to regard Adam with a beaming smile. In return Adam's look said much more than any words.

'Now,' said General Kildare, moving briskly to new business. 'What about your own plans. How did you get to Rome? Are you on leave?'

Adam told him about shuttling between the two Convalescent Camps. Now he was beginning to see his future plain and he talked about his plans. 'I'd like to see Jonesy, then once things are settled I'd like to get back to the unit as soon as possible.'

'Yes. Well, from all reports they can use you. The new offensive is due to start in a few days.'

The General's face assumed a musing look. 'I'll have Newgate post you to my own staff for temporary duty; then we can send you to the field whenever you're ready. In the meantime, if you're going to be in Rome, come to dinner with me and meet some of my friends. We might even get drunk together, at least once. . . .'

Adam laughed; at the moment that was just what he felt like doing. The idea of having dinner with General Kildare suddenly seemed the most pleasant prospect in the world.

The two fighting friends chatted a few minutes more. At his request the General granted Adam one last favour: a signed sheet of paper authorizing him to see the prisoner Jones at any time desired. When he walked through the marble corridors, out into the sunshine, and down the sweeping flight of steps, Adam moved with a lightness of step that *Il Duce* in his prime might have envied.

4

BACK at the hotel Bazin looked disbelieving at first. Adam had to launch into a full account of his interview with General Kildare, but Bazin stopped him before he was half through. His long face was transfigured. 'Thank God!' said Bazin. Then, an instant later, with new and even greater excitement: 'That means I can go back now—I'll leave today!'

While Adam and the Padre listened Bazin told how badly affairs were going with the Rifles: not only were the companies under strength; the shortage of officers was critical; and the new push would be starting any day. Colonel Bond had urged him to hurry back. Adam's face grew dark as he heard these details. 'What about "B" Company?' he asked grimly.

'Your successor's name is Green. He seems able enough but he's never been in action before.'

'Look,' Adam stated, 'I'll be back myself in a matter of days. Tell the C.O. I'll expect Green to be sent L.O.B. when I arrive.'

'Yes, *sir*,' said Bazin, grinning. Then he turned. 'How about you, Philip?' he asked casually. 'We're even without a Padre.'

'I'll come with John,' the Padre answered at once. He looked at Adam inquiringly. 'That is—if you can fix it with your friend the General?'

Bazin snorted. 'Kildare will give him the city of Rome, and all Italy too if he wants it. Let's have a drink. Let's have several drinks.'

Later, Sergeant-Major Mitchell came knocking at their hotel-room door, searching for Major Adam. Adam took one look in his face and knew at once what he wanted. 'All right, Mitch,' he said with resignation. 'You can go too. Just look after the Company for me until I arrive. Now come on in and have a drink.'

It was a day of many drinks, of happy, confused comings and goings. There was a liquid luncheon; after which, with much unnecessary laughter, Major Bazin was loaded into his jeep. Mitchell looked competent behind the wheel, but when the jeep pulled away from the kerb Bazin was singing in a lusty voice, with a wild glint in his eyes. It was a day of bright sunshine and celebration.

The news about Jonesy, presumably leaked by someone on Colonel Newgate's staff, raced like wildfire to every Canadian in Rome. Everywhere it was heard with relief and satisfaction. Everyone, with the possible exception of Major Armstrong, the Assistant Provost Marshal, felt the same way. It was simply not right to shoot a kid like Jonesy: he was not really guilty; and, anyway, he was one of their own. At the pine-ringed prison on the outskirts of Rome the small detachment heard the news with an even deeper sense of relief—and for a deeper reason. . . .

The big Sergeant, whose name was Burnside, took the good news to Jonesy at once. But it seemed to make no difference; Jonesy listened with the same polite, good-natured smile, and did not seem affected in the least, one way or the other. The Sergeant walked away shaking his head. He could only conclude that the boy had never believed in the possibility of his own death; the thought that some of his fellows might take him out and shoot him was probably too terrible an abstraction for Jonesy ever to comprehend. Anyway, Sergeant Burnside decided, to hell with all that. . . . He went out looking for a bottle of beer.

Much later still, back at the hotel, Adam and Padre Doorn arranged to drive out and see Jonesy in the morning. Then Adam went to bed, and fell soundly asleep at once.

5

DAPPLING sunlight poked through the pine trees; birds sang on the branches overhead. Adam sat with his eyes closed, enjoying the slow sensation of coming awake to this pleasant day. He was quite content to leave the Padre, seated behind the wheel of their jeep, to parley with the sentries at the barbed-wire gate.

There was delay. The red-capped M.P.s were polite, but firm: the Canadian guard commander would have to be summoned. So they sat in the pine-scented sunshine and waited.

A burly Sergeant appeared at the Padre's side of the jeep. He saluted and stood with a glum, hangdog air. 'Sorry, sir,' the Sergeant told the Padre, 'but Major Armstrong will have to be called.'

Again they waited; two relays of messengers were dispatched about this business. Beside him Adam could feel the Padre shift impatiently in his seat. At last, with no appearance of haste whatsoever, a big, pistol-holstered figure came strolling across the parade square.

'Oh, it's you, Padre,' Major Armstrong observed sourly, when he stopped at last beside the jeep. 'Well, I'm bloody well not allowing any visitors today!'

He laughed; although the noise came from deep inside his body it still sounded coarse and externally rasping.

Adam opened his eyes sufficiently to observe this phenomenon. Major Armstrong was a big, powerful-looking man, grossly over-fleshed. His face was fat, his eyes tiny. It was still early morning but his face was prickled with sweat, his bush-shirt blotted with damp patches.

Now the Provost Major rested his forearm on the jeep's lowered windshield. His small, cupid's mouth made a constant sucking noise, as though he were chewing jujubes.

Padre Doorn regarded him without warmth.

'Say,' Major Armstrong announced, before the Padre could even state his business. 'You hear yet that the Yanks beat us to the punch?'

The Padre frowned and said nothing.

'Yeah,' Armstrong went on, relishing the effect he was about to make. 'They shot their boy Zacco this morning.'

The Padre gaped at him, appalled. Quietly Adam sat up straight in his seat. He was wide awake now.

The big Provost Major sucked at his gums reflectively. 'At that, of course, we won't be far behind. We'll have our boy Jones tied to a chair and duly processed by the end of the week—that is, if Ottawa can only shake the lead out—'

The Padre was trembling, his face white. He lashed out: 'Armstrong—what are you saying? Last night the General—'

'Oh, sure,' said Armstrong, 'that was yesterday. This is today. McGuire, the Provost Marshal, called me this morning to say the sentence had been confirmed, awaiting final word from Ottawa. "Apply maximum security regulations," McGuire said.'

Behind Armstrong the Sergeant stood with a tired, helpless expression on his face.

Those tiny eyes glittered. 'And to me, Padre, "maximum security" means no visitors. Come the execution I'll give you a free pass. But right now I got a lot of details to attend to. So, if you don't mind—get the hell out of here!'

Again Major Armstrong laughed his hollow, sucking laugh.

Quietly Adam put one leg over the side of the jeep. He stepped out and walked round the front until he stood within inches of the Provost Major, so close that Armstrong had to turn, move back a pace and face him. His fat face filled with surprise.

The two men stood in a glare of harsh sunlight. Adam was balanced easily on the balls of his feet, hands light at his side. 'Armstrong,' he said, in the softest of voices. 'We're going through this gate. But before we do I want you to know that you're a piece of garbage—a stinking, offensive piece of garbage.'

Armstrong's mouth opened; he backed away another step.

At once Adam closed the space between them.

'Another thing, Armstrong,' he said, in the same soft tone. 'Open that fat obscene mouth of yours again, and I'll close it for ever. I'll start by rubbing your face in that barbed-wire over there.'

Adam's glance bored steadily at Armstrong's face. Beyond the Provost Major the burly Sergeant showed an expression of intense, incredulous delight. Seconds of silence ticked by while the two men stood locked in the same attitude.

Armstrong was bigger and heavier than Adam. There was power as well as fat in that big body; in addition to rank he was accustomed to use his physical strength to quell anyone who questioned his superiority.

The big man stared at Adam, tiny eyes blinking, lips slack; and a quiver passed through his body. In that moment he knew that the man facing him meant exactly what he said. He would not be deterred by consequences. He would be prepared to have his own body hurt to whatever extent was necessary to effect his purpose; he would go on smashing until he cut his opponent down, and he really would use that barbed-wire. Armstrong recognized the kind of man he was up against. He became sick with fear.

'Start the jeep,' Adam ordered over his shoulder. '*You*,' he said to Armstrong, his voice dripping with contempt. 'Read this!'

The Provost Major peered at the piece of paper held before him; he saw the signature, and joyfully he leaped at this means of escape. 'Of course,' he said, his voice piping high. 'If the *General* says so, of course. . . . Sergeant Burnside—jump to it! Escort these officers to see the prisoner.'

He moved two quick paces to the rear. This time Adam did not close the space; instead he turned back to the jeep. The Sergeant gazed at Adam with a glance of wonderful respect.

The Padre brought the jeep to a stop outside a wooden-frame hut where the Sergeant indicated. The engine noise sputtered out, but neither man made a move to descend; Adam and Padre Doorn sat silently in the jeep. They looked at each other with an agony of uncertainty in their glance.

At last Adam sat forward. 'Sergeant Burnside,' he demanded. 'What *is* this all about?'

The big Sergeant looked at the ground unhappily. 'I'm afraid, sir, it's like Armstrong said—' no one noted the missing title of respect—'He did get that message from Headquarters this morning. It seems they're really going to do it. . . .'

'But that's impossible!' Adam burst out. His glance returned to rake the Padre's face. 'When I left Kildare yesterday everything was decided. And he meant it, no doubt of that—I heard him give Newgate the necessary orders.'

'John,' said the Padre in a low voice, 'I don't know. I only know I'm going in to see Jonesy now.'

For the first time then Adam looked at the wooden building. Inside it somewhere was a cell containing a prisoner guarded by nervous sentries. Only minutes before he had looked forward to seeing Jonesy; it would have been like a holiday visit—knowing at last that Jonesy was safe, even guaranteed to survive the war. Now, instead, when he saw him, it would be a matter of trying to tell Jonesy that some morning soon these same guards of his were going to take him outside and shoot him. . . .

'No,' Adam declared flatly. 'At least, *you* go and see him. I'm going out to find Kildare.'

Adam pushed at the Padre in his hurry to get behind the wheel of the jeep. The Padre climbed out; he and Sergeant Burnside moved to one side. Adam swung the jeep in a tight circle, and accelerated toward the prison gate.

6

ADAM spent the rest of the day attempting to see General Kildare. He was not in his office; no one at Headquarters could, or would, tell him where he was. Even Colonel Newgate was not available. It was made quite plain in the Colonel's office that Adam had lost any status as a privileged visitor.

Adam quickly discovered, however, that the sentence of Rifleman Jones really had been confirmed. It was the talk of every clerk and orderly who passed by in the marble corridors. This was a Wednesday; betting had it that the execution would take place on Saturday. Adam heard this talk with a stony face.

Outside what seemed to be a central office, loud with clacking typewriters, Adam sat down on a bench. He forced himself to sit still. The hot anger burning inside him would accomplish nothing: what was needed now was cold, calculating intelligence. Kildare, for unknown reasons, had reversed his decision; but

200

none the less he remained the only person with any power over the event. Therefore Kildare had to be reached; and somehow he had to be made to act.

Gradually Adam's breathing became calmer. He was glad now he had not been able to find Kildare at once. Bursting in on him, raging with righteous indignation would have been useless folly. Adam closed his eyes. Sitting on that bench he filled with a breathless, burning urgency of purpose.

Adam stood up then. He walked along a corridor until he found a washroom. In the mirror he held inspection of himself. His face looked pale and drawn; but outwardly he was an able, efficient-looking officer. While hurrying soldiers brushed by his bench he had suddenly remembered that he had every right himself to be in this building; the General's own order had posted him here for 'temporary duty'. And now he was going to inspect his new place of military assignment.

Adam removed his cap and hung it on a peg in the washroom. He took a random piece of paper from his pocket which he held carefully in one hand. He tugged the belt of his battle-dress tight, and he strode briskly out into the corridor.

With a severe, preoccupied look on his face Adam marched into the large central office. The clerks took one glance and bent to their typewriters with new energy. This stern, frowning officer, standing among them with a piece of paper in his hand, looked as though he might be planning some vast reorganization of the whole establishment. And there were still a few of them who might, just possibly, be remustered to infantry. The typewriters clacked furiously.

Adam moved from office to office, never pausing too long, always with the same grave, appraising air. He avoided the inner offices occupied by officers because he knew he would not find there what he wanted. Most of the men he observed at work wore General List or Staff Clerk badges; but there were some with regimental flashes on their shoulders, and it was these he looked at most closely. In a large headquarters staff like this, Adam knew, it was only a matter of time until he discovered the right man.

Before long he was rewarded. From a doorway he looked into a smaller office of the 'Q' Department. At a desk, obviously in charge, sat an elderly Staff-Sergeant peering through thick spectacles. And this Staff-Sergeant wore the shoulder flash of the 2nd Rifles. Adam walked in.

'Good day, Staff,' he said warmly. 'It's certainly good to find another Rifleman here. My name's Adam.' And he held out his hand.

The Staff-Sergeant stood up. He was a thin man, with sparse grey hair, and he stood quiveringly to attention like the very old soldier he was. Through thick spectacle lenses he peered at Adam, at the Rifles' flash which announced fellow membership in an honoured regiment. He had been an aging regular at the outbreak of war; the Regiment had been his life and treasure. He peered at Adam's Divisional patch, his glance lingered as though fascinated on the coloured chest ribbons; and a beatific smile possessed his face. Although he was already at attention he moved his boots apart for the purpose of banging them together again, and he stood ramrod stiff. 'It's a pleasure to see *you*, sir!' he sang out. He accepted Adam's extended hand.

By now Adam had estimated the man's age as close to sixty; it probably took an Order-in-Council, he thought, to keep him even this near to the front.

'When did you leave the unit?' Adam asked in a tone of interest. 'Weren't you with "D" Company on the Hitler Line?'

The old man's leathery cheeks flushed red with pleasure. ' 'Fraid not, sir,' he said apologetically. 'Fact is, I'm Category—haven't seen the unit in quite some time.'

He peered at Adam myopically; apparently he felt more explanation was required, for he added: 'Fact is, sir—I've a bit of trouble in the joints. . . .'

'What rotten luck!' Adam said with quick sympathy. 'But I hope you'll come up and visit us whenever you can—'

Adam broke off; he peered around the room. The Staff-Sergeant followed his glance with concerned attention.

'Staff,' Adam said, 'I'm new here. Is there any place we can have a cup of coffee together?'

'Yes, *sir*—there's a very good canteen downstairs.'

'Fine! But—you're sure it won't interfere with your duties?'

'Not in the least, sir. It will be my pleasure. Smith,'—this over his shoulder, without turning his head—'Carry on! '

In the corridor they fell into step and marched together to the

202

canteen. A respectful circle cleared round their table; and curious glances were cast at the Staff-Sergeant sitting with the important-looking officer. The old man's name was Perkins. He led a barren, functional life back here at Headquarters; and, in fact, this was the first Rifles' officer from the field he'd ever spoken to in Italy. By the end of their second cup of coffee he would have given anything, up to and including his life, for Adam.

Adam became deadly serious when he started to talk about Jones. Perkins knew all about it, of course. He thought it unbearable shame that a Rifleman—

'He's more than a Rifleman, Perkins. He was in my Company. Also, he's my friend.'

'Of course, sir.' Perkins nodded in quick agreement.

Adam explained that the only hope, however slight it might be, was to persuade General Kildare to take some new and drastic action. But the General would not see him—everyone at Head-quarters refused to tell him where he was. Did Perkins know any way of finding out?

Perkins sat and brooded. 'Just to find out where he is, sir—say, by tonight?'

'That's it.'

Perkins's old eyes gleamed behind his spectacles. 'That shouldn't be too hard, sir. I know his personal driver—young chap who owes me a few favours. . . .'

Adam's own face lighted up. This was just what he had been looking for. Adam told Perkins to call him by military telephone at the hotel as soon as he got word.

'Yes, sir.' Perkins hesitated. 'I would consider it an honour, sir, to offer my own services—in any way possible.'

'Thanks,' Adam said. He looked at the loyal old soldier and he felt stirred by real affection. 'Thanks, Perkins—I'll certainly remember that.'

7

HALF an hour after Perkins telephoned Adam stood outside the street address he had been given. It was an expensive-looking apartment house, high above the city, in the most expensive part of Rome. Adam went inside, found the right apartment number, and pressed the bell.

After a few moments the door was opened by a British Brigadier, a handsome, ruddy-faced man. 'Yes?' the Brigadier asked.

Adam hesitated. 'General Kildare wanted to see me, sir,' he said.

'Oh—well, come in, old chap; I'll tell him you're here.' The Brigadier went away, smiling cheerfully.

Adam stood in a rotunda with a domed ceiling. Directly ahead an entrance-way led into an immense, spreading room; it was a vista of sleek opulence. A table was spread with cups and liqueur glasses. There were rich clouds of cigar smoke, the chattering of women's voices. Adam walked forward.

He halted on the threshold. In his battle-dress and boots he felt heavy, almost boorish, at the fringe of this civilized room; but he stood as though entirely sure of himself.

Kildare was rising from a deep chair; on each side of him a bare-shouldered woman held a liqueur glass in her fingers. Kildare caught sight of Adam. His face darkened, and then turned purple. He looked as though he might choke or explode.

'Good evening, sir,' said Adam. 'Sorry I couldn't make it for dinner, but I found I was able to take advantage of your kind invitation after all. . . .' His glance was utterly assured and respectful.

The two women, neither of them young, but both attractive, regarded him with interest. Through a haze of cigarette smoke the British Brigadier looked amused. And General Kildare glared.

Adam waited in the same politely smiling attitude. After another few seconds, as though despite himself, General Kildare's expression softened. He might have been thinking that Adam was pulling the thing off beautifully—just the way he would have done it himself. He began to chuckle loudly.

The General strode forward and seized Adam's hand. 'Well, you're here,' he said. 'Come and meet my friends. The Countess Ciotti—may I present Major Adam? And Mrs. Hicks—Major Adam. . . .'

Adam bowed and made polite sounds. He was smiling and attentive, perfectly at ease. He accepted the liqueur glass which the Brigadier handed him.

There was light conversation then, but all the time the General kept watching Adam and his glance became increasingly sombre.

After another few minutes he asked the others to excuse them. He led the way out of the room; Adam followed him onto an enclosed porch which ran the length of the apartment building. The star-studded sky of Rome, with towers and domes faintly outlined, formed a blue velvet backdrop. Adam took the chair that Kildare indicated. The big man sat down opposite him, a lighted cigar clenched in his fist.

'All right,' said Kildare. 'Let's have it. I suppose you're angry that I could not stop the execution?'

'It *must* be stopped,' Adam said steadily.

In the half darkness the cigar pulled away from the General's mouth. 'Adam—it *can't* be stopped. Try to get that one fact into your bloody thick head. Nobody in the world can stop the thing now.'

'I'm doing my damnedest,' said Adam. 'But you're the one with the power.'

The General swore.

'Don't talk like a schoolboy,' he said. 'I told you before that at times one can only accept circumstances; and this is one of those times. There's nothing anyone can do—'

'Except the General Officer Commanding!'

The General was silent for several seconds. 'Adam,' he said. 'I don't know why I put up with you. Your least endearing habit of all is to make me explain myself. All right, I'll spell it out for you: that Colonel from London you saw in my office was a messenger-boy, sent to keep me in line. London had decided that my confirmation was to be purely automatic. If I proved difficult the Colonel had one word to put on the wire and my dismissal came back by return. Not that it made the least damn difference anyway, because the confirmation had *already* gone to Ottawa— before I could act at all! ' He laughed; it was a pained, bitter laugh that hurt him. 'So much for the power you think I have.'

Adam was silent. Then: 'I'm sorry, sir. I did not realize that; I have no right to ask—'

'Adam—within my power, you can have any other goddam thing you want! '

'But that's the *only* thing I want.'

'Don't be a fool, boy.' The General stood up. 'Why don't you get right back to the Rifles? For your information, the Divisional attack starts on Friday. I'll make the posting, give you a jeep. And tonight you could go out and get good and drunk.'

Again Adam was silent. 'Sir—when will the execution take place?'

When the General spoke again it was in a tired, spent voice. 'Word from Ottawa is expected tomorrow. If that word is received the execution will take place Saturday morning.'

Adam stood up. For a moment the two men stayed together in the half-darkness of the porch.

The General laid a huge hand on Adam's arm. He spoke with the concentrated concern that a father might use. 'Now, Adam— you understand the thing's beyond affecting, don't you?'

'I understand,' Adam said. 'Good-bye, sir.'

When he walked off the porch General Kildare's big hunched-up figure stood still, his glance staring after him anxiously.

Adam opened the door of the apartment and stepped into the Roman night. At least, he thought, one thing was accomplished: every other possible course of action was eliminated. If Jonesy was to be saved, if there *was* any possible way—now it was up to him. Adam found his parked jeep and he drove away.

8

LATE Friday morning Padre Philip Doorn sat alone in his hotel room, listless, waiting. He had left Jonesy at the prison an hour before. While there he had learned that the execution would take place tomorrow—Saturday morning. And now he sat here, awaiting Adam's return.

He sat looking at his wrist-watch. Its ticks were pulse-beats, a striking metronome on his eardrums. Time seemed to be a torturingly slow, ponderous weight; and yet, whenever a clock was able to register its message with him, he was grieved to discover another giant slab of time removed. As he looked at his watch his eyes watered. For the past two days Padre Doorn had felt himself constantly on the brink of tears; it was something he had to fight against; he feared the least thing might set him to crying.

It was the other things, apart from the one central, terrible problem of Jonesy, which made him want to cry. The thought of his friend John Adam, for instance.

He was not at all sure that his friend was even sane. For the past two days Adam had busied himself with secret comings and goings. His face had assumed a brooding, indrawn look— trance-like, as though he had lost all touch with reality. Last night he had not been to bed: the Padre knew because he kept watch from the adjoining room. And now Adam had an inseparable companion: a half-blind old Staff-Sergeant called Perkins, a peculiar old man with a wild air about him.

The Padre stared sightlessly at his watch. While he sat with his thoughts another slab of irrecoverable time rolled away.

Outside the door there were clumping noises. Then Adam, followed by Staff-Sergeant Perkins, came marching into the room. Both men looked dusty and rumpled; their uniforms were marked with earth and grass stains. Adam unslung a pair of binoculars and tossed them on a bureau. 'Drinks, Perkins,' he ordered.

'Sah!' the Staff-Sergeant acknowledged.

The old man moved about to collect bottle and glasses; to the Padre it seemed that he walked stiffly, as though suffering from arthritis in his joints. For some reason the Padre felt like crying every time he looked at this devoted old campaigner.

'Bring your note-book too, Perkins.'

'Sah!'

Drinks arranged, the old man sat down at the table opposite Adam. He riffled through the pages of a Field Service Message Book until he found the right place, then he held his pencil poised between crabbed fingers. The Padre regarded the two men with a look of sorrow.

Adam held one hand to his head, eyes closed, frowning in con-centration. He started to dictate: 'From supplies, delete bangalore torpedoes, and substitute two pairs of wire-cutters, plus two pairs of heavy gloves. Also add: burnt cork for blackening faces.'

The Staff-Sergeant's pencil scribbled busily.

'John,' the Padre said, in a low voice. 'Have you heard? It's tomorrow morning. . . .'

'Two flashlights, six igniters, pencil type. Yes, I heard—' Adam's eyes were still closed. 'Perkins, I don't trust that Italian boatman: we'll have to scare him, as well as bribe him. Note that down.'

'*Tomorrow!*' The Padre's voice rose to a higher pitch.

'I know.' Now Adam opened his eyes. 'That's why we have to

get the operational detail settled at once. Plan "A" goes into effect tonight. Perkins, hand me the Log.'

The Padre knew that Adam had spent all last night compiling this Log. It was an exhaustive charting of vehicle and personnel traffic through the prison gates, diagrams showing sentry changes and beats, and other notations which he did not understand. The Padre gazed at Adam, his friend, and his glance became more deeply sorrowful. John, John, he wanted to call out: come back to me, come back to reality. This is a fantasy you have erected to hold reality away from yourself, but in the end it will only be crueller still. John—come back. . . .

In his agitation the Padre stood up and paced over to the window. Behind him the voice of clipped military detail continued. Maybe it's worse than fantasy, the Padre thought: maybe he's really going to do it—and God knows what will happen then, except that others will be destroyed also, and it will be that much more terrible for Jonesy. . . .

The Padre turned and saw the two men poring over the notes spread on the table. Their drinks remained untouched.

Adam looked up at the Padre thoughtfully. 'Philip,' he said, 'we'll hold a formal "O" Group later, of course, but in the meantime perhaps we should run over your own assignment.'

The Padre sat down again, in the same chair. He felt a familiar smarting sensation in his eyes.

'It may seem that we're not giving you much to do, Philip, but I assure you your own role is vital.' Now Adam leaned forward, his eyes agleam. 'Please listen carefully. You will be in Jonesy's cell at 0100 hours when the first explosion occurs. You stay there, of course, until the fire on the west side of the Camp—that's farthest from the river—is well under way, and by then most of the guards will be over there fighting it. Stay there, in fact, until I throw the smoke grenade into the hut. Then you get him to the doorway, and I take over from there. I expect to have him through the hole in the wire and into the motor-boat in less than twenty-eight seconds—'

'John—' this in a beseeching voice—'I was with him today. He asked why you had not come to see him.'

Adam's lips moved, but no sound emerged. '—By then,' like

an engine his voice caught, and chugged on of its own accord—'by then, of course, his cell door will be unlocked—'

'John—Jonesy is worried, he's frightened, but he doesn't *know* yet! They don't promulgate the sentence until two hours before the execution—at 0500 hours.'

Adam's voice ran down completely then. He looked crumpled and broken. From across the table Perkins, the loyal adjutant, peered anxiously through his spectacles. 'Sir,' Perkins reminded him, 'you were detailing Major Doorn's assignment.'

'Of course.' Adam shook his head, as though to bring himself awake. 'Padre,' he said. 'You must understand that every detail of this plan is vitally important.'

The Padre sat forward, hands clasped together, his eyes pleading on Adam's face. 'John, listen to me,' he said. '*Please* listen. This plan of yours is impossible; it can only end in making Jonesy's suffering even greater. No—' His voice went higher, and harder, to cut off protest. 'Just *listen*—that prison camp is swarming with Provost Corps men, as well as the regular staff. But even assuming you did get him out—what then? Could you hide him—hide *Jonesy*? Anyone else in the world, perhaps, but not Jonesy. And think—the American police, the Italians—the *carabinieri*—every soldier in southern Italy would be called out to hunt him down. Then, when they did get him, his death and suffering would be that much harder. To say nothing, of course, of anyone else who might get killed during the escape, your own court-martial and that of Perkins. John, John—come back to reason. You must understand this—believe me!'

Perkins, at mention of his name, had come to his feet. His fists were balled at his side, his face stern and working. *He* was committed to the venture: for days he had lived and breathed and thought of nothing but this matter of Jonesy's rescue; it was the most important purpose he had known in his life. He was prepared to die for the cause if necessary; he was outraged by the Padre's words—they were traitorous. . . . He opened his mouth to speak.

Adam glanced up and motioned him to silence. Adam's face was stony; he stared ahead, unseeing. He knew—or *had* known, at the beginning—the truth of everything the Padre said; but he had suppressed it in his mind because to accept was to know that his task, which had to be accomplished, was impossible of accomplishment. Now full realization of this truth seeped back in. All the fire and the decision faded from his face.

The Padre wanted to reach out and touch him. Instead, he said in a detached, objective tone: 'I'm going to see him tonight. I'm going to try to tell him before Armstrong marches in with the promulgation order. And then I'll stay beside him—until the end.'

Adam merely frowned; he did not yet grasp the full meaning of what the Padre said. Then he looked up, and suddenly he exploded. 'You mean you're going to *participate*?'

'I'll be the Chaplain,' the Padre said steadily, 'if that's what you mean.'

Adam stared at him, shocked and disbelieving. Philip Doorn, his friend, was going to take part in the execution: he was going to further the evil instead of fighting it. And yet, he sat there now like a man who has made an honest decision, judging it to be right. . . .

'John,' the Padre began again in a pleading tone.

'Come, Perkins,' Adam ordered savagely. 'Let's get out of here.'

In silence, except for the clumping of their boots, the two men moved about the room, collecting their notes and impedimenta. They left with no glance for the one remaining behind. When the door slammed the Padre let his head fall forward on his arms.

Down on the sidewalk, in the bright sunshine, neither man found anything to say. Together they walked slowly to the parked jeep and there they came to a halt. Adam paused irresolutely.

His mind clamoured with the one vital thing the Padre had said: Jonesy had asked for him, and he had not yet gone to see him. He suffered an agony of impatience now; he wanted to get out to the prison at once. But, first, there was Perkins.

Adam glanced in the face of the man beside him and he saw immediately that Perkins knew. Both men knew; and in that instant each one looked quickly away.

But just as quickly Adam looked back again. His faithful ally was stooped over; uncharacteristically he leaned with one hand to support him on the hood of the jeep. The old man's face was drawn and grey. He looked ill.

'Perkins,' he cried in alarm. 'Are you all right?'

'Yes, sir. Just a little tired. Not too accustomed to field conditions, I'm afraid. The night air and wet grass. . . .'

Now, with the impetus of purpose removed, Perkins was feeling an old man's complaints. Adam looked at this man who was old enough to be his father, this gallant ally, and he filled with futile anger against himself. He grasped Perkins's arm firmly and he led him back to the hotel entrance, then through the lobby and into the bar. There he seated him in a chair and stood by his side. This was an officers' bar, but no one thought to question Adam. 'Two double cognacs,' he ordered.

They drank their cognacs and in a few minutes the colour came back to Perkins's cheeks.

'That did the trick, sir,' Perkins said, wiping his lips. 'Think I'd better get back to Headquarters now.'

'I'll drive you.'

They drove through the streets of Rome in silence. There was much that each one could have said, and wanted to say, but they sensed that this silence was better.

Adam let him out in front of the big marble edifice.

'Good-bye, Perkins,' he said.

Staff-Sergeant Perkins brought himself to a stiff attitude of attention. His eyes blinked, he seemed to have trouble seeing through his thick spectacles, but he held himself erect and he produced the smartest salute of all his years of service. 'Good-bye, sir,' Perkins cried, in a ringing voice.

He stayed at rigid attention. He remained standing at the kerb while Adam turned the jeep round and swung on to the road which led to the prison.

9

IT WAS not a cell really: merely a room in a barracks block with a door that locked. An iron-grilled window gave glimpse of the muddy Tiber; outside was the scent and rustle of pine trees.

Jonesy was sprawled boyishly on his cot. He looked up, his face lighted with instant joy, and he leaped to his feet.

'Jonesy!' Adam cried, feeling a flood of deepest pleasure.

At once Jonesy's own voice was a happy babble, filling the room. They clasped hands, then they sat down together on the iron cot; the springs creaked with their weight.

It was as though there had been no interruption of time. Without pause Jonesy's voice raced happily along, picking up the threads of a thousand tiny events and happenings they had known together. For him their relationship had never been broken; there had been no parting; that terribly decisive, intervening event might never have occurred. Adam looked in Jonesy's radiant face; and he found himself laughing and talking too, merely content with the present moment.

From the first instant of greeting, in fact, Adam had made his decision. The first glimpse of Jonesy's face had pulled him back to reality, and washed his mind with cooling draughts of reason. He saw now there was only one possible course of action: and that was to stay with Jonesy until the end, and envelop him with a cocoon of protecting comfort. He must shield Jonesy. That was the necessity the Padre had already discovered. It was no longer a question of fighting against execution, but merely of holding away its horror from Jonesy's understanding.

Adam listened to the gay, prattling voice, but his mind was busy with other things. The—arrangements, for instance. . . . Suddenly it became loathsome, unbearable, to think of the sweating Armstrong coming to place his obscene straps on Jonesy's body. For an instant a haze of anger obscured Adam's vision. No, he swore silently: *he* would do that—whatever had to be done; and at every step of the way the strength of his own body would be there to support, and sustain.

'You know what, sir?' Jonesy's question came in a tone of secret triumph; it broke in on Adam's brooding.

'No, Jonesy—what?'

'I've learned how to play rummy. The Sergeant taught me.'

'Well—that's fine. . . .'

'Would you like a game, sir?'

There was a small table in the cell. There, where Jonesy pointed, was a pack of cards amid piled magazines.

Adam cleared his throat. 'Well, right now I've got some business to attend to. But I'll come back in a little while, and I'll bring the Padre with me, and then we can play a three-handed game.'

'All right, sir.' But at the prospect of being left alone some of the sparkle faded from Jonesy's eyes.

212

Adam was in a hurry to get away. He stood up and moved to the door. He had his hand on the latch when Jonesy spoke.

'Sir,' he said. 'Why are they going to shoot me?'

Adam was slow in turning about. He looked in Jonesy's eyes; he returned that serious, inquiring gaze; and he was gripped by despair. What—with God's help—could he say to this? It was like one of those rare, but momentously serious questions posed by a child, which one wonders whether to answer in earnest. Well, would it help him to explain that this was the familiar equation of sin and punishment? Jonesy expected that. After all, he continually made mistakes, and stood ready to accept whatever punishment his mistakes merited. But—that was not the truth. The truth was that Jonesy had done nothing wrong at all, unless perhaps it was to be born what he was, to *be* what he was.

Adam stood with his hands at his side. 'Jonesy,' he said. 'You've done nothing wrong. You've never done anything wrong in your life. Now, you're not to think of that any more; just forget it completely. Pretty soon the Padre and I will be back for that game of cards.'

Adam stood there, striving with all his being to convey a message greater than his words; he tried to will a message of love and trust and assurance.

Then, in the next instant, Jonesy's face cleared magically; again he was all smiles and contentment. He picked up the deck of cards from the table and sat down with them on his cot. 'I'll be waiting, sir,' he said.

Adam closed the door behind him.

Standing on the tarmac outside the prison hut was a short, dapper man smoking a cigarette. He wore battle-dress, with belt and revolver holster, and the rank badges of a Lieutenant-Colonel. He stood smoking his cigarette without haste, as though waiting for Adam's appearance. And Adam knew who he must be.

Adam approached and halted in front of the Lieutenant-Colonel. Cool grey eyes regarded him steadily.

'Colonel McGuire?' Adam asked.

'Yes.'

'Do you know who I am?'

'Yes—I know you, Adam.'

'Sir—I want to stay with Jones now; I want to be with him

during the execution. And I'd like to be put in charge of the—arrangements.'

The grey eyes regarded him unblinkingly. 'Adam, I was prepared to place you under arrest tonight. Your plans were hardly secret.'

'Oh, that. . . . Well, it's all over with now. Arrest me later, if you want. But I *have* to do this.'

There was a flicker of feeling in those grey eyes. 'No need to talk of arrest, Adam. For what you ask, however, I just haven't the authority.'

'But if General Kildare says so?'

'In that case—of course.'

'Will you come with me to a telephone, sir?'

Colonel McGuire flicked his cigarette away. 'Be glad to. There's one in the Camp office.'

The two officers turned and fell into step as they walked together toward the main building of the prison camp.

10

IT WAS another bare room in a bare hut. A naked electric light bulb dangled above a trestle table.

It was late afternoon; the day was not warm, but Major Armstrong's bush-shirt was damp, almost blotted to his torso. From time to time his fingers reached up to strop a beard of sweat from his chin. He was watching while Adam read from two typewritten sheets lying on the table. He made a sucking noise through his teeth; his fat face was arranged in what he considered to be an agreeable expression. His whole attitude suggested the utmost deference.

Now he sat forward and stabbed a moist finger at the typescript. 'There,' he said. 'That's the part—under "Procedure".' He read aloud: ' "The prisoner may be shot either standing up or strapped to a post fixed in the ground, if available, or sitting down strapped to a chair. . . ." And since there's no post available, I've arranged to have him strapped in a chair.' He spoke in a voice of friendliest good reason.

Adam had been reading the neatly typed pages with a look of loathing, as though it sickened him to find such obscenity cast in military terms and set down on paper. At Armstrong's remark he looked up. His face was storm-ridden, a muscle throbbed tautly in his neck. He stared at Armstrong; his glance ate into Armstrong.

'Listen,' Adam said, softly, viciously. 'I don't care if it takes the whole goddam Provost Corps all night—but you'll get a proper stake, and fix it properly in the ground. Understand?'

'Yes,' Armstrong answered.

He was unable to disengage his glance, and he almost added 'Yes, *sir*.' In a moment he might bluster to compensate for this abasement; but right now he sat up straight; he was genuinely frightened of the man who sat beside him.

Adam glanced away. For him Armstrong had no more meaning than the chair he sat on: they were both mere instruments to be used for a purpose.

'Get out your note-book,' Adam ordered, 'and pay attention. I'm going to run over every item on the list.'

Freed from Adam's scrutiny Armstrong's face relapsed into ugliness; one fist opened and closed on the table. Then Adam looked at him again.

'Very well,' Armstrong said quickly. He reassembled his smile. 'Very well; whatever you say. . . .' Obediently his note-book opened.

Adam went on speaking, as though to an inanimate object. 'There will be no black cap,' he dictated. 'It will be a blindfold, and I'll put it on myself.'

Major Armstrong wrote in his book.

'The M.O. will *not* affix the aiming mark over his heart—*I* will.' Adam's eyes were closed, his face tight with concentration. 'And throw away those goddamned straps and ropes—they won't be needed.'

Then he opened his eyes and looked at Armstrong. 'One other thing—what about the firing-squad?'

'Ah, yes—the firing-squad.' Armstrong sat up and spoke in a tone of relish. 'Ten rank and file, a sergeant, and a lieutenant. I've had them out rehearsing all day. You see, it's quite a tricky piece of drill. They have to ground arms, be marched away, then I reload their rifles, putting blanks in two of them—'

'For Christ's sake!' Adam's voice was a roar. 'Never mind that. Who's the lieutenant?'

After a moment Armstrong managed another smile. 'Well,' he said, 'the lieutenant's a useless-looking tit. Arrived last night from Avellino. He's taking on this job to clear off an adverse report, and work his passage home to Canada.'

'What's his name?'

'De Rougemont.'

Adam leaned forward. 'Not *Bernard* de Rougemont?'

'I think that's it. Do you know him?'

Adam made no reply. He sat back in his chair again. He did not hear whatever else Armstrong was saying. Instead, he was remembering the night he arrived at Bazin's castle and was met by Lieutenant Benny de Rougemont, resplendent in breeches and clanking spurs. And from there his mind leaped to the moment of meeting with Toni, the fireworks on the terrace, and afterwards. . . . He suffered a piercing, desolating moment of pain; then ruthlessly he wrenched his thoughts back to the present.

'Anyway,' he heard Armstrong saying, 'this de Rougemont doesn't matter a damn. I've briefed Sergeant Burnside on exactly what to do.'

Adam sat there in silence, staring at the rough wood of the table-top. After a moment he stirred and he picked up the typewritten pages again.

'I'll go over the whole thing from the beginning,' Adam stated. 'Then I want you to call the firing-squad and your Provost people together and check every detail.'

He looked down at the typescript. 'First item, Promulgation— you can come to the cell at 0500 hours, but you're not to say or read anything unless I tell you. . . .'

Adam's voice, clipped, decisive, sounded on. The two men sat at the table and went over every sentence.

In the prison camp outside now it was dusk: soft, velvety dusk; the guard was changing and the night's activities were commencing. In one small, secluded portion of the Camp grounds a squad, consisting of ten soldiers, a sergeant, and a lieutenant, stood bunched together, smoking cigarettes as darkness bloomed around them. They were reluctant to resume the strange drill they had to practise.

11

THE morning was clean and fragrant. The dew was still fresh on the grass. A light ground mist rolled away before the heat of the climbing sun.

On this edge of the prison camp a U-shaped space had been cut from the forest. The base of the U was a red-brick wall, and down each side marched a precise line of sentinel pines. In the forest clearing the neat groups of soldiers looked clean and compact; coloured flashes on their battle-dress showed bright against the green of pines. In front of the brick wall a stake was fixed in the ground, and this stake was the centre of its universe: it commanded the unwavering regard of every soldier.

The firing-squad stood 'at ease', but without the least stir or motion. Sergeant Burnside was on their right; Lieutenant de Rougemont several paces apart on their left, aligned at right angles to his ten-man rank. He looked pale and sleepless; he blinked in the sunlight and continually wet his lips as though thirsty. Behind him, drawn up before the pines in positions prescribed by Colonel McGuire, were all those others whose duty compelled them to be present. A cordon of military policemen stayed at rigid attention along the top and down each side of the U.

It was a precise, well-ordered scene: a parade efficient and purposeful in every way; but there was not one person there who did not wish himself elsewhere.

The nearest wooden-frame building was no more than one hundred yards distant. That was where the prisoner was lodged, but no head turned in its direction. Every officer and soldier stood motionless, waiting, his glance fixed on the stake in the ground.

There was a noise which no one affected to hear: the creak of a door opening, the shuffle of boots on wood. Lieutenant de Rougemont made a signal with his hand and the men of the firing-squad came quietly to attention. There would only be one spoken command today: the word 'Fire!'; then the volley would follow at once; and the purpose of this assembly would be concluded.

A group of khaki-clad figures appeared in the doorway of the hut, descended the steps, and extending into file began to march toward the forest clearing. The group numbered six. Two Provost Sergeants marched in front; next came a file of three—in the centre, the prisoner Jones, hatless, blindfolded with a white handkerchief

—with Padre Doorn on one side, Major Adam on the other. Major Armstrong brought up the rear.

The procession was walking rather than marching, with no appearance of haste, its speed apparently geared to that of the prisoner. Jonesy's blond hair gleamed golden in the sunlight; his battle-dress was freshly creased, his boots brilliantly polished. He walked with his head held back as though his nostrils would sniff the freshness of this day which he could not see. He walked unaware of the piece of paper with a painted black ball that was pinned over his heart. Adam and Padre Doorn stayed close on each side of him; no daylight showed between the three.

On Adam's face as he walked was a frown: a look, almost, of worried puzzlement. He was filled with a new wonder, possessed by it to the point where the agony he had expected to suffer at this moment did not exist. From the beginning his intention, agreed to in every particular by the Padre, had been to prevent Jonesy from knowing what was happening. They would simply not allow him to comprehend what the preparations and the final event meant. They would interpose themselves protectively until the last second, and then Jonesy would die without fear, unaware, even, there had ever been cause for fear. And last night in Jonesy's cell, while the game of rummy went on for ever, they thought they had succeeded. But there came a moment, a lonely unguarded moment at three o'clock in the morning, when the cards lay unregarded on the table, and neither man could keep his despair from showing; and Jonesy, concerned, glanced from one to the other.

'Look, sir,' he said slowly to Adam, his glance speaking to both of them. 'Please don't worry about me. I am not afraid.'

In that moment Adam and the Padre knew that Jonesy had understood all along; and after that it was almost as though Jonesy were trying to comfort *them*. He kept the talk going unflaggingly, he cracked weak jokes, and tried to make them join in his laughter. Adam had filled with astonishment and wonder— which remained with him now as they walked together toward the place of execution. Jonesy was trying to make it easier for them; and he had produced a dignity of his own which was stronger than the terror and the brute degradation of the coming moment.

This same wonder showed on the Padre's face too. He walked

at Jonesy's side with a firm step, his face alight, and he peered at the blue sky above them. He kept one hand securely under Jonesy's elbow.

They were within thirty yards of the stake when from somewhere a late rooster crowed. The call came clear and sweet in the morning air, full of rich promise for the autumn day which stretched ahead. In this place it was an incongruous sound, suggestive of ducks, and calm mill-ponds, and barn-yards.

Across Jonesy's blindfolded face Adam and the Padre shared a glance. To them perhaps the sound recalled other barn-yards, especially that first one they had known in far-off Sicily.

At the rooster crow Adam had paused. His boot struck an uneven piece of ground; he stumbled and almost fell. But Jonesy's hand reached out at once and Adam used it to steady himself. There was only that momentary pause, then their advance continued.

The procession reached the stake at last. Adam had planned things so that once Jonesy was in position the others would simply keep on marching; then, the moment they were passed, the order to fire would be given. And now the others did march away— everyone except Adam. Jonesy's back touched the stake, as planned, but Adam remained standing before him. Jonesy stayed erect, his head back, his face under its blindfold seeming to search for the warmth of morning sun.

Adam remained locked in that attitude as though he could not move. After another few seconds Jonesy shifted his head slightly and spoke from the corner of his mouth. 'Sir,' his voice said, making its last communication with the world. 'I think you'd better go now.'

Adam's glance fell. He made an about-turn and walked unsteadily in the direction of the trees. There the Padre's hand reached out to stop him, and drew him to his side.

The order to fire should have been delivered as soon as Adam moved, but it was not. There was nothing but silence again.

Lieutenant de Rougemont, commander of the firing-squad, stood staring at the prisoner, his mouth opening and closing in spasms. Lieutenant de Rougemont was seeing himself. For the first time in his life he was face to face with himself, and he discovered in that moment that he was not willing to pay the price of his passage home. After another few seconds he solved the problem, or had it solved for him, by fainting. His knees buckled, touched on the ground, and he fell forward.

The whole delay had now lasted perhaps ten or twelve seconds. In the forest clearing there was a rolling murmur of sound; every eye flashed toward Major Armstrong, whose task it now was to get this thing done. But Armstrong stood paralysed. He stared at de Rougemont's sprawled body with a protesting, incredulous look.

At the stake Jonesy's body was still erect, but now there was a perceptible tremor in his legs. The black ball of an aiming mark fixed over his heart began to wobble.

Adam stepped one pace forward from the trees.

The rifles of the firing-squad wavered in the air. Sergeant Burnside was glaring at Major Armstrong's useless hulk with a look of outrage, then he looked back at his ten riflemen.

'Squad,' Sergeant Burnside commanded. This word of command steadied the rifles, brought the muzzles centring once more on their target.

'Fire!' Sergeant Burnside shouted.

The volley shattered the morning calm. Jonesy's head nodded to his chest. His body stayed upright for another second, then it slumped and pitched forward to the ground. In the same instant Adam was running, with the Medical Officer close behind.

Sergeant Burnside stayed where he was. His head dropped and his shoulders shook, racked by huge sobs. He was crying; tears scarred his cheeks. Padre Doorn saw this and came hastening to his side. He placed both hands on Burnside's shoulders.

In front of the stake Jonesy's body lay quite still.

The neat military groupings broke in all directions. Adam and the Medical Officer knelt together on the ground. After a moment the Medical Officer straightened and stood up. He signalled with his hand to two stretcher-bearers stationed beside a waiting ambulance. They came at the double, unlimbering their stretcher as they ran.

Adam remained kneeling where he was. The Padre left Sergeant Burnside then and went to stand at Adam's side.

220

12

FAT, opulent farm land of the Campagna went skimming past. The jeep tugged in its slip-stream; it had the deserted road to itself because all other vehicles had already gone north to the battle which had been raging for two days. The jeep seemed the only moving thing in the world, swooping bird-like over the highway.

Adam's knuckles showed white on the wheel; with both hands the Padre clung to his seat. They were spinning through space, the wind a flat pressure on their faces. They were silent; they had not exchanged a word for thirty miles. Each one sat alone with his thoughts, yet aware of the other, aware of the communion they shared: the sense of wonder they puzzled at between them.

Their silence remained intact when they came bursting, suddenly, into Tuscany. Here was wild, pitching terrain, crenellated to the sky with castles and jagged hilltop towns; the jeep seemed a-toss on a sea of vineyards. Adam held the accelerator pressed to the floor. It was mid-afternoon now; there was still a long distance to go.

But then he had to slow behind an ox-drawn cart which was labouring up a hill. The cart was laden with bulging wicker-laced bottles, undoubtedly filled with local red-rich Chianti.

At the crest of the hill the jeep was barely moving: they stood poised on the brink of a new valley, a new breadth of world spreading out below. On one side, before the ground fell away, was a meadow studded in the centre with three oak trees; and under these oaks a black mare watched pridefully while her knock-kneed colt frisked on the emerald grass.

Adam braked the jeep. He pulled to the side of the road and shut the engine off. He sat for a moment unclenching his fingers on the steering-wheel. Then he took out his cigarettes and lighted one. He and the Padre regarded the scene before them.

The valley, and the world it contained, marched to a skyline which was afire in afternoon sunlight with the distant flash of tower and turret window. It was an incredibly clear-etched scene: as though each least impurity, each least defect of definition, had been filtered out. Closer, in the smaller frame of the meadow, the colt teased at its indulgent mother.

Adam was first to break the silence. 'I don't know why,' he said.

'But I feel all right now. And yet, I thought—I believed—when the execution was over everything would be over—'

The Padre was watching the colt's awkward arabesques. 'I know,' he said, 'I feel the same way.'

'*Why?*'

Adam's voice expressed all the urgency of wonder that they shared and puzzled at between them.

'Because Jonesy wanted it that way,' the Padre said. His tone of calm belief added that this was all the explanation he would ever need. His glance continued to follow the frisking colt.

Adam thought: that's one reason, there are probably others; there's no one answer, and it really doesn't matter. . . . The foreground profile of his friend Philip Doorn was framed in the meadow, and it seemed to Adam now that the Padre looked younger. Why, he looks like a man of God again, Adam thought: one who has been away, and has at last returned. And what about himself—did he wear any different outward appearance? For there was no doubt that each of them was changed, in a sense, perhaps, restored to whatever they had been before Sicily.

For an instant Adam was even able to think about Toni, with calm detachment and love; he wondered where she was and what she was doing; and he thought: there might still come the day—

But Adam stopped thinking then. At this moment he only knew that he was going where he was needed, to do the best he could; and that in itself was sufficient: there was no need to search out more.

Adam sent his cigarette tumbling end over end to the roadway. 'All set?' he asked.

The Padre nodded his head. He took his glance away from the meadow scene, and he smiled. 'Ready,' he said.

Adam shifted gears. The jeep picked up speed, and then they went swooping, hawk-like, into the waiting valley.

13

THE entrance to Battalion Headquarters was crowded with jeeps and carriers and signals equipment; it was a familiar sight, such as Adam and the Padre had seen a hundred times before. Eight hundred yards to the front, they had been told, the rifle companies were dug in; two hundred yards beyond them was a ridge, the crest of which formed the Start Line for an attack by the Rifles tomorrow morning. Adam and Padre Doorn climbed out of their jeep and went inside.

They found the C.O. standing over a map-strewn table. The instant he saw them Colonel Bond's weary face lighted up. To him Adam's coming was like receiving a company of reinforcements; there was much, even, that the Padre could do; and the Colonel told them so. Then, when the greetings were done, there came a pause. The Colonel looked in both their faces; his eyes asked a question; and for a moment the name of Jones trembled on all their lips. The word of Jonesy's death had already flashed to the front, even before their arrival; but here, with the immediacy of tomorrow morning pressing ever closer, it seemed something remote, an event already set down in past history. It was the death of only one man, after all, and back in a static setting, whereas— tomorrow morning. . . . Jonesy's name was not mentioned.

Grey afternoon light filtered through the sand-bagged windows. Colonel Bond was tired. He passed a hand across his face; then he launched into an account of the present tactical situation. This was the biggest attempt yet, he said, to smash German resistance in northern Italy and allow the armour to sweep over the Lombardy plain. Several Allied Corps were participating; there were one or two new wrinkles: our aircraft were dropping some kind of burning jelly stuff called napalm, we had tanks equipped with flame-throwers. But, still, it remained an infantry battle; and progress was slow everywhere against strong enemy resistance.

Colonel Bond's clipped recital continued. Now, for the Battalion. The attack was set for 0800 hours tomorrow morning, and 'B' Company—the Colonel smiled wryly at their under-strength condition—was commanded by Lieutenant Sankey; Major Green had been evacuated with jaundice last night. The other companies—

All at once the Colonel's voice stopped. A look of tired recollection appeared on his face. He stared first at Adam, then at the Padre; and he turned to the table in the centre of the room, where his fingers plucked idly at a stack of air photographs. 'Look,' he said, in a low voice, 'I'm afraid I've a piece of bad news.'

Adam and the Padre exchanged an aching flash of a glance.

They both knew, in that instant, what the news must be. There was only one thing, one *more* thing that it could be.

'Bunny?' Adam asked, from between clenched teeth.

'Yes.'

'How—and when?'

'Last evening,' said Colonel Bond, in the same subdued tone. 'He was up on the crest making a recce. Apparently he stood up to get a better look through his glasses. There was a sniper in the window of one of the houses down the slope. He was shot through the head.'

The Padre let out all his breath.

Adam made no sound. His mind registered the information, but he suffered no pain of grief, or anything at all. He glanced at Philip Doorn, saw into his dark, saddened eyes, and knew it was the same with him also. He thought: we always knew it had to happen. Bunny knew, and we knew; the only question was when. The Padre's eyes spoke with his: they recalled how Bunny once said he could not stay at his Field Punishment Camp or he would begin to believe he had escaped his destiny. . . . It was something that had to happen some time, and now it had, and that was all. Adam did not wonder at his own lack of grief; that would come later—when there was time to suffer grief; soon enough would come the flood of grief. . . .

The silence lengthened, and one thought, a sad and wildly irrelevant thought, entered Adam's mind. That sniper in his lofty window. Was it possible—could he imaginably, as he squeezed off that fatal round, have been conjugating the Latin verb to love? Reciting, as he sighted his rifle: '*Amo, amas, amat. . . .*'? How Bunny would have relished some such beautifully conceived stroke of fate. . . .

But then Adam stopped thinking of Bunny. He cleared his mind for matters of immediate concern. He and Padre Doorn both looked back at the Colonel again, ready, expectant.

Colonel Bond sensed and shared their mood. He began talking again, picking up the threads from where he had left off. He started to outline the plan for tomorrow morning's attack.

Half an hour later Adam and the Padre stood in gathering darkness outside Battalion Headquarters. They were both smoking cigarettes, holding the lighted ends shielded in their hands while they waited for the runner who would guide Adam to the 'B' Company position.

The runner appeared, identified himself, and then stood waiting out on the roadway.

They finished their cigarettes. 'Good-night, John,' the Padre said then. 'Until tomorrow. I'll be up there, close behind you.'

In the darkness Adam placed one hand on the Padre's shoulder. 'Good-night, Philip,' he said. He turned toward the waiting runner on the roadway.

It was a short walk to the Company position. When he arrived, Adam was welcomed back like a voyager who has been long away from home, whose return has been anxiously awaited.

Sergeant-Major Mitchell was the first to greet him. Adam at once recognized the squat, compact figure standing on the crown of the roadway. The two men reached for each other's hands; for a moment they stood in the darkness regarding one another with quiet pleasure. Then they went inside Company Headquarters, a stone hut set deep in the hillside which had once been used to store vats of *vino*. Here there was candlelight, the tang of damp earth, and a ring of grinning faces. Adam shook hands with each man there, because each man seemed to want it so.

He sat down with Mitchell and Lieutenant Sankey on the earth floor; by spluttering candlelight they bent their heads over maps and air photographs. Adam listened to the plan of attack they had devised, and at once his mind began to work out alternatives and improvements: advance the Forming-Up Place a hundred yards, and be safer from enemy D.F.s; send the tanks round by that track, and they would not draw fire on the infantry. Yes, the plan could be improved. . . .

'All right, Mitch,' Adam said, after another few minutes. 'Call an "O" Group for one hour from now. Right now I want to visit the platoons. Is there anyone to guide me?'

'Yes, sir. Corporal Ewart is standing by. And we have your equipment ready too.'

Adam looked at the wall where Mitchell pointed and he saw his own web equipment hanging from a nail: pistol, binoculars, pack, blanket and gas-cape—all neatly strapped and secured. He had completely forgotten such mundane details, and he flashed a glance of appreciation at Mitchell.

He had not heard the name of the corporal who was to guide him and when Adam turned he blinked in the face of the short, ferret-sharp little man who stood before him.

'Ewart?' he said in amazement. He looked in Ewart's beaming face, and he stared at the two stripes on his denim sleeves with sheer disbelief. *'Corporal* Ewart?'

'Yes, sir,' said Ewart, standing proudly at attention.

'Yes, sir,' added Sergeant-Major Mitchell. 'Promoted lance-corporal six weeks ago, full corporal three weeks ago—now a section commander in Ten Platoon.'

'Well!'

Quickly Adam wiped the amazement from his face; Mitchell could explain this transformation to him later. He smiled. 'It's good to see you, Ewart. Let's go and make our rounds.'

Adam was eager to get out and see the men of the platoons: that would finally position him, and make his home-coming complete. Then he would hold his 'O' Group with the platoon commanders, talk to Mitchell—probably over a drink of issue rum —and then to sleep. He and Mitchell had done this together many times before.

Corporal Ewart made a smart about-turn, and Adam followed behind him to the doorway. There the two men stopped for a moment, then they moved out into the darkness.

14

THE morning was dull, the sky streaked with slaty grey.

Adam and Corporal Ewart lay stretched out together in the grass, at the highest point of the ridge. Behind them the three platoons were deployed across the reverse slope, with the tanks formed line-ahead on their right. It was still ten minutes to H-hour; the men lay on their weapons and smoked a last cigarette.

In his ear Ewart's voice went on and on, talking interminably, but Adam scarcely heard. His eyes regarded the sweeping second-hand of his watch; his mind was quite detached from this time and place.

Adam lay on the grass, at peace with himself. Today he possessed a slow, sad certainty of knowledge. The mystery of man and his plight lay revealed before him. He knew man because he *was* man. Today he felt himself to exist at the central suffering core of all humanity. He was filled with a huge compassion and love and understanding for every man who had ever lived.

Ewart's voice was only a minor distraction. The name 'Krasnick' was constantly repeated; it seemed to Adam he had heard the account of Krasnick's death a hundred times already. And still Ewart's voice persisted on, forever talking of Krasnick, the man whom he discovered in the moment of his death to be his friend.

Now Ewart sounded aggrieved. 'Some say Simpson was better,' he argued. 'But the Sergeant-Major agrees with me that Krasnick was the best Bren gunner in the Battalion. What do you think, sir?'

Adam heard this question, and he thought about it.

'I say Krasnick was the best,' he said. 'But say more than that, Ewart. Krasnick was more than a good Bren gunner—say he was a good man too.'

And so they all are, Adam was thinking: Each one of them, in his fashion, was a good man. The trouble was that they *were* men, and being such, they were caught up in the strangling nets which man's plight cast over them: they could not always act the way their goodness wanted them to.

'Oh, yes,' Ewart said eagerly, his glance afire. 'Krasnick was a good man, all right. I know that because I was his Number Two and I lived with him so long.'

But Adam did not hear. It must have been at about this spot that Bazin was killed, he thought. His glance journeyed upward to a tall tree which had its base on the opposite, enemy side of the ridge.

'You know what I remember best about Krasnick, sir?'

Adam had discovered a bird, a large, raffish, dissolute-looking bird, perching on the top branch of the tree. What a peculiar place to perch, he thought: and what a jolt that bird will get when the barrage opens. . . .

'What I remember best about Krasnick?' Ewart repeated doggedly.

'No,' said Adam, hearing this time. 'What was that?'

'You remember that castle place back in Sicily? The first day?'

'Yes. Oh, yes.'

'And the attack. You were leading. We were the fire section. Krasnick and I had the Bren.'

'I remember,' Adam said.

'Well, there were a lot of horses milling round the castle gates. And Krasnick refused to shoot them. That's what I remember best about Krasnick. He shot a lot of Germans—but he would never shoot horses.'

The large bird, wings a-whirr, shot from its branch, and went speeding in a tight spiral to the top of the sky; it became a black dot, and then it disappeared. Adam lay watching and waiting and thinking.

Ewart said it again, aggrieved he had not been heard. 'Krasnick would never shoot horses,' he insisted.

'Of course,' Adam replied. 'None of us would.'